Praise for *A Life Once Dreamed*

"Rachel Fordham has crafted a tender tale of compassion and grace that authentically depicts a mother's heart and touches on questions of family and identity and the nature of real love."

Carolyn Miller, award-winning author of the Regency Brides series

Praise for *Yours Truly, Thomas*

"Fordham's wholesome tale will hit all the right notes for fans of Christian historical novels"

Publishers Weekly

"Fordham's writing exemplifies emotional intimacy, renews fascinating historical settings, and exudes uplifting Christian wisdom."

Booklist

"I want to live in Azure Springs with the friends we get to meet in Rachel Fordham's *Yours Truly, Thomas*. This story is a cup of romance, a pinch of mystery, and a savory plot seasoned with memorable characters (including a wayward dog) all trying to find their way in worlds turned upside down. *Yours Truly, Thomas* is the perfect read to lift your spirits. It did mine!"

Jane Kirkpatrick, award-winning author of *Everything She Didn't Say*

Praise for *The Hope of Azure Springs*

"In her promising first novel, Fordham assembles an endearing cast of characters in the rugged Midwest plains for a tale about surviving and thriving."

Booklist

"With unusual charm and warmth, Rachel Fordham opens the door to Azure Springs, a place as memorable as the people who inhabit it—namely the unique Em, a hero of a sheriff, and an assortment of heart-tugging, endearing townsfolk. A memorable story of faith, family, and happy endings!"

Laura Frantz, author of *The Lacemaker*

"This delightful book about the resilience of the human spirit and the power of love will keep you turning pages until the very end. After you read Rachel Fordham's satisfying story, you'll want to give the world a hug."

Jennifer Beckstrand, author of *A Courtship on Huckleberry Hill*

A Life Once Dreamed

Other Books by Rachel Fordham

The Hope of Azure Springs

Yours Truly, Thomas

A Life Once Dreamed

Rachel Fordham

Revell
a division of Baker Publishing Group
Grand Rapids, Michigan

Published by Revell
a division of Baker Publishing Group
PO Box 6287, Grand Rapids, MI 49516-6287
www.revellbooks.com

Printed in the United States of America

Library of Congress Cataloging-in-Publication Data
Names: Fordham, Rachel, 1984– author.
Title: A life once dreamed / Rachel Fordham.
Description: Grand Rapids, Michigan : Revell, a division of Baker Publishing Group, [2020]
Identifiers: LCCN 2019041863 | ISBN 9780800735395 (paperback)
Subjects: LCSH: Secrets—Fiction. | GSAFD: Mystery fiction.
Classification: LCC PS3606.O747335 L54 2020 | DDC 813/.6—dc23
ISBN 9780800738662 (casebound)

This is a work of historical reconstruction; the appearances of certain historical figures are therefore inevitable. All other characters, however, are products of the author's imagination, and any resemblance to actual persons, living or dead, is coincidental.

20 21 22 23 24 25 26 7 6 5 4 3 2 1

For my babies:

Garret, who teaches me to go for my goals with tenacity.
Spencer, who challenges me to think deeply.
Adele, who shows me what real charity looks like.
Titus, who models pure optimism for me.
Gideon, who offers me an abundance of kindness.
Walter, who reminds me to laugh.
My foster loves, who teach me that every day matters.

I'll love you all forever.

Prologue

Buffalo, New York, 1874

Fearful, *timid*, *reserved*. Agnes had been described as such since she was old enough to pay attention to the words of the adults around her. She looked again at the advertisement on the wrinkled sheet of newspaper. The Dakota Territory. Schoolteacher. Contract. Her head spun as she considered the venture. Nothing about it naturally called to her, yet she was fairly certain she had no other options.

"Good morning class, I'm your teacher, Miss Pratt," she said to her reflection. A large mirror hung above her dressing table, giving her a perfect view of herself and her spacious bedroom. Agnes looked hard at her brown eyes with their dark lashes. Could they be described as anything other than reserved? James had always brought out her spirit and eased her worries. Often, he told her that her eyes sparkled, and when she lost her temper with him, he told her they were full of fire. Without him, could she be bold and strong? She leaned in closer, cleared her throat, and said, "I'm Miss

Pratt. Take your seats." She attempted an authoritative edge. "Hurry up."

Her shoulders slumped. She had not sounded commanding. Teaching may not come naturally to her, but she had done well for her tutors, excelling. Nodding her head, she embraced the fact that—academically, at least—she was qualified.

She pulled the pins out of her hair and let her auburn curls fall past her shoulders, running her fingers through the strands. James had always loved her curls. When they would stand at the fence ready to bid each other good night, he would often weave his fingers into her hair. Then he'd lean in and—

She groaned. It would do no good to entertain such thoughts. Rather than think of tender kisses and love that would never be again, she picked up the embellished brass hairbrush her father had gifted her two years prior for her sixteenth birthday. With more force than necessary, she brushed the loose curls back and smoothed her hair against her scalp. At the nape of her neck she twisted her hair into a tight bun and glared at her reflection. "I'm Miss Pratt." She mimicked the voice of the stern Miss Jenks, who'd tutored her in French. "And I'll never be anything but Miss Pratt. There will be no more dreams of romance. No more longing to be anything but a teacher."

Despite her melancholy, fears, and broken heart, she laughed. Laughter would have been a good sign, an indication that the future might somehow work out, but this wasn't her airy, light laugh like the one James had so often evoked. Tonight, she laughed in discouragement and utter remorse for the change in her life plans.

How had this happened? She looked again at her reflection. Days ago she'd been happy and full of promise. The world had been right. It had been more than right—it'd been perfect. But it had all been a lie. Everything had fallen apart. Her whole world had been snatched away.

"Aggie." A rock clink against her window. "Aggie, come talk to me. Whatever it is, we'll work it out."

Tears pricked her eyes as she turned her back to the window and stepped farther into the shadows of her bedroom. Soon she'd be gone, and she'd never again hear James's voice. Their years together were over. She'd go to the Dakota Territory. She'd teach. She had no other options. She'd sign the contract and she'd be Miss Agnes Pratt, the schoolteacher, forever.

CHAPTER ONE

Penance, Dakota Territory, 1880

"Miss Aggie!" Tommy Smith yelled as he came through the schoolhouse door. "Are you a spinster?"

Agnes turned quickly—so quickly that her knee slammed into the side of her desk. She winced. The pain stole her voice.

"My pa says he don't understand why you ain't married. He says some folks are destined to be old maids, but he don't know why you are. Why ain't you married?" Tommy set his tin pail against the wall and swung his arms by his sides as he went to his seat. "You're pretty enough to be married. My pa said that too. He said you're the finest-lookin' woman in all of Penance, after my ma, of course."

The normal ruckus of the morning all but vanished. Agnes felt dozens of eyes turn on her. Running her hands over her skirts, she scrambled for the right words. "Tommy, it is impolite to ask after someone's personal life in a setting such as this."

Let that be enough, she prayed.

Facing the slate board, she quickly wrote several equations. The noises of children began again—feet scuffling, books thumping on desks, and voices lowly murmuring. Good, she didn't want to spend the day answering questions that were none of these children's business.

Just as she was about to begin lessons, she heard, "Miss Aggie?"

"Yes, Tommy?" She gritted her teeth and slowly turned to face him. "Did you have a new question? A different one?"

"Well, I thought you said since you was our teacher, we could ask you anything. I 'member you sayin' you would do your best to answer any question we had. I wanna know why you ain't married. That's my question. It don't make no sense to me. My pa's a smart man, and he don't know either."

Clara Belkins, a busybody in the making, decided to join in. "I remember you saying that too." She pursed her lips and waited. The room grew still and quiet. Only the ticking of the windup clock could be heard.

"Clara, Tommy, all of you, listen up." Agnes forced a smile. "Children, as your teacher, I *will* try to answer your questions. You must know that. But there are some questions that are called personal questions. Personal questions are impolite to ask others, especially in a public setting. My choice to remain *independent* is personal."

Tommy shot his hand into the air again. Avoiding his gaze, Agnes straightened a stack of books on her desk. The chubby arm waved more frantically. Despite her best efforts, she could not ignore the boy's flapping arm any more than she'd have been able to ignore a lion's roar.

Agnes resigned herself to her fate. "Yes, Tommy?"

"Is being independent the same as being a spinster?"

Knocking the books she'd been straightening onto the floor, she sucked in a hurried breath of air before bending to pick them up. Standing again, she spoke in a rather firm voice. "That's enough questions. We need to begin our lessons. I've many wonderful things to teach you today. We'll begin with our math groups. Group five, come to the board. We are going to work these multiplication problems together."

The normal noises of the classroom replaced the speculative whispers. Soon the day felt like every other. Arithmetic, reading, science, and history. Little hands raised with questions, naughty boys pulled braids, and girls chattered together whenever she turned from them.

When the last student left for the day, Agnes walked through her classroom picking up stray slates, stacking books, and erasing the board. The one-room schoolhouse was simple but warm and welcoming. The stove in the middle provided physical heat, and the colorful drawings and prints on the walls added warmth that sparked the imagination and touched the soul. This was her life. Colorful and simple. Comfortable and predictable. Running her hand along one of the wooden desks, she smiled. Her heart burst with gratitude at the thought of such beautiful children, full of promise. Her hand stopped on Tommy's desk. The boy was so unpredictable. Always asking questions.

Without meaning to, he had her asking herself if all of this was enough.

The classroom. The children. The town.

Normally she answered in the affirmative. Agnes enjoyed teaching. She'd been afraid at first, but now she found great joy and purpose in it, and when the school day ended, she didn't mind the quiet of her home. She'd woven herself into the fabric of the town, serving and loving the townsfolk and making a life for herself in Penance. Why did sweet, baby-faced Tommy have to ask her those questions? For six years she'd fought to accept her lot and make peace with her choice to come to the Black Hills of the Dakota Territory. Leaving had been for the best. And her life here was good. So, why wouldn't the familiar ache go away?

Tommy's question plagued her long after she left the schoolroom. *Spinster. Spinster.* She heard his voice say the word over and over again in her mind. *Spinster.* Someday she'd accept the title. After all, it was merely the natural consequence of her choice. It meant unmarried, did it not?

After arriving home, she sat at her small table and busied herself by making plans for the next day's lessons. First, she decided which sums she'd begin the day with, then she went to work on a reading lesson. As she reviewed the plans, she realized a poem was needed to help break up the monotony, so she found one she hoped would make the children laugh.

Her orange cat, Tiger, rubbed his body against her leg. He purred as he pressed his thick coat against her. Giving in to his demands, she picked him up and held him in her lap. The dear old cat had been her companion even before she'd made the rash but necessary decision to leave her lavish life for a more primitive one in the West.

"That Tommy Smith and his questions! He sure knows how to knock me off my feet." She laughed as she petted the cat's creamy orange hair, and he squirmed and pressed his body closer to her. A low purr earned him a smile. "You like that, don't you? You always have. Even when you were just a kitten."

"Do you remember James?" She shook her head, trying to knock the wistful longing from her heart. "I know I shouldn't complain. But I do wonder sometimes if there could have been a way for things to be different." Tiger looked at her. His eyes had seen so much. They knew her story, unlike her friends in Penance, who only knew that she'd come seeking a job. "It wouldn't have been fair to James though. You know it has to be this way, don't you?" She sighed. "It doesn't matter anyway. I'm sure he's married and probably has a dark-haired baby or two. One that looks just like him, with a solid jaw and dark brows. And I'm a teacher. I've my students to brighten my days." She scratched Tiger's ears. "It's a good ending for us all." She scratched harder. "But if Tommy calls me a spinster again, I might have to take a switch to him."

Upon hearing the word *switch*, Tiger jumped down and ran away.

"I was only playing. You know I could never strike that precocious child. But I've been tempted. You can't blame me for that. You would understand if you had to answer all his questions."

Tiger's long tail swayed behind him as he slunk beneath a chair and turned away from her. She thought of going after him but stopped herself. Daylight would be gone soon, and she still needed to hang her wash, iron, and fix a meal. Work, she'd learned, was a blessing most people failed to acknowledge.

Determined to keep the children busy, Agnes overprepared for class the next day. The students moved from one activity to the next like a wheel in perpetual motion, so busy they had no time for flippant questions. It was Friday, and by Monday everyone would have forgotten Miss Aggie's status as an independent spinster, or so she hoped.

"Are you coming to our house to eat Saturday night?" Ruby Lawrence asked at the end of the day. "I've been looking forward to it all week." Ruby's name fit her perfectly. She had the fairest skin, but her cheeks were always ruby red no matter the weather.

"Of course I'm coming. I hardly ever miss our Saturday reading time." Agnes smiled at the excited eight-year-old. Ruby belonged to her dearest friend, Hannah, and although Agnes would never admit she had a favorite student, she could never deny that Ruby possessed a special place in her heart.

"Will you bring some of your books with you?" Ruby picked up a piece of chalk and returned it to the tray on the blackboard. "The ones with the pictures?"

"Would you like me to?"

"Yes! I can only remember living here in Penance. I know I lived somewhere else before, but I was little. When I look at those pictures, I can imagine other places." Ruby crossed the floor to her lunch tin. During the day the children kept them near the back of the room where they hung their coats. "Do you miss the city? I'd love to see the tall buildings and go to a store that sells nothing but candy. I'd love to wear a fancy dress and go to a dance. It must have been the most exciting place to live."

"I miss things about it. People, mostly. But there are things I don't miss too." Agnes thought a moment before speaking again. "Ruby, it doesn't matter so much where you live as how you live. And even though I do miss things, I love being a teacher and I'm needed here. You'll understand someday how good it feels to know you're needed. Just the other day, I was able to watch Beth Higley's baby so she could rest, and I help Old McHenry haul water. I am glad I am here to help and to teach all my students."

Ruby looked perplexed. Finally, shaking her head, she said, "I don't like hauling water, but I like babies and I like McHenry's stories. I'm awful glad you decided to come here even if you did have to leave the big city. Clara told me that in her old town, before she moved here, she had a teacher who kept a switch by his desk and found a reason to use it every day. I don't think I'd like school one bit if you were like that."

"I've also heard tales of such teachers. But I'll never use the switch." The very thought sent a shiver down her spine. The children were far too dear to her to ever strike. She cupped her hand by her mouth and whispered, "I've a confession. I'm afraid of the switch myself. All the threats I've ever made were far from earnest. I'm not sure I'd be brave enough to use it."

Ruby giggled. "You're very brave. You came all the way across the country without any family. I'd never be that brave. I still get scared at night sometimes, but I know I'm not alone like you. I think you're the bravest around to live all by yourself." Ruby's eyes grew big when she spoke. "Were your teachers nice when you were little? Did they use a switch?"

"I had tutors who came to my house. My mother would not have tolerated my being swatted or switched, but I do remember a few who rarely smiled." Agnes put a hand on the girl's shoulder. "You better get going. Don't want your mama worrying."

Before stepping through the door, Ruby said, "Tommy is

right. You're real beautiful. I wish I had your auburn curls. My hair is so straight."

"But your cheeks are always rosy, and your eyes are the bluest blue." She nudged Ruby toward the door. "I suppose we're all beautiful in our own way. Hurry home before your mama comes looking for you."

CHAPTER TWO

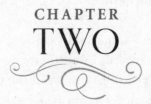

The Lawrences lived outside of town a little over a mile into the hills. It would have been a quick ride, but with the weather so fair, Agnes walked, taking her time and enjoying the spring flowers and gentle breeze. The stubby evergreens displayed bright new growth on the tips of each branch as birds sang from their lofty boughs, and through the trees she caught a glimpse of deer nibbling the spring bounty. Agnes savored the walk, grateful she could flee to this lovely place.

Ruby's father, Joshua, worked hard in the mines. Four years ago, he'd moved to Penance with his family, hoping to find steady work. They'd come late in the season, weary and dirty from their travels. Somehow, he had found the time to not only build his family a sturdy cabin but also cultivate their piece of earth and build a barn for the animals.

Agnes had watched Ruby while Hannah worked with Joshua to prepare for their first winter in the territory. The small gesture had bonded Agnes and Hannah, proving that time and sacrifice could produce love and friendship.

"Ruby, are your chores done so you can sit and read?" Agnes yelled to Ruby when she poked her head above the garden fence. Dirt and sweat adorned her cheeks, yet her rosy hue still shone through. They waved at each other, both smiling. "I've brought the books I promised. They're in my pack."

"I'm done now. Mama said I could wash up and come in as soon as you arrived. I was hoping you would show up earlier. I wouldn't have had to weed the peas then." Ruby brushed her hands on her apron as she walked toward Agnes. "I'm glad you're here."

"I wouldn't miss it. Do you want to read inside or outside?" Agnes looked toward the log they often sat on. Joshua easily could have made it into firewood, but he left it for Ruby.

"Inside. I think Mama likes to listen while she works."

"Wonderful idea." Agnes reached out to Ruby as they headed to the house. "Come along."

Simple furniture made from Black Hills timber filled the main room—a table with one long bench on each side and two chairs in front of the fireplace. Even with all the rich brown of the wood, the family had found a way to make the small room bright. Ruby's school projects were on the wall next to finely stitched samplers. Rag rugs adorned the floor, each handmade and filled with bits and pieces of memories woven into the fabric. Pink from a dress of Ruby's, blue from baby Grace's faded blanket, yellow from a well-worn skirt of Hannah's.

"Aggie, you've saved Ruby from the weeds!" Hannah said

from beside the stove where she stood stirring a pot. "No doubt she was glad."

"I'm told I should have come earlier." Agnes breathed in the hearty smell of simmering soup, causing her mouth to water in eager expectancy. "Smells delicious. Need any help?"

Hannah shook her head. "Go ahead and read with Ruby. She tells me it is her favorite part of the week."

"Very well. Holler if you need me." Agnes and Ruby sat in the chairs near the empty fireplace. They pulled them close together so they could both look at the pictures in the book. Agnes projected her voice loud enough so Hannah could hear. After three long stories, her mouth felt dry. "It's your turn now," she said to Ruby as she handed her a thin book with easier words. "Remember, I don't mind if you stumble over words. Just try your best."

The little girl made a face but took the book and began. Slowly she made her way through the story. When the call for supper came, Agnes heard Ruby sigh.

"It's so hard." She closed the book and handed it back.

"It'll get easier. Don't give up. One day we will read together, and the words will come easily. I've a feeling once you take off, we'll have to beg you to pull your nose from the books." Agnes put an arm around her. "You can do this."

"I wish it weren't so hard."

"I know. But just because something is hard doesn't mean we should give up. Sometimes the hardest things are the very best things. I think hearing you read a whole book with no errors will be all the sweeter because you've had to struggle to get there."

"I won't give up." She leaned in to Agnes's embrace. "But I do want to."

"That is a sentiment I can understand. When I first came to Penance, sometimes I wanted to curl up and cry. I didn't think I'd ever fit in here, and now it's home. Reading will come. I know it will."

"Come on, you two," Hannah called. "Sit at the table. I've fixed us a feast."

Joshua came in from outside for supper. He hung his hat on the hook near the door and brushed off the dust that had settled on his shoulders. He smiled a greeting at them all before crossing the room to Hannah and giving her a swift kiss on the cheek. Each week a bittersweet sting settled deeper into Agnes's heart as she watched them together. Hannah, Joshua, and Ruby had one another. Indeed, she was happy for them. A home full of warmth and love had once been her fondest dream. A dream that tapped on its thick cage within her, begging to be set free as she sat in the warmth of the Lawrences' cabin.

"I went by Grace's grave." Joshua's deep voice pulled Agnes from her reverie. She watched as Joshua's eyes found Hannah's. "I added a few stones. I wanted to make sure it was covered well."

Hannah's face paled. "That was good of you."

"I'm sorry, I know it's hard to talk about." Agnes watched as Joshua rubbed his thumb back and forth over Hannah's knuckles. "I thought you'd want to know."

"I'm glad you told me." Hannah's face puckered like it always did when she was reminded of her loss. "I'll sleep better knowing it."

An uncomfortable silence filled the room. Rarely were there lulls in conversation unless Grace was mentioned. They ate slowly, but Agnes tasted little as she remembered the family's loss. Even Ruby sat in stoic silence. It'd not been long ago that the silence would have been filled with Grace's happy gurgling. Agnes's eyes wandered to where the baby should be sitting. She imagined Grace's once-plump arms waving at the family or flinging food as she ate. There was a hollowness where she should have been. Why, Agnes asked herself, must there be so much heartache and loss? But she knew why—pain and longing were the only possible by-products of a heart torn from one it had bonded to.

Eventually, the meal ended, and the dishes were washed and put away. Joshua stepped toward his wife. "I got everything done outside. Why don't you and Aggie take a walk. Ruby and I will cause some mischief here while you're gone."

Hannah met Joshua's gaze and gave a silent nod. A moment later, the two women left the small cabin and set out through the hills together, meandering among the wildflowers and rocky crags. The paths were well worn from their many nights strolling together in the hills.

"Joshua's trying so hard to make everything right. He's always been so good to me, but especially since we lost Grace." Hannah sighed. "It still hurts so badly. I wake up and walk to her bed to check on her. And she's never there."

Agnes put a hand on her friend's back. "You were a good mother to her."

"It's always empty, and I hurt all over again." With a tight smile on her face, she continued. "But then I look around and remember I have Ruby and Joshua. I tell myself to be thankful for the good I still have. But sometimes I feel like I cannot breathe."

Grappling for words, Agnes wished she knew a way to make it right. Since coming to Penance, she'd found a great deal of confidence and strength, but she still did not understand many things. "I wish she could come back so you could hold her."

With tears in her eyes, Hannah pointed. "Look there. I haven't seen merrybells yet this year." She stopped and picked the dainty flower. "When Grace was first born, Joshua said her hair looked this color. She didn't have a lot of it, but so much more than Ruby had as a baby. It was enough that we marveled over it." She held the flower to her heart. "Lately, I've felt like God's telling me she is well and free of her pain. I don't doubt she's found peace. My faith is firm. But I long to hold her. I ache for it." Tucking the flower into her pocket, Hannah brightened. "Let's show Ruby the flower. I'll have more aches and burdens to carry if I miss my chance to make her smile. And you ought to tell me any news you have. I want to hear it."

They turned back toward the house, walking slowly as they went. "I've just been teaching, and I've gone to help McHenry a couple times a week. The poor man can't get around well with his leg broken. He entertains me with his stories." She brushed a loose hair from her face. "I took Joshua's advice and asked Sam Landon to make some repairs on the schoolhouse. Maybe next term I won't worry that the wind will blow the school down."

"We wouldn't want you blowing away." Hannah laughed. Then she grew serious. "Joshua speaks highly of Sam. Seems he's a good man."

"He seems nice enough. I've only talked to him a handful of times." She shrugged. "He's just another logger."

"I don't think all loggers and miners are the same." Hannah spoke softly. "It might not hurt you to try to discover the differences in some of them. Or at least one of them. Sam, for instance, is quiet but seems thoughtful."

"I'm sure he'll do fine work on the schoolhouse. That's all I need to know about him."

Hannah opened her mouth, then closed it. In the gentlest of ways, Hannah had tried to open Agnes's mind and heart to the possibility of finding love in Penance. Each time Agnes rejected the efforts, wishing she were brave enough to tell Hannah everything about her past, but she understood enough about the way the world worked to know that it'd do no good.

Agnes stopped walking and looked toward the horizon. "When I'd been here a week, Laurel's family invited me to supper. I went thinking they wanted to get to know me, and perhaps they did, but I believe more than anything they wanted me to meet their uncle Charles." She cringed. Charles had poor manners and worse hygiene. He'd been bold and put his arm around her. She shivered even now. "It's been constant ever since. Everyone is always trying to be a matchmaker. I politely tell them I'm committed to teaching, and at first I could tell them my contract did not allow me to marry for at least a year. Even now it says I'd have to give up my position if I married. I can't have teaching and a family. I think everyone ought to be content having me teach."

"No one doubts you're a good teacher." Hannah picked another flower. "Joshua is a good man, and he's a miner. They may not all be revolting. You could court a few and have your pick. There must be a good man out there. I know you love teaching and you've done well with it, but a family—"

"You sound like Minnie." Agnes laughed. Minnie had

endeared herself to Agnes despite her nosey and overbearing nature, but she certainly didn't need two friends foisting their opinions on her. "She found me after school yesterday and told me I just had to meet the new doctor. She said he looked like a Grecian god. You should have heard her." Agnes rolled her eyes. "I told her I found it highly unlikely a man like that would move to Penance, but even if he did, I didn't want him. Too bad she's married to Lem, or I could tell her to chase the doctor around town."

"Lem's a patient man." Hannah grinned. "I know you've said it before, but will you really never want anyone? Don't you want a family, children?"

An ache seized her chest. Babies, with their little toes and sweet-smelling hair, had always called to her. She'd yearned to hold a child and know she didn't have to give him back to his mother's waiting arms. She blinked quickly. "I like babies well enough. Minnie's expecting another one. That'll be nine. Can you imagine? I'll have to go hold one of hers when I get an itching to."

Hannah shook her head. "We tried so long for another baby after Ruby. We felt blessed when Grace came, but now she's gone. Seems unfair that Minnie has so many." She covered her mouth. "I'm sorry. That was callous of me. Minnie can have all the babies she wants. All babies are blessings. I should not have said that."

"Don't fret over it. I've thought plenty of the same thoughts before. I find myself wondering how it is that one woman's trial is to have a baby a year and another's is to have years of yearning."

"Nonetheless. I should be more charitable. Forgive me?"

Agnes nodded. "Of course."

"Let's get you back before it's dark. After you meet the doctor, you'll have to tell me if he truly looks like a Grecian god or if Minnie's just spinning one of her tales again."

"If I were the betting type, I'd wager that she's just enjoying all the excitement and hasn't stopped flitting about long enough to take a good look."

Agnes's and Hannah's laughter mixed together as they walked arm in arm back to the cabin where they parted ways—Hannah to her family and Agnes to her empty home. As she walked among the trees and flora, she did all she could to focus on the world around her and not on babies and beaus.

CHAPTER THREE

James Harris let out a deep and audible sigh as he unloaded a second box of supplies into the one small cabinet at the back of the office. He let the empty crate fall to the ground. There wouldn't be room for everything he needed in this tiny space, but he'd find a way to make it work. He let out another sigh. Penance was going to be his home—not forever, but for now.

A City Destined for Greatness Nestled in the Heart of the Black Hills, the newspaper had read. The latter was true. They were surrounded by hills, but he wasn't convinced any pending greatness existed. Still, with no competing doctors in town, he would get to hone his skills without anyone looking over his shoulder. Someday he would return East to civilization, refinement, and familiarity. In fact, if things went according to plan, he'd head back with more than what he'd arrived with.

He opened the last crate and found a few textbooks, several rolls of bandages, and his old journals. Holding one of the thick leather journals in his hand, he wondered anew why he hadn't left them back in Buffalo. Perhaps it was because writing in them had always brought a bit of peace and leaving them would have felt like leaving his sanity behind.

He flipped through one of the thick volumes, scouring the pages for something, anything that felt like home.

September 18, 1869

The boys dared me to walk through Forest Lawn Cemetery today. I didn't like going, but I didn't let them see that. I just smiled and tried to look brave. I walked right past them and heard George whisper that he thought I wouldn't take the dare. Once inside, I started thinking about dying and began wishing I hadn't gone in. Even now I keep thinking about it. Once I came out, I told the boys it was not scary, but it was. I left them and ran next door to see if girls were afraid of dying too. Aggie said she wasn't afraid of dying, just of not living. I don't know what she meant, but I was glad she didn't tease me.

Now I'm sitting here wondering what things I want to do with my life. I've never thought much about it. I figured I'd grow up and do the same things as Father does. Maybe I won't though. Maybe I'll do something different.

Closing the book, he laughed. At fourteen he'd had no idea how his life would play out. Eleven years later, he was nowhere near Buffalo or his father.

He glanced once more around his little clinic, with its bare table and small cabinet, then he stepped outside into the bright sunlight. Blinking his eyes, he tried to help them adjust. When they did, he noticed several people on the street staring in his direction. Openly gawking, one man even pointed. Looking behind him, he saw nothing unusual. It had to be him they were staring at. His clothes were all in order, nothing was amiss there. Running a hand along his broad jaw, he felt his smooth skin. He'd recently shaved, and he felt no missed spots. His dark hair was combed. He'd even spent extra time smoothing down the stubborn patch at the crown of his head that always tried to reach for the sky. Shrugging, he grabbed his trusted medical bag, just in case, and headed to the mayor's home where he was due for supper.

"The town is buzzing about your arrival," Mayor Paul Clint said after welcoming him inside. "Everywhere I turn, someone is talking about the new big-city doctor."

"I have noticed a bit of a stir."

"It's not every day we get someone so exotic in town." Mayor Clint led the way to the dining room, where his wife and children were already seated and waiting. He made brief introductions as he and James took their seats, then continued with his conversation. "You're from a place different in most every way from Penance."

"Buffalo is hardly exotic."

"To these backwoods folks it is. Some of these people have never lived anywhere with more than one main street. What part of New York is Buffalo in?"

"Western, where the winter lasts half the year. It's on Lake Erie, near the canal." Just the mention of the city filled James's mind with images of home. Of the more-than-comfortable brick houses, the rows and rows of shops that sold anything a person could possibly need. The trees with their leaves that changed colors four times before falling.

And of course, he thought of the snow. "It's a fine place, despite the winter."

"Well, you're here now and that's what matters. We're mighty glad you answered the committee's advertisement for a doctor. We got more than we had hoped for with you." Mayor Clint sat back deeper into his chair. He ran his fingers over his short mustache. "If you don't mind me asking, what about the job appealed to you?"

"It's hard to say what it was that drew me here. Wasn't the name. That much I'm sure of." He laughed, hoping his joke would keep them from digging too deep for his motives. "Buffalo, and any big city, has a certain appeal, I won't deny that. I suppose I want to stretch my legs a bit before I settle down."

"Stretch your legs, huh? I'm not sure I like the sound of that. We'll have to do our best to convince you to stay here. What do you think?" He smiled at his children. "What could we do to keep the doctor in town?"

The two little girls shrugged.

"Maybe a Penance bride will do the trick." Mayor Clint laughed.

"Paul!" Rose Clint, the mayor's wife, said with her eyebrows raised. "No matchmaking. Leave the man alone."

"It's all right, Rose. Finding a doctor is not easy. I'm willing to do what it takes to keep him around."

James set down his fork. "I heard women were being recruited too. I figured that meant you had a bit of a shortage."

"That's the truth. There were a few years when I could go weeks without seeing a skirt other than Rose's. It's changed some, but it won't settle down around here until we marry up a few more of these miners. But don't you worry about the competition. We've a few selective ladies who think they're a bit too good for a miner or a lumberjack. I think they're waiting around for someone a little more refined." The mayor pointed at him. "Someone like you."

James squirmed in his seat. He'd only recently left his mother and her persistent attempts to find him a suitable match. He didn't need the mayor taking over that role. Besides, he had his own plans for his heart. "For now, I just want to hear about Penance. You can only learn so much from a one-column advertisement. If this is to be my home, I ought to know a thing or two about it."

"This town hasn't been around long. I know because I was one of the first to settle these Black Hills. Just a few years back, in the late sixties, we decided to get this place running. Mostly miners, we had a bit of gold fever for a few years, and now we have lumberjacks swarming in too. But businessmen are coming, wanting their piece of it all." Mayor Clint reached for a serving bowl and piled his plate with potatoes and vegetables. "I think this place might become something yet."

"Why Penance? Why not name it something a little more pleasant sounding?"

"Well, we were all sitting around one night. A whole table of us old-timers talking about the hard first years, how we should have all left long ago. We decided we'd done our penance and it was time for this town to take off. We started laughing about blizzards that came out of nowhere, hailstorms that wiped out our meager crops, and the lack of women. The more we talked, the more we liked the sound of it. We figured anyone moving out here would have to have a sense of humor. If they can't laugh about the name, they probably don't have the kind of spirit it takes to make it in these hills. And after all these years, we feel like our penance, those hard years, have paid off and were worth it. It may be small and rough around the edges, but it's a good place."

James thought about his own penance. The lonely, miserable penance he'd been inflicting on himself. Maybe in this rugged place he'd finally be able to put it all behind him. "I aim to be one of those who can make it here. If I leave, it won't be because the land was too rough. Tell me more. What all've you got in Penance?"

"Well, we got saloons. I'm sure you've seen them. These men seem to think the way to survive Penance is by drinking. It's my hope some God-fearing women will tame the lot of them." With that, Mayor Clint picked up his glass and gulped down the liquid inside. "Rose isn't keen on drinking, so it's water for me."

James grimaced. Penance wasn't the only place where men drank to get through life. He'd seen it his whole life. There had been nights he'd longed to join them.

Clint kept talking. "Then there's the usual places—dry goods, mercantile, saddlery. Same as you've got back in Buffalo, only not so many and not so grand. And now we've got a few women coming in, even some families and children. The single women either take a job at the saloon or they marry up with a bachelor."

James cut in then. "Better not try to line me up with a saloon girl. My kin would disown me over that." Suddenly embarrassed that he had said such a thing with children around, he looked to Rose Clint. "I'm sorry, ma'am. I spoke out of turn."

"These children have spent their lives around rough

workingmen. No apology needed," the mayor answered for his wife. "We'll find you a bride, one way or the other."

One of the little girls looked up from her meal and said, "What about Miss Aggie? She's not married."

Rose said softly, "That's enough. Miss Aggie is a fine woman, and if she decides to marry, she'll manage on her own." Rose turned to James. "She's our schoolteacher. She's a lovely woman."

"Not Aggie." Clint wiped his face but didn't do a thorough job and potatoes clung to the tip of his mustache. "Finding a teacher is about as hard as finding a doctor. If he convinces Miss Aggie to marry him, I'll have to replace her too."

Aggie Pratt. James set down his fork, his throat tight—so tight he wasn't sure he could swallow a bite until the strange feeling went away. Of course they knew her. She lived here, among these people. Still, the sound of her name on their lips sent his heart racing.

Rose passed the rolls around the table. "She's from back East like yourself. I can't remember for certain which city. She's been here so long I hardly remember her coming, and she's not one to talk of the past."

"No one cares about the past here." Clint tore a piece of his bread and wiped his plate with it. "Half this town is running from something. She could be too. We're just glad she's here."

"This town has plenty of upstanding people, and Agnes is one of them." Rose's voice was soft and kind.

Clearing his throat, James hoped his voice would stay steady. "I'll be sure to stop in and say hello. I'd like to meet everyone if I can."

James ate in silence, looking from his food to the window to avoid eye contact with anyone who might suspect he shared a history with Aggie Pratt. Desperately, he searched for something else, anything besides Aggie to talk about. How was it she still had such a hold on him? It had been six years since he'd seen her face.

From the window he saw miners with grimy faces wandering the street. One man walked heavily to one side. A limp from an injury, or perhaps he'd walked that way since birth. "Do you have much call for medicine?"

"More than we'd like. Usually small injuries. Cuts, burns. But we've had big losses too."

"I'll do what I can to keep that from happening again. You can count on that."

"I expect no less, and these people deserve no less." Clint stopped eating, and his voice took on a serious tone. "These people are my people. They may not have old money or grand mansions, but they matter. You remember that when you look in their eyes."

"I will."

With a full stomach and a weary body, James reclined on his lumpy mattress and stared at the ceiling of the little room above the clinic. Rough wooden beams adorned in cobwebs and dust met his gaze. The wind raged outside the thin walls, howling as it went. James listened, searching for a pattern, looking to see if any sense could be made of it. Often over the last few years he had searched for his own direction. Wondering if life would ever feel right again. Was there rhyme or reason to any of it?

But now he was here in Penance, and he had to believe the Lord had a hand in it. Aggie Pratt resided here, in this very town. Somewhere out there the same howling wind pricked her ears. The same sky painted with stars was above them. It was the first time in a very long time that they shared the same sights and sounds. Had her life found a pattern, or did she, too, struggle to navigate the chaos? Would she want to see him? In his dreams she always did. He had so many questions. So many things he yearned to know, so much he *needed* to know.

Rolling onto his side, he grasped his pillow, balled it up, and shoved it under his neck. He was this close to her, this close to the answers he sought. Soon enough he'd find the right way to approach her, then perhaps the hole in his heart could finally heal.

CHAPTER FOUR

Dear Father,

Spring is upon us in Penance, and it has me thinking of spring in Buffalo. I can almost smell the fresh air and see the white world slowly give way to luscious green. I long to go back in time somehow, to before. Isn't that a lovely thought? Lovely and tragic all at the same time. I know that it'd never be the same and I'd never feel the same ease there as I once did, but I'd be near you.

Most of the time I am happy here. And yet at other times I'm not. If I had not left, I would have been there when Mother died. I could have learned how to make her orange rolls and asked her to push me on the swing one more time. The other night I dreamed we were all together and she was singing her silly song about birds in the treetops. I'd love to put my arms around her and tell her my fondest dream is to be good like her.

I did not set out to write you a sad letter. I suppose we all have melancholy days when we want to change our lot. Don't worry over me. I am well and my days are full. I want you to smile when you read my words. Truly, I am happy.

I will tell you the news around town. We've a new doctor. I've not met him, but I am grateful he's come. The town needs more than McHenry to take care of their needs. He does not know the latest treatments and medical thinking. Minnie has already decided the doctor is the man for me. No doubt you can picture the sort of busybody she is from my many letters. I told her I had no interest in the doctor and was content teaching. Even if I felt inclined to care for the doctor, he's from back East and no doubt thinks the same way as the sort I ran from.

I've kept busy with the schoolchildren. They are memorizing poetry for their upcoming afternoon of recitations. I already feel so proud of them, and they've not even performed. I've spent the little free time I have with Hannah. She's doing better, though the ache in her heart is still there, I am sure of it. I can see her reaching for happiness, but there's a shadow of sadness about her. Sorrow, I fear, is a plague that cannot be avoided, only navigated.

Write me and tell me your news.

Your daughter,
Aggie

Agnes folded and sealed her letter. Then she pressed her lips to it, hoping with all of her being that the love she felt would travel the long road to her father.

She made her way into the heart of town. With any luck she'd catch the mail coach, and her somber words could begin their journey across the beautiful and vast land that separated her from her beloved father and the world she'd once called her own.

Agnes slowed her swift gait when she neared the mercantile. Warren and Osa, the town's only twins, ran outside to greet her.

"Hello, Miss Aggie!" Osa shouted much louder than necessary. "Mama let me and Warren buy a piece of penny candy because it's our birthday tomorrow. We're going to be seven."

Warren held out his piece for her to see. The little peppermint stick sat on his dirty palm. "I'm just licking mine. I want it to last."

"How wise to savor it." Agnes put a hand on a shoulder of each child. "I hope tomorrow is very special for you."

"Every year on our birthday Mama makes us flapjacks, and instead of them being plain circles, she makes them into little shapes." Osa danced around as she talked. "I hope mine is a horse. I love horses."

"That is something very special. You will have to report to me on Monday and tell me what they looked like."

"We will," Warren said before taking another tiny lick of his dirty candy.

"Did your mama make your birthday special?" Osa stopped prancing around long enough to look at her.

The lavish birthdays she'd celebrated as a child flashed through her mind. The gifts and the food. The guests and the ball gowns. Such warm memories. She smiled down at the children. "Just like your mama, mine tried to make me feel like a queen."

Osa smiled brightly, boasting missing teeth and a pink gumline. "I'm glad. I think birthdays are my favorite days. Even better than Christmas."

"And you are very lucky to get to share it with your brother. Better give me a quick hug. The next time I see you, you'll be so old that you might not want to."

"We won't be too old," they both said.

Warren looked toward the store and groaned. "Mama said she'd hurry, but she always takes a long time in the store. I think she's talking to Charlotte's mama."

Osa nodded. "They always talk forever."

Agnes put a finger on her chin. "When I was a little girl, there was a boy who lived right next door to me. We saw each other every day. When my friend and I had to wait for something, we would play a game called I'm Going to the Moon."

Osa laughed. "Sounds ridiculous. No one could ever go to the moon."

"It does seem unbelievable. But imagining such things is exciting. Let me tell you the rules. Listen careful, I've a feeling you'll like it and it'll help pass the time." They listened attentively. "One person is the leader and gets to decide a commonality for the things that come to the moon while the others must put the clues together to discover what they have that is alike."

The children nodded as she explained the rules. Then they played a round together. Agnes kept it simple so the children could feel the satisfaction of solving a puzzle. Clapping her hands, she declared, "You're right. Only things that started with the letter *P* could come. Now, Warren, since you guessed it, you think up one."

When they were thoroughly engrossed in the next round, she left them to the game and walked away with memories rolling about inside of her. Memories of hot, humid summer afternoons spent lying on her back in the thick green grass. James beside her. Both looking at the cloudless blue sky. Taking turns leading round after round of I'm Going to the Moon. Their game only ending when the waiting ceased or one of them became so stumped by a clue, they lost their patience or their temper. Remembering their feisty disputes brought a genuine smile to her face. Oh, how the two of them could go at each other. As a child she'd been timid at times but never with him.

Yet no matter how fierce the words between them, they always came back together. Well, they always had, until she'd left.

Agnes grasped the letter tighter, reminding herself of her purposes for being in town.

"Agnes!" loud and overzealous Minnie shouted as she bounced down the street toward her. "Agnes!"

Pretending she hadn't heard, Agnes took another step. Since the doctor had arrived, Minnie had become preoccupied with matchmaking, and Agnes wanted none of it. Eventually, she would have to meet the man, she knew that. But she was in no hurry to do so. Better to let someone else snatch him up first. It made no difference to her.

"Agnes!" Minnie stepped near her, her breathing heavy due to the quickening of her pace.

Admitting defeat, she turned. "Hi, Minnie."

"The new doctor's here talking to Lem and a few others. We spotted him leaving his office." Minnie waved her hands in front of her face. It did no good, and her face remained flushed and wet with perspiration. "I want to introduce him to you. You've got to see him."

"Perhaps I'll say hello another time." Agnes looked down the road for the mail coach. She didn't see it.

"Come and meet him," Minnie pleaded. "Just one little look. It won't hurt anything."

"I already told you how I felt about meeting the new doctor," Agnes snapped. "If I break a bone, I promise I'll call on him. Until then, I have other things to do. I don't care to gawk at the man. Let it be."

Minnie took a step back as though Agnes's words had assaulted her. "I know you think you're too good for marriage, but I didn't realize you were above *meeting* someone new. Can't even say hello to a stranger." She put her hands on her large hips. "Weren't you the one who gave us all a lecture on welcoming newcomers, being kind to everyone? Better eat the cake you served and go welcome him. You wanted a doctor here as bad as the rest of us."

Agnes fought to keep herself from slumping in discouragement. She wasn't above any of it. Why must Minnie push so incessantly? "Fine," she barked back. "I'll meet him. I'll go say hello. I'll thank him for the skills he brings, but then you leave it be. No matchmaking. No scheming."

Minnie, a victorious smile on her face, grabbed her arm and pulled her toward the crowd. "I knew you would come," she whispered. "I just knew you couldn't resist. You won't be sorry, not in the least."

Agnes rolled her eyes but continued walking. Arriving at the outskirts of the group, she peered between the shoulders of the two large men who stood in front of her. Through the gap she caught glimpses of the esteemed doctor. Dark hair, expensive suit. A gold chain hung from his pocket. A big-city boy. Perhaps his fancy duds and slicked hair won him admittance into society's finer circles, but here they simply meant he was unseasoned. He wouldn't last. Not out here. Pomp and arrogance did not ensure survival. He'd turn tail and run back to the ease of the East. It was only a matter of time. She folded her arms across her chest. It wouldn't be long, and the town would be doctorless again.

The man in front of her stepped away, and her view opened. Her breath caught in her chest. *It's impossible. It can't be him*. Heat rose to her face. Above the expensive suit rested the face of James. The handsome, beautiful face of the man she'd loved. Her heart beat wildly, faster than she'd ever felt it beat before. Penance, with its clapboard buildings and dirt streets, began to spin.

It can't be James. She pressed a hand to her head, trying to slow the thudding she felt within. James, her James, wasn't a doctor. He was back in Buffalo following in his father's footsteps, wasn't he? Her mind struggled to believe what her eyes saw and her heart felt.

Staring dumbfounded, she watched as James Harris interacted with *her* people. His dark hair fell across his forehead as he bent low to talk to an old woman. He pushed it away with the same strong hands she'd held so often. Then he smiled at the woman and the small dimple to the right of his lip showed. Over the last six years, she'd often wondered if she'd still know him if their paths were to cross. And now there he stood. She'd know that smile anywhere. He was a little broader through the shoulders than he'd been in her memories, but he was the same James Harris.

Certain now that the man before her was James, she clutched her letter to her heart and fled.

"Agnes, wait," Minnie called after her. This time Agnes did not acknowledge her friend. She only moved faster, weaving around miners, past loggers, around any obstacle in her path.

Struggling to think clearly, she looked to her left and right, then dashed toward the school.

"You been doctoring long? Cause if you have, you probably seen what I got," a man to James's right said. "I got a mighty bad rash along my stomach you're gonna wanna take a look at. It's been festering, and it itches something awful." The man started untucking his shirt right there under the overhang of James's clinic.

James stopped the man, appalled that he would undress in front of women. "I'll gladly take a look at it inside the clinic. Why don't you come back later this afternoon?"

The man nodded before shoving his shirttail back into his pants. "So, how long you been doctorin'?"

"This is my first position," James answered honestly. Several muted whispers resonated around him. "But I was in the top of my class," he added quickly. "We treated many patients at the hospitals in the city while we trained."

"Well, new or not, he's got to be better'n Old McHenry. Probably ain't so funny, though, and not so cheap," a dirty-faced woman with an eye patch said.

A younger woman with a clean dress and easy smile spoke above the din. "I think it's a fine thing that you've chosen our town." Her words saved him from acknowledging the previous comment.

"I'm glad to be here," he responded, even though everything in him questioned his decision. Glancing around, he wondered how long he needed to visit before he could break free and search for Aggie. He'd decided only the night before to forgo waiting for the perfect opportunity and go find her. He'd waited long enough. His nerves, his fears, they were not reasons to hesitate. He'd been in town days already. He wanted to see Aggie.

A sudden movement caught his eye. Looking up, he saw a woman quickly dart away from the group. Alarmed, he continued to watch her, trying to sense what she ran from.

"Agnes, wait," another woman called, then threw her arms out, huffed, and walked in the opposite direction.

Agnes! His Aggie? Could it be?

"Excuse me." He tried to part the crowd. "I have to go."

His eyes and then his feet followed the familiar auburn curls, knowing but not caring that the gaggle of people would be talking to his back.

With his heart racing, he sped to close the gap between himself and Aggie. Her gait, her figure, all of her was so familiar, it was almost as though time had not stolen so many years from them and they were merely playing a game of chase. She beat him to the schoolhouse and disappeared within its walls.

For a moment, he stood there. The wooden door was inches from his forehead, so close he could see the patterns of the wood grain. He wondered what to do. What to say. A shiver raced through him. Years of wondering, and now in a matter of moments he would see her, he would have answers. Perhaps he'd touch her. The wondering would end. The distance would vanish.

One deep breath later, he had his hand on the knob. He twisted, then with gusto he shoved it open.

Aggie stood on the far side of the schoolroom, a hand pressed against her heart. Words escaped him. All his planned speeches were gone. His limbs were weak, but his eyes were awake and well. They took in the sight of her, the reality of her presence, the beauty of her person. Then they met her gaze. The same almond eyes he knew so well were looking back at him.

Knowing he had to say something, he opened his mouth, but all that escaped was a soft "Aggie?"

"James?" she answered, her voice as breathless as his own.

No one else had ever said his name the way she did. To his great pleasure, she repeated herself, only softer this time. "James."

All the expressions he loved and missed passed over her face. Surprise turned to happiness and then just as quickly to joy. Too soon it left, replaced with confusion. And then that, too, fled.

He watched her take a deep breath, saw her purse her lips.

"What are you doing here?" she snapped. "What kind of trickery is this? You're not even a doctor."

"Aggie."

"Don't Aggie me." She moved a step closer. "Tell me why you're here. Penance is not exactly a place you happen upon. What are you doing here?"

Battered by her words as soundly as if her hand had struck him, he took a step back. This was not the reunion he'd envisioned. His defenses flared in rebellion. "It's not your town. I'm free to live and go as I please. I'm not tied to anything. I'm here because I answered an advertisement.

And if you'd bothered to correspond with me, you'd know that I am indeed a doctor." He could not suppress the stubborn pride that rose in him. Hurt fueled his words. "I never would have come to this post had I known I'd find you here." As quickly as the lie came, he wished he could pull it back inside. Instead, he pressed on. "I caught on plenty quick that you didn't want to see me when you left without saying goodbye."

A flash of pain crossed her face before she masked it. Six years hadn't changed her all that much. He knew these looks, knew them well. Next, she would stomp her foot, grit her teeth, and start moving around the room in frustration.

"Oh, how could you," she said before stomping a heel on the wooden floor. Then she took a couple steps left and then right as she muttered through her clenched jaw. "This is my home now. I know these people. I love them, and you just show up and think you can weasel your way in as though you're one of them."

He leaned against the wall. Waiting.

"I came here to get away. To start over. And now you show up." Her hands moved as she spoke. Her cheeks flushed a deep crimson. "I don't understand. It's wrong and cruel. I can't live with you in the same town."

"This town needs a doctor. If you love this place so much, you ought to thank me." Ready to put the flames out and move on to the happy part of their reunion, he stepped closer and put a hand on her shoulder. "Stop, Aggie, and listen to me."

She stopped pacing, but her head continued to shake. "No. I can't." Brushing his arm away, she said, "I can't make you go, I know that. But . . . I can't pretend like the last six years didn't happen. Things are different now, but some things are the same. I can't do this."

"Aggie," he pleaded. "Give me a chance. At least talk to me."

Her voice was quiet. "No. Leave." She wouldn't meet his gaze. "Just go."

"What are we to do? Live as though we're strangers and don't share a past?" James shifted until she could not avoid his eyes. "Let's talk. There must be a better answer."

"You don't know me now. And it's obvious I no longer know you. We may as well be strangers." She looked away, but before she did, he thought he saw tears pooling in her eyes. Then her words came soft and slow. "I can't do this. Leave."

"But Aggie."

She buried her face in her hands. "Please. Go."

Narrowing his eyes, he watched her a moment. She didn't waver. Backing away, he made for the door. Suddenly angry, he stomped out, throwing the door back behind him. Hearing it slam, he felt one moment of satisfaction, followed immediately by deep anguish, hurt, and confusion.

"Doctor Harris!" someone shouted.

He didn't care who it was or what they needed. What sort of a doctor was he if he couldn't even fix the one wounded person he so desperately wanted to heal? Head lowered, he walked the back way to his small apartment above the clinic, all the while wishing for a way to somehow reverse time and play the scene again, to do it differently. If he'd had his way, he would have rushed in, taken her in his arms, and told her how he'd come all the way here to be with her, and they could talk about the past and make promises for the future. But time had a cruel way of moving forward, regardless of circumstances. He'd lied. It was uncharacteristic of him. He fought off the remorse that surfaced, telling himself it made no difference. Let her think what she would.

CHAPTER FIVE

"Hannah!" Agnes shouted when she rounded the bend. "Hannah!"

Hannah stepped away from the washing line. "You're here early. Trying to get Ruby out of her chores?"

"Of course not." She clasped her empty hands together, suddenly aware she'd brought no books. She'd planned to deliver her letter, return home for the books, and then come to Hannah's. Desperation had simply moved her feet one step at a time until she'd arrived. Slowing her tread, she asked, "Where's Ruby?"

"She and Joshua decided to see if they could catch anything at the creek. We weren't expecting you so early. Not very ladylike, her fishing, but when you don't have a son . . ." Hannah shrugged. "Come inside. I could use a cool drink. I've been out here for hours."

The warm days of spring had Agnes tugging at her dress,

trying to pry it away from her damp skin. Today seemed extra bad, but maybe it wasn't just the heat that had her perspiring. "I'd like that."

Once inside, the two women sat. "I think it's going to be a hot one this summer. I don't remember the heat ever coming on this strong this early. I'm glad the snow is gone though. I'd take heat over the freezing temperatures."

Agnes stared at the cup in front her. Talk of weather seemed so trivial. She could hardly focus. Hot, cold, it changed nothing.

"You all right, Aggie?"

Agnes took a slow drink of water, hoping she'd know how to explain her woes to her friend. Despite the water, her throat still felt dry. "I came to Penance and left everything behind, and today my worlds came crashing together." She set down her cup and groaned. "You ever wonder if life is working out the way it's supposed to or if it's just some kind of cruel joke?" She wiped the corners of her eyes. "On days like today, and even before, I've sometimes wondered why I've been dealt the hand I have. I feel guilty, but that's the truth. Some days I wonder why. Why was I born where I was when I was? Don't you ever wonder?"

Hannah scrunched up her face as she studied her friend. Then she laughed softly. "I have some days of wondering and some days of contentment. I see Ruby and Joshua, and I think my life is blessed beyond measure. Other days I see the weeds, the laundry, and . . ." Hannah straightened in her seat. "And I think of Grace, and well, those days are harder to make peace with."

"Today is one of my harder days," Agnes said flatly as she pushed back from the table and stood. "I came to Penance because I was certain it was the right choice to make. Today I'm not sure about anything." She paused. "That's not true." She closed her eyes, trying to clear her mind. "I love the children and everyone here, but . . . Well, it's other things. Questions fill my head, and sometimes I want to scream. Or throw myself on the floor like Minnie's youngest always does."

"For my family and many others, you've made a difference. Your contribution to the town has been significant." Hannah put a comforting hand on Agnes's arm. "Perhaps Penance was part of the plan but not all of it?"

"I don't know. I thought this was everything. I can't deny the good things. The friends here have been a gift, and I've learned so much. I see the world differently since coming here. In many ways I've found myself here. But sometimes the past still hovers over me. I've told you about my parents and our home, but I've not dared tell a soul about why I really left. It hurt too much, so I've tried to forget it." Agnes pulled at her tight collar.

"Would it hurt less if you talked about it?"

Agnes walked to the front window and looked out. "I ran because it was the only choice I could make. I was at a crossroads. I could watch the world move on around me or go find my own future." She swallowed. It'd been so long since she'd put a voice to her struggle. She'd locked it up so deeply by the time Hannah had arrived in town, she'd never dredged it up. "There was a man I loved, but it couldn't be. I'm sorry, I should have told you."

"No. Don't say that. If you needed to hold this secret in your heart, there's no need to apologize."

"I pretended it away, but now, today, I remembered it all

so clearly. I remembered the joy and how I adored him. But then the pain I felt when I left came rushing back."

"Why?" Hannah whispered. "Why did you leave a man you loved?"

"I knew his parents would not approve, not if they knew the truth about me. They are the type to hold to tradition, even when they ought not to. It was complicated. But there's no room for understanding when you are one of the wealthiest families in the area—and his family was." She folded her arms across her chest, wishing she could will it all away somehow. "I tried to do what was right. I didn't want him to have to choose between me and everything else." Tears ran down her face. "Will I always be haunted by what might have been?"

Hannah didn't answer right away. She went to Agnes and pulled her close. "I don't know the story, and even if I did, I doubt I could give you an easy answer. Try to have a soft heart toward whatever's ahead. That's how I get through a hard day. I tell myself to pull out the weeds, scrub the laundry, and keep hoping. Because I don't know what's ahead and neither do you. But when we get there, to whatever it is that is next, we have to be ready to welcome it, not scrambling to catch up."

Agnes stood in silence. Was there truth in Hannah's words? Could there be something more ahead for her?

"I'm not the type to pry." Hannah spoke the truth. She'd always been there to listen but had never tried to wrestle words from Agnes that she was reluctant to voice. "I've known you had a story of your own. We all do. Sometimes not talking is the easiest and best way. Other times we need a friend who will listen and not judge us. I'll be your friend no matter what you need." Her eyes soft and kind, Hannah smiled at Agnes. "Heaven knows you've listened to my troubles." At the mention of her own hardship, Hannah's eyes grew dim. "You were there"—she sniffled—"when I needed you."

"It's not right of me to complain." Agnes wiped her face. "I've never had a loss like you've had with little Grace." Sorry for her insensitive plea for pity, she let her thoughts wander from her own worries to those of her friend. "Another day I'll tell you more of my past. It doesn't seem right today. Not now while you're still grieving Grace."

"Listen to me, Aggie. Sorrow is not a cake or a pot of oats. It doesn't run out just because one of us took a hefty serving. There is endless sorrow to go around. Yours is as real as mine. Why bicker over who took more? Your hurt, whatever the source, is real—as is mine." Hannah took Agnes's hand and squeezed it. "You have been a true comfort to me since losing Grace. Before then, even. Perhaps you came to Penance because I needed you. And for that I am thankful."

Agnes nodded, despite the growing lump in her throat. Grace had touched so many lives in her short time on earth. "I'm glad I was here then."

"And I'm glad I'm here now." Hannah pulled Agnes through the front door and away from the house. "When you're ready, I'll listen. For now, let's walk toward the fishing hole and see if Ruby's caught anything. I know she'd love to show you if she has."

"You are the dearest of friends." Agnes wiped at a rebellious tear. She smiled despite her inner turmoil, thankful for a friend as dear to her as kin.

"Life is not a cruel joke." Hannah's soft voice was full of

passion. "There's purpose to it. I believe it. Even the pain has purpose. And there's joy to be had. Let's find Ruby. I've no doubt we'll see joy on her face when she sees you're here."

Agnes followed Hannah down the narrow path between the cabin and the creek, making their way carefully over roots and ruts that tried to knock them off course.

Ruby caught sight of them when they crossed over a little rise. She ran toward them, her braids bouncing up and down as she approached. "I caught one, Mama. Wanna see my fish?"

Hannah looked over her shoulder. "Joy," she mouthed to Agnes. Then she turned back toward Ruby. "Is it a big one?"

"Naw, it's a little thing. But Pa said since it's the first one I caught all by myself, we have to bring it home and cook it up."

"He's right. I've heard no fish ever tastes better than the first one you catch. Do you think there will be enough for Miss Aggie too?" Hannah bent down and spoke directly to her daughter.

Ruby pulled her mouth to one side. "If we all take small bites, there will be. But you might want to cook something else for supper too."

"I've caught a few of my own. I think there'll be enough fish to go around," Joshua said from the edge of the creek.

Ruby raced ahead and stuck her hand into the bucket of fish. Water splashed out, but she didn't seem to notice. A bit more digging, and she pulled out her fish. It was small, tiny even, but the smile on her face was exquisite. Hannah made quite the fuss over the small fish, causing the little girl's smile to grow even bigger.

At the table that night, Agnes took her time chewing her bite of fish. "Oh, Ruby. This is the best fish I've ever tasted."

Everyone agreed. The flavor did not last long in Agnes's mouth, but she hoped the sweet memory would linger with her always.

Before Agnes left that night, she and Hannah were alone again scrubbing dishes.

"Have you caught a glimpse of the new doctor?" Hannah handed Agnes a stack of plates. "Surely, you've seen him around town."

Agnes scrubbed harder. "Mm-hmm," she mumbled.

"Do you think since he's from back East and went to one of them fancy schools, he might know what was wrong with Grace? I want to understand what happened."

Agnes stopped washing. "I suppose he might. You could ask."

"I haven't met him yet. I've been so nervous since I heard he'd come. Have you spoken to him? Does he seem like the type I could talk to? I'm not so bold as you. I get flustered talking about hard things, and to a stranger . . ."

Agnes shifted on her feet. "I saw him today. He was talking to Lem and some others. He seemed the sort to listen to you."

"Why, Agnes Pratt, your cheeks are bright red. Now, you must tell me more about this doctor." Hannah leaned in close. "Was Minnie right? Is he handsome?"

"You catch Minnie in the right mood, and she'll tell you her horse is handsome. I hardly noticed the doctor's appearance." She pulled her hands from the water and dried them off. "He seemed nice enough."

"Was he what had you all flustered? Did he resemble your man from before?"

"Well, he did . . . he did. The doctor did affect me, but not for the reasons you're thinking." Agnes untied her apron and hung it on a hook. "I need to be heading back. Go talk to him. I think you should. I don't like you thinking that you've done something wrong. No one ever mothered a baby the way you mothered Grace."

She dared a look at her friend.

Hannah smirked at her. "Be safe walking back," she said. "And when you're ready, I'll enjoy hearing what it was about the doctor that had you rushing over here questioning everything."

Agnes made no attempt to hide her remorse. "It's not a happy tale."

CHAPTER SIX

"You didn't leave a good impression. Now we've got to find a way to fix that." Mayor Clint, his hands folded across his chest, stood in the dim clinic, mere days after James and Agnes's reunion in the schoolhouse. "I expected this to go better."

James slammed the textbook shut. "If they're sick, they'll come. Broken bones, fevers. I fix those things. I wasn't brought here to keep everyone happy."

"You're wrong. These people aren't going to spend a penny on a doctor they don't trust. They'll just keep traipsing up the hills to McHenry. It's a shame, too, because they've already spent so much on you."

"What do you mean?" James asked.

"We all knew we needed a doctor, but it was the schoolteacher who went door to door getting money so we could put advertisements in all the big papers. Might not sound like much to you, but for this town that was a sacrifice." Mayor

Clint took a handkerchief from his pocket and wiped his brow. His hair was thinning but still dark. "We need a doctor. They know it, but they're stubborn. Once they let you in, you're in. Until then you have to be careful."

"I don't understand why they've got anything against me." James had stood in the hot sun for hours greeting the citizens of Penance. He'd taken their complaints seriously. "I don't know what they expect from me."

"There's a lot you don't know. I'll tell you one thing. Slamming the door of the schoolhouse on Miss Aggie doesn't bode well. She's been here longer than half the town, and I can't think of a soul who doesn't like her. She's respected. Sure, there's talk about her independence, but they admire her and will rally around her at all costs." The mayor narrowed his eyes. "I don't know what you got against her, but I'd get over it right quick. No one's going to stand by and let you disrespect her."

"I don't have anything against Agnes Pratt," James said. "I don't. That was all a misunderstanding."

"Well, the wrong people saw you come out of the school, and already I've had three requests for a new doctor." The mayor put a hand on the doorknob. "I expect you to make this right. I take complaints seriously. People need to trust you."

James nodded, resigned to his fate. "I'll see what I can do."

"I'm about to go have a word with Miss Aggie herself." Mayor Clint motioned for him to follow. "Come on."

"I'm not going to see her." James leaned back in his chair and began thumbing through his book again, pretending to be studying hard. "I can handle this on my own."

"Look, people been dying around here over little things. They need a doctor. Miss Aggie knows everyone, and even though she can be a bit of a spitfire, they love her. I'll be asking her to travel with you, introduce you to everyone. Once people see the two of you together, the rumors will end and this will die down." The mayor gave James a moment before saying, "Get up, James. I said I was heading over now. There's a recitation I'm already late for. My girls will frown for a week if I miss it."

James, tempted to be stubborn just to show the man he wouldn't be bullied, gripped the arm of his chair. But the more he thought about the mayor's plan, the more he liked it. Aggie and him traveling around. They'd get to spend time alone. They'd get another chance to reconnect and set things right.

"Oh, all right. I'll do it." James followed the mayor out of the building.

Agnes stood off to the side at the front of the crowded schoolroom. Parents and students filled all the seats and even stood along the walls. She tried to keep her eyes on the students and not glance back at the mayor and James, who had arrived late and crept into the corner.

Osa stood at the front, prepared to recite. Each student had worked hard to memorize a piece of poetry. Some wrote their own, while others recited famous poems.

Osa had chosen to recite a poem she'd written herself. She cleared her throat, giggled, then began.

> The sky is blue, the grass is green.
> The prettiest day I've ever seen.
> The cows are fat and ready to milk.

> They feel soft and warm, as soft as silk.
> The chickens are scratching and looking for food.
> The little ones are running and in a good mood.
> Mama's cooking breakfast, Papa's in the shed.
> The baby just woke up, I better get out of bed
> And enjoy this day God has given me.
> Everything is perfect as perfect as can be.

Muffled giggles filled the room, followed quickly by applause from parents and visitors. Agnes glared discreetly at the big boys beside her and whispered for them to stop laughing. Then she stepped to the center.

"Fine job, Osa. You're a clever girl." Agnes smiled at the child as she took her seat. "We've only one recitation left. Beth, will you come and say your poem?"

Beth tiptoed to the front more timidly than most of the students. She spoke in a soft voice as she recited a poem by Thomas North. She gave a bashful smile, then quietly went back to her seat to the sound of applause.

"I am so proud of each of you. You all did such a fine job," Agnes said.

Everyone clapped again.

"You may all gather your belongings and go with your parents. Thank you again for your hard work. We only have a few days left, and then the term will be over. It's been wonderful." She'd planned to say more, but the sight of the room full of students and parents threatened to steal her voice. She smiled at them and, with a quivering voice, dismissed everyone.

Several students came to bid her farewell, and a few parents thanked her for the presentation. Slowly the din of the crowd died. But unlike her regular school days when the room emptied and she stood alone, today she felt the presence of others. Without even looking at them, she knew Mayor Clint and James remained in the room.

"Miss Aggie, do you have a moment?" Clint asked, his voice forcing her to acknowledge their presence. "I hate to bother you. Especially when I know you've been busy with your presentations. You've done fine work."

She smiled her thanks and waited. Clint nudged James forward a bit. She looked between the two of them and finally asked, "Was there something you needed?"

"I, well, we came to ask a favor of you." Mayor Clint smiled beneath his mustache.

Agnes tried not to look skeptical, but she couldn't help wondering how James had already found himself an ally in Mayor Clint. "What can I do for you?"

Her eyes betrayed her with every look in James's direction. They wanted to search his handsome face for answers to the questions that had been troubling her. They wanted to see into his soul and know how he truly fared. Was he well? Did he miss her? *Don't do it*, she told herself and studied the floor instead.

"Seems a few rumors are spewing around town about the good doctor here." Clint slapped James heartily on the back.

"That so?" she said, fighting the smile that tempted to form. She focused harder on her shoes and the floorboards.

"Well, some folks are saying he's no gentleman and a scoundrel, and they don't trust him."

Agnes's head shot up then. She looked at James without intending to. *A scoundrel? James?* "Why would they say that?"

"When I stopped in to say hello to you the other day, a few of Penance's finest saw me close the schoolhouse door a bit too rough. Rumor is I'm not in your good graces." He smirked. "Seems your approval is awfully important."

"Agnes," Clint said, "you've been here long enough to know the people need a doctor. Wasn't too long ago you stood in the rain on my doorstep sobbing about it."

Agnes felt tears sting her eyes at the memory of Grace and her battle to survive. She'd died that horrible night. Agnes had been there; she'd heard Hannah's anguished cries and seen the lost look on Joshua's face. She'd left, racing with all her might to the mayor's house. When he'd opened his door, she'd pounded on his chest with her fists, sobbing as she pleaded for him to get a doctor. "Don't speak of Grace," she whispered.

"I didn't mean—"

"Don't apologize." Agnes rubbed her forearms in an effort to soothe her nerves. "You're right. I know we need a doctor. McHenry is a dear man and he's done his best, but there are so many situations beyond his knowledge." Agnes dared a glance at James, only to find him watching her. "He can set a break and make a poultice, but we need more."

"We needed a doctor for the miners and for Grace," Clint said. "We need one now too."

"What do you want me to do?" she asked.

"I want you to go with James and visit as many people as you can. Introduce him, let them see you trust him. I'm confident they will too."

Traveling with James would ruin everything. Being near him would make keeping her resolve ever so hard. Even being this close to him stirred something in her. She wanted to cry and scream and run into his arms all at the same time. "I'm not sure I can do that. Perhaps someone else could ride along?"

"No one else will do." The mayor's voice sounded determined. "School will be out this week, so there's no reason you can't ride with him. Unless, of course, the rumors are true? If that's the case, let's throw him out. I've no need for another scoundrel in this town."

Again, she allowed her eyes to find James's. The boy who'd teased her, danced with her, and kissed her hadn't grown into a scoundrel, had he? The same dark eyes that had always told her so much met hers. They told her that his fate rested in her hands.

"He's not a scoundrel. Not that I know of," she said. "I'm a good judge of character. I see a man out of place but not a bad man."

"I'd appreciate your help." James's voice was gentle. "I'd like to be a good doctor for these people. Someone I admired a great deal told me when I was younger that I could do great things. I'm a doctor now, and I'd like to be a great one for the people of Penance. I don't know about Grace or the miners, but I know that if I'm given a chance, I'll help this town as well as I'm able."

"Greatness"—she let her eyes find his—"is what this town deserves. I'll do it. I'll introduce you."

The mayor clapped his hands. "Good. I'm glad that's settled. I'll leave the two of you to work out the details."

"But . . . ," Agnes blurted. "You can't . . ."

It did no good. The mayor left, and they were alone again. She wasn't ready for this. Not yet.

"I'm sorry, Aggie," she heard James say under his breath. "I didn't know a door slam was going to put us in this fix.

Just think of all the trouble we'd have gotten into as children if a little thing like that had gotten people riled up."

"Don't be sorry." She sighed. "It's not your fault. Well, maybe it is. You did show up out of nowhere."

His eyes darted to the floor. "I'm still getting used to the idea myself."

Could she believe him? She wasn't sure. It all felt surreal. After all this time apart, they were together under the same roof. So close they could see each other, hear each other, and touch one another if they chose.

James looked at her, a friendly smile on his face, his dimple making an appearance. "I was hoping we could talk. I didn't realize it'd be today, but what do you say? Will you take a walk with me?" He held out his arm. It hung in the air, tempting her.

How was he so comfortable around her? It was all confusing and exciting and infuriating. It was everything, and at the same time it was nothing. This could not be. There would be no picking up where they left off. There'd be no strolling around town or stolen kisses.

"There will be plenty of time to talk while we are riding through the hills together." Agnes took a step back, putting more distance between them. "Let's wait until then."

"I was hoping we could talk now, put a few things behind us. Answer a few ques—"

"I have to go."

He reached out again as though he were going to take her hand.

She backed farther away, suddenly afraid that if he touched her, she'd forget herself. "I'm meeting someone. I can't talk right now. I'm . . . I'm sorry."

"Someone?"

"I have a life here." Her voice rose without her permission.

"All right," he said, backing off. "What's our plan?"

"Meet me here Monday morning, eight o'clock. I'm not free before then." Agnes grabbed her books, hugging them tight against her chest as she moved to the door, hoping he would follow her lead so she could lock up and slink away.

He walked right to her. Then he touched her cheek ever so gently and ever so quickly. "Your cheeks still turn pink when you're flustered." A smirk formed on his face. "Have fun with your *someone*."

"Ohhh . . . ," she fumed to his back as he walked away. After locking the door and stomping home, she threw her books on the bed and scooped up Tiger. Hand on his back, she aired her frustrations. "I do have a life here. And you are *someone*. At least to me you are."

A low purr crept from the orange cat.

"You love me, don't you?" She buried her head in his soft fur. "We've a good life here. Why did he have to come and disturb it all? Why is he here?" she whispered. "You'll have to see him. He's as handsome and ornery as ever. That's not true. He's more handsome than before, and I've a feeling he's as perfectly ornery and utterly adorable as ever. And now he's a doctor. Can you imagine?"

She groaned and pressed her hand to the place on her face he'd touched. "I don't know if I can do this again."

Two hours of walking the dusty roads and trails of Penance hadn't been enough to clear James's mind. Why had he even come? He'd wanted answers, and still all he had was questions.

Wildflowers danced in the relentless breeze of an open meadow. They were different from the flowers of Buffalo, but he knew Aggie would love them, at least he believed she would. In Buffalo, they'd often ridden outside the city and walked in the fields.

"They make me happy," she'd said to him one vibrant spring day. "It's like God's way of saying we made it through winter, and spring is going to be beautiful and good to us."

James bent and carefully gathered an armful of the brightest-colored flowers he could find. Maybe she wasn't ready for him to put the flowers directly in her arms. But he could leave them for her. Maybe she needed a sign, a happy sign. Maybe they both did. Winter had been long enough. It was time for *their* spring.

He left the flowers on the doorstep of the teacher's house without so much as a knock. With a solemn heart and hopeful resolve, he turned and walked away.

CHAPTER SEVEN

Sam Landon made his way over to the schoolhouse, toolbox in one hand, lunch tin in the other. He'd been logging for years now, getting up each day and trudging off to work. He worked for money and for distraction, but there wasn't much pleasure to be had in it. Getting up this morning had been easier, less motivated by duty. A hawk circled above him. He stopped and stared up at it. In graceful, large circles, around and around it flew. Effortlessly gliding through the windless air.

For years, he'd heard the men at the camp talk about Miss Aggie, but he'd never paid attention to her until she'd asked him about making repairs on the school. He'd not hesitated in agreeing. Working alone, using his carpenter skills, appealed to him. Plus, she'd looked him in the eye when she'd asked, and she'd been gracious. Or maybe it was the way she'd smiled at him that'd convinced him. He swung his lunch pail like he'd done as a boy and told himself the reasoning didn't matter and decided to just enjoy the respite from the busy logging camp.

"Miss Aggie, I didn't expect to see you here," Sam said when he caught sight of her sitting on the porch, mindlessly twirling one of her curls around her finger.

"Hello, Sam."

He set his load down and eyed the space beside her on the step. "School's out. Can't be kids you're waiting for."

"Mayor Clint suggested I show the new doctor around. You know how hard it is being new in town." Aggie bent and plucked a dandelion from the ground. "It's different here, and unlike the loggers, he doesn't have a camp full of men to welcome him. I want to help him get settled in."

"Settled down is more like it."

She sat up quickly. "What?"

He shrugged, feeling sheepish for being so blunt. "Everyone I've run into is talking about the fancy new doctor and his good looks and expensive clothes. I figured you might be as interested in him as the rest."

"Sam!" Aggie balked at the suggestion. "I'm not after the doctor. I never would have guessed you were one of those busybodies who decides who everyone ought to be paired with."

"I've never been called a busybody before. I just figure you might wake up one of these days and decide you want to be more than just the teach. Folks are always talking about you getting married someday." Sam pulled off his hat, his unkempt hair now visible. Wishing he had spent a little more time on his appearance, he ran his hands through it. His efforts did little good. He could still feel it lying in complete disorder. "Maybe you should give him a chance—or at least someone."

"Teaching's a worthy calling."

"I guess it's the peaceful morning. It has my tongue wagging. I apologize." He swallowed. All this talk wasn't like him. When he'd been back home, he'd been comfortable talking. But since setting out on his own, he'd become more reserved. He shifted his weight from side to side. "I'd like to be your friend. I didn't mean to overstep. And you're right. Being the teach is somethin' to be proud of."

He picked at a hole in his shirt, then decided there wasn't anything wrong with sitting by her, so he sat. It was foolish to believe she would become his friend, but could it hurt to try? Maybe having someone to talk to wouldn't be so bad.

She smiled at him. "And just between the two of us, I tend to speak my mind when I shouldn't. I suppose we have that in common."

"Well, it's nice to be in the company of someone I share so much with." He cleared his throat. "I hear you're a good teacher. The best there is."

She laughed then, a soft little laugh. He liked the sound of it, and something warm swelled inside of him knowing he'd been the cause of it. "Thank you. I was so afraid when I first came here. I'd never taught before, but I've found a genuine love for it. I'd feel lost out here without my students."

"You ever need anything else, be sure and let me know." Sam looked at the woman sitting next to him. Her back was straight and proud, but he figured that deep down, she wasn't so different from other girls. "I got a few sisters I haven't seen in a while. I hope someone's looking out for them. I'm sure you got a family somewhere that's hoping you have someone around to give you a hand when you need it. I'd do that for you."

She stared at him, and he found himself wishing he knew

what she was thinking. He'd only ever courted Ruth, but he was young then and often wrong when he guessed her thoughts. Aggie nodded. "I think my father would be glad to know it." She threw the dandelion she'd been holding on the ground. "So, um . . ."

Sam's head jerked around, then he smirked. "Looks like your doctor's coming. Have fun helping him settle down . . . I mean *in*." Feeling bold, he winked. "I'd better get busy. I got a whole list of repairs to make."

"Thank you for taking the job."

"My pleasure." He picked up his tools and lunch and walked toward the back of the schoolhouse, where he planned to start by replacing the rotten siding.

Don't look back, he reminded himself, despite the strong pull he felt to glance again at Miss Aggie. Would her eyes follow him? Since leaving home, he'd rarely been around respectable women. Not since Ruth had he felt much of anything for a woman. Shaking his head, he tried to clear it, but ever since he'd heard from his mother that Ruth and her husband would be having a baby, he'd felt out of sorts.

Agnes watched James as he rode up on his tall, spotted mare. Sitting erect, he looked at ease, his body moving with the rhythm of the horse. Would she ever get used to seeing him again?

"Hey there, Ag. It's been a long time since I caught you staring at me." He grinned. "Best sight I've seen in ages. A beautiful girl looking my way."

"I was admiring your horse," Agnes said, rising from the porch and walking toward the horse. She stopped and patted the animal's nose. "I bet you're glad you stuck with your riding lessons. There's no way you'd make it out here if you hadn't."

"I'm glad to see you haven't lost any of your wit. As a matter of fact, I am glad I stuck with those dreadful lessons. But here's the truth, you are probably still a better rider than me." James smirked. "You ready?"

"You were so afraid when you were little, but you did it." She brought the reins around her horse. "I thought we would start with the families and men to the south of us."

"South, it is."

Agnes's horse stamped his foot and snorted in a most impatient way. Her usual horse was nursing a leg injury, and the livery had only this massive beast to spare. With no mounting block, her getting up in the saddle with any type of dignity seemed an impossible task. She put her hands on her hips and eyed the saddle.

"You coming?" James asked, a playful twinkle in his eyes.

"James?" she said, hating having to ask him for help.

"Need something?" he asked with a look of mock innocence.

Tempted to swallow her pride and plead for help, she nodded once but stopped when she saw Sam approach. He stepped toward her and laced his fingers together. "Looks like you need a hand up."

"Thank you, Sam," she said, giving him her most dazzling smile. "You're such a gentleman. It's a shame Penance doesn't have a few more of you around."

"Course. Like I said earlier, I'm happy to help anytime you need it." Sam boosted her up, then stood next to the horse and ran a hand up and down the animal's neck.

"Sam, have you met the new doctor? James Harris."

Sam shook his head. "Can't say that I have. Nice to meet you, Doctor. My name's Sam Landon. I work at the logging camp. It'll be good having you here."

"I'm happy to be here." James pulled his reins to the right. "Let's go, Aggie."

"Thanks for fixing up the schoolhouse," she said to Sam as she set off down the road.

All weekend James had wondered how to handle this outing, and already he'd botched it. His lame attempt at humor had backfired when that Sam fellow came along and put his hands out, *helping* Aggie onto the horse. James wouldn't make the same mistake twice. Sam might have shared a few moments with her, maybe they even cared for each other. It wouldn't make a difference. It couldn't.

What James and Aggie had ran deeper.

Didn't it?

James's horse followed Aggie's past the town and into the foothills.

She turned in her saddle and said, "We can visit the people closest to the city in the evenings. I thought we would spend the daylight hours with those farther out. It's never wise to get stuck in the hills too late."

"You know where everyone lives?"

"No, not everyone. There are men and families tucked in these hills, living in places I've never been to. I do know most everyone who wants to be known."

"You've changed, haven't you? The timid you is gone," James said. "The old Aggie wouldn't have known where backwoods trappers and rugged loggers lived."

"I knew no one when I came here, and there was no one else to rely on. I did what I had to do. I suppose I've changed, in a way. I had to overcome my nervous nature. But mostly I think I'm still me. Just a little older and more independent." Aggie said the last part quietly. "You've changed too. You're a doctor now. You never spoke of such dreams."

James didn't speak right away. If only they could go back and have all the time they'd missed. Things were easier then, when he knew everything about Aggie Pratt and when she'd known all of his dreams. He'd imagined that same girl would greet him when he rode into Penance. Ever since learning her location, he'd dreamed of who she'd been. The sweet girl he could laugh with, fight with, and even cry with. Did that girl still exist? He looked at the woman in front of him and mourned for a moment the loss of time, the loss of familiarity.

"Was it hard? These last years?" he asked. He watched her with great interest. He wanted to know this Aggie like he'd known the girl in his past. "Were the last six years as hard for you as they were for me?"

She didn't answer. If only the path were wider and he could ride beside her. Then he could see her face, search it for answers.

Was she sniffling? Her tears had always been his undoing. Everything in him had always wanted to take away her pain and make the world easy and bright for her. What if he could not fix this? Whatever *this* was.

When she still did not answer him, he decided to be content simply being in her presence. *"Be gentle and patient. She's built a wall around her heart. It's thick with reasoning she thinks is valid. Tear it down gently, if she'll let you."*

James could hear the sage words of Aggie's mother, Catherine Pratt, encouraging him to be patient. He'd always respected the elderly woman, but following her counsel would prove challenging when he so desperately wanted to understand the divide that existed between him and Aggie.

Her horse led the way up the winding path. Evergreens offered them some shade, though they were nothing compared to the leafy maples of Buffalo.

James allowed his mind to wander back to the last time he and Aggie had been alone in Buffalo. Her normally sunny countenance had been dark. A strange foreboding had filled him when he looked at her. She'd walked beside him with swollen, tear-filled eyes. Her arm, tucked in his own, had been tense and shaking, not comfortable and relaxed.

When they were away from peeping neighbors and local gossips, he broke the silence.

"You all right, Ag?" he asked, putting an arm around her waist and pulling her close.

Her eyes pooled with tears. "I can't marry you," she sobbed.

"Can't marry me?"

"I can't do it. I . . . I can't. I'm sorry."

"Is it too soon? We don't have to get married now. We can wait." James pulled her tighter to him, hoping his strength would somehow reassure her. Together there was nothing they couldn't face.

"It's not that. I loved being asked. I've wanted to marry you since our first kiss." Aggie chuckled a little, despite her tears.

"Aggie, you were six," James reminded her. "Your hair was still hanging in those two long braids."

"I know. But even then, I knew. We were saying goodbye

over the fence and you kissed me. I swore I'd never kiss anyone else as long as I lived." Aggie laid her head on his shoulder. "And I won't. I won't ever kiss anyone again. I promise I won't."

James put a hand under her chin and tilted her head up before pressing a kiss to her forehead. "You don't have to. It's going to be me and you forever. Just like we are now, and like we've always been. We'll be there for each other, no matter what comes."

"James I *really* can't marry you. But it's not your fault." She moved away, just inches, but it felt like so much more. "Promise me you won't ever blame yourself. Be angry with me if you must, but don't blame yourself. Promise me you'll have a good life."

"The only promise I'm making is that you are the only girl for me. Tell me what's going on." James tried to take her back into his arms, but she only stepped farther away.

"I can't say. It will only hurt you. And I won't hurt the people I love. I won't hurt you like that. I won't put you in a position where you have to choose." She stepped even farther away, her eyes unwilling to meet his. "I'll always love you, James Harris. No matter how much we've fought, you've always been my dearest friend. You've been more than that. So much more."

A strange new look he'd never seen before found its way to her face. Resignation? Defeat? What did it mean? When he tried to get more out of her, she fled. She refused to see him after that, and then one day she was gone.

Still, all these years later, he wanted answers. He needed them. Whatever happened six years ago still seemed to plague her. He'd never been very tactful with her—he hadn't needed to be. They'd grown up together, talking to each other as openly as family would. But with six years of questions between them, he knew the rules had changed.

"McHenry lives around this corner. I thought we'd start there." Aggie slowed her horse and turned up a little path. "He worked alongside a doctor for a few years when he was in California. He came out here and learned a few tricks from the Indians. He's the closest these folks have to a doctor."

"What will he think of me?"

She studied him. "He'll approve. He knows he's old, and he knows change is part of life. In fact, if you sit beside his fire, he's bound to tell you a few tales. He's seen this place change, lived through things we can only imagine. Be warned though. He can be a bit gruff."

"Strange, isn't it? You being the one to warn me. Our roles have switched."

She smiled. "You were good to stand by my side when I felt out of place at the many dances we attended. I'll help you here." She pointed. "See there. That's McHenry's cabin."

They rode toward the small rectangular cabin and then dismounted.

"I'm going to fill his water buckets for him. He took a fall not long ago and isn't getting around very well." She grabbed the buckets from the side of the cabin and walked toward the stream, James not far behind her. Carefully, she filled them with water. Without asking, he took the buckets from her and they made their way back to the small cabin.

Aggie knocked on the door. When there was no answer, she pushed the door open and let herself in. "McHenry. It's Agnes. I've brought you water."

A loud *thunk* drew their eyes to the corner. McHenry swore, then picked up the cane he'd knocked over. "You tryin' to scare me to death, girl?"

"It hasn't worked before." She laughed. "I've brought someone for you to meet."

"You finally settled on a man?" McHenry scratched at his bearded face. "I thought you were still considering taking up with me."

"Of course I am, but a girl can only wait so long to be asked."

James stared at Aggie. He couldn't reconcile this witty woman with the shy girl of his youth. She'd always had plenty of spunk, but it'd been reserved for him. And now here she was sharing friendly banter with a man older than her father.

"This is Doctor James Harris. He answered our advertisement."

McHenry's eyes left Aggie and found him. He studied James a moment, then patted the seat beside him. "Come and sit. Let me tell you about your new home."

"I'd like that." James sat on the stiff wooden chair and faced the aged man who, in a sense, he was replacing. His white hair was pulled back and tied with rawhide. His beard was long and tangled. There was nothing about him that resembled the doctors he'd worked with in school. They'd believed in presentation and decorum. This man lacked formal wear, but something about his creased face and well-worn hands screamed of experience.

"I been doctoring here in my own way since the fifties. It was a different land then." He took Aggie's hand in a fatherly way. "They need you now. These people need you. You young folks are Penance's future."

For an hour, McHenry talked of herbs, snowstorms, and death. He told of fevers, battle wounds, and pride. When at last James and Aggie stood to leave, James watched as Aggie planted a kiss on the weary old man's cheek. "I'll be by soon to fill your water, and I'll sweep this place for you then."

"Does it look like I can't take care of myself?" McHenry asked.

"No. You look fit as a fiddle. I just use the water as an excuse so I can say hello." She winked at him. "I enjoy your stories. Selfish motives bring me here."

"So long as you aren't telling the town that I'm on my last leg, you can come whenever you like." He looked at James. "Take care of this girl. She's as stubborn as they come, but I'm rather fond of her."

"I'll do my best to take care of everyone."

Once they were out of the cabin and out of earshot of McHenry, he leaned closer to Aggie and said, "The mayor was right. You're the perfect person to show me around. The way you looked at him . . . you care."

"He's easy to care for."

"Let me help you," James said when she neared her horse. Then he put both hands around her waist, his hands lingering only a moment before he lifted her to the saddle. The feel of her was so familiar, it sent his heart beating faster. He patted the horse's side, doing his best to appear unaffected. "There you are."

"Thank you," she said from atop her horse.

"You're welcome." He continued patting the horse a moment, then he grinned at her. "When you introduce me to the livery owner, remind me to thank him for loaning you such a tall horse." James heard her guffaw at the suggestion as he walked away and mounted his own horse.

"Tell me, how is it that you've become such good friends with McHenry?" James asked as they started off down the path.

She kept her gaze straight ahead. "I ran into him at the edge of town when I first moved in. I was upset and lonely. I'd never felt more out of place. Everyone and everything felt so different here." Then over her shoulder, she said, "And I hated knowing that back home life rolled along without me. I felt so horrible about it all. He listened when I sobbed and told him how I missed my home. He tried to ease my pain by telling me his own story. He told me many tales. Some of them full of sadness."

"And you've been friends since?"

"We have. I suppose that first night I met him, I realized we are all alike despite our upbringings. Same hurts, same joys. I listened to his story and felt less alone. That night changed the way I saw the people of Penance. It changed how I saw the world."

James grimaced at the thought of his Aggie in tears. Alone in this rustic place. If only he could have been there, he would have made everything right for her. But would she have learned to love these people if he'd been here to rescue her? "I've never felt more out of place in my life than I have the few days I've lived in Penance. And I do know someone here. I can only imagine what it was like for you all those years ago."

"It was not all bad. I found friends and purpose. And I've learned a great many things. I can start a fire and shoot a gun, and I can cook. Well, I'm still working on cooking." She laughed. "My tears helped me meet McHenry, so I suppose they were not in vain. My years here have not been aimless wandering. I've led a good life. Truly, I've been happy."

"I'd forgotten what an optimist you can be. And so many skills. Cooking? What would your old cook Ingrid say?"

Aggie laughed again—a happy laugh full of heart. "I think she'd be shocked. Everyone back in Buffalo would be shocked if they saw how we live here. Just look at me in my homespun dress, and my hair is always so plain. I don't even know what the fashions are anymore. I've calluses on my hands from churning butter with Minnie and twice as many on my feet because I need new boots." She smiled and straightened herself taller. "I don't mind it though. This hard life is rich and full. I think of the people I'm with here, and I never would have known them if I'd just lived in my wealthy Buffalo world. I suppose I'll take the homespun dress and calluses and dear friends and all of it." She shrugged. "This is who I am now. I'm sure it's shocking to you, but it's a life I love."

He wished he could weave his fingers through her curls and pull her close. No fashionable dress or coiffed hair could have made her any more perfect. She did look different. Her cheeks were full of color. Her hands seemed less nervous and more confident. If anything, her beauty had grown. "Tell me about the next family," he said, changing the subject.

Aggie signaled to her horse. "You'll find out when we get there." With that, she raced off through the trees.

Digging his heels into his spotted mare, he followed her.

Agnes rode quickly through the trees, loving the feel of the wind in her hair and the warmth of the sun on her face. The path to Tommy Smith's house consisted of a steep but easy ride.

The first eighteen years of her life, she'd shared every happy thing with James. Today she would share another piece of her joy with him—Tommy Smith.

Even on her unfamiliar horse, she outrode James. Pulling back slightly, she slowed. Her intention was to beat him, not lose him in the Black Hills.

The Smiths lived in a little log cabin at the top of a ridge. Their pa had his own claim and worked it alone. He spent most of his time below ground, chipping away at the rock. Occasionally, he'd come up for air with a piece worth a fair price, always vowing that one day he would hit a big vein. She'd never heard a member of the family doubt him.

Just before reaching the Smiths' cabin, Agnes pulled her horse to a complete stop.

"You don't have to let me win. You could have ridden harder," Agnes teased James. "Next time, go ahead and give it your all. I like a little competition."

"I'll let my horse have free rein on the way down." James leaned over and whispered to the horse, "Run like the wind. We'll show Aggie what we're made of." He looked up then and smiled. "But then you'll have to write my mother and tell her I slid off the side of a ridge. Be sure to tell her it was all your fault."

Agnes scrunched up her nose. "Never mind, let's not race down. You know I've always been afraid of your mother. Some things have changed, but that has not. I will just have to wait and race you on flatter ground."

"Six years later and you still enjoy winning. I thought perhaps you would have grown out of that." He frowned, but his eyes twinkled.

"I think I've matured," Agnes said, defending herself. "But a few things will never change." *Like loving you*, she thought.

James stared at her like he was looking for a hidden meaning in her words. "There are some things I never want to have change. Some things I hope have not changed."

Agnes kicked her horse ahead a little, suddenly afraid he could read her mind. That he knew how her heart ached for him.

"The Smiths' house is around this corner. Tommy, their little boy, is one of my students. I've never met a boy quite like him. He's . . . unpredictable."

James came alongside her. "He sounds intriguing."

"I have to warn you. He says the most inappropriate things. His questions are pointed, and . . . well, even just the other week if you'd heard the things he said, you'd understand."

"You've piqued my curiosity. What did Tommy say that has you all pink in the face?"

Agnes sighed. "You'll laugh."

"I won't." James pulled his mouth into a straight line. "I'll be very serious."

"In front of the whole class, he asked me why I never married. When I told him it was my personal choice to remain independent, he asked if *spinster* and *independent* were the same thing."

James did laugh. She wanted to tell him to stop, to keep his word and be serious. But like his laugh had always done, it made her smile, then chuckle, and soon she was laughing with him.

"You said you wouldn't laugh," she managed to say when she caught her breath. "You're horrible."

James put a hand over his mouth. "I had no idea Tommy would ask such an excellent question. I think I'll like your Tommy Smith."

Agnes knew she still liked her James Harris. If only she could tell him so.

James secured his horse in front of the Smith cabin, then he walked to the side of Aggie's horse and helped her down. Before releasing her, he whispered in her ear, "You certainly don't look like a spinster. I'll have to tell your Tommy a thing or two about women."

"James," she said, smacking his arm. "Be serious. You are here to make a good impression."

"I was being completely serious," he replied as he walked toward the little home. "I've seen plenty of spinsters, and none of them have looked a thing like you."

Aggie stepped around him and knocked on the door. "Be good. There's nothing wrong with independence," she said to him under her breath while they waited for the door to open.

A stout little boy with round cheeks and dark brown eyes opened the door.

Aggie waved at him. "Hi Tommy. I brought the new doctor by to meet you."

"How do you do, Doctor?" Tommy said, reaching out his grimy hand.

James took it, trying to keep a straight face as the little boy shook his hand. "I'm doing really well. I've been looking forward to meeting you. Miss Aggie tells me you ask excellent questions in class. I've always thought a man who can ask good questions was destined for big things."

"Well, sometimes I ask her questions she can't answer. I asked her once how it was that babies got inside of their mamas," Tommy said matter-of-factly. "She told me to speak to my mama about it. Mama told me to talk to her when I was older. But I kept asking and she finally told me how things work. It didn't seem so complicated. I don't know why Miss Aggie didn't know how to answer that question. I thought she was smarter than all that."

James covered a laugh with a cough and looked at Aggie, wondering how she contained her own laughter. Chubby Tommy pulled at his trousers as he kept talking. "Another time I asked her why she weren't married. Said that was a personal question. What do you think, why ain't she married?"

James brought a fist to his mouth and cleared his throat. "Well, maybe she was waiting for the perfect man to ride into town. I've never thought it was wise to settle for a match that's less than ideal."

"We got loads of men in this town. I don't think that's it." Tommy fiddled with the button on his suspender. "I think she's waiting for me to grow up. Wouldn't be right us marrying, with me being so young."

Aggie began making all sorts of strange sounds like she was choking and snorting at the same time. James patted her on the back. "Poor teacher must be a little winded from our ride here."

James fought with all his might to keep from laughing himself.

"She does that." Tommy shook his head. "She talks to us about manners, but she's always making these strange sounds."

Once Aggie regained control, they both turned their attention on the boy.

Tommy kept talking as though he'd never been interrupted. "She does answer lots of questions for me. We all think she's a real good teach even if she don't know everything. But Mama says you have to go to lots of school to be a doctor. I been thinking that since you been to so much schooling, maybe when I have a question Miss Aggie won't answer, I could come your way and get my answers."

"I think that's an excellent idea," Aggie said. She clasped her hands together as though she were excited. "Perhaps we could put together a list of all the questions I've had trouble with. I'd love to come along and listen to the answers. Maybe I'd learn something too."

"I'd let you come along." Tommy put out his hand. "Unless, of course, it was a topic suited only for us men."

James met Aggie's eye. A silent message passed between the two of them. A simple look, and it was as though they'd shared an entire conversation.

Accepting his fate, James said to Tommy, "I'll gladly answer any question I can. Come on by my clinic anytime you want."

CHAPTER EIGHT

Two days of riding through the Black Hills of the Dakota Territory and they'd made over twenty stops. Lots of single men, a few men bunking together, and four families. They'd returned to their homes late each night and gotten up early each day. The family visits had been the best and the worst for Agnes.

She and James had both always loved children. At the Monroes' home, he'd met little Golden, or Goldy, as everyone called her. When she entered this world, her pa named her Golden, knowing no piece of gold pulled from a mountain could be more precious.

Upon their arrival, James crouched down in front of the little girl and complimented her fine manners and lovely name. While Agnes talked to the adults, James showed Goldy a magic trick. He picked a pebble off the ground and asked her if she thought he could push it through his head.

"Of course not," said little Goldy. "No one can do that."

"I think I'll give it a try," said James. "I'm pretty sure that if

I push really, really hard, it'll go through." Then he proceeded to moan and groan as though the rock were truly cutting through his head. Goldy's pale face grew whiter. At last, he sneezed, and the rock appeared to fly from his mouth.

With her mouth ajar, she walked to him and felt the back of his head and looked in his mouth.

"How'd you do that?" she demanded. "There ain't no hole."

James bent low again and tapped the tip of her nose. "Magic."

"Do it again. Please."

And James did. He performed his rock trick over and over. Each time, Goldy marveled in amazement.

She put both hands on her hips. "I declare, it really and truly must be magic."

Her dramatic statement brought laughter from the adults.

Some of the homes they visited had caused James to cringe as he witnessed the conditions. And now they rode back together, satisfied with the day they'd put in.

"Aggie, I've been riding around these hills with you for two whole days," James said as they headed back toward Penance. "I've been doing my best to watch my tongue. I think I've done pretty well. But it doesn't feel right, being near you and not saying what I think." James scratched the back of his neck as he rode. "Considering our history, don't you think we ought to answer a few questions from the past? It'd ease my mind a lot if I could put a few things to rest."

Agnes's fears were coming to fruition, despite her wishes and hopes to go on in this light and easy way. Whenever she pictured their roles reversed, she got a glimpse of his frustration. But even understanding his pain did not change reality. "The truth is, there are some things I won't ever answer. But there's plenty I will."

He scowled. "Fair enough. Why'd you leave?"

Agnes glared at him. "Why'd you pick that one? You know I can't answer it."

"Why'd you leave without telling me where you were going? Without even a goodbye?" James said. "I went to your house and all anyone would say was you were gone, and it was what you wanted. They wouldn't tell me where you were or why you left."

"Oh, James, I wanted to say goodbye. But I had to go. If I'd told you where I was, you'd have cornered me and demanded answers. Just like you're doing now."

James's voice took on a sharp edge. It was low and piercing. She could feel his hurt, the pain that was seeming to intensify. "Why are you keeping secrets from me? You told me you'd marry me. You promised it, and then you took it back, only to disappear. Now we're together, and all you'll give me are pretty little answers that skirt around the truth."

"James, you have to believe me—"

"No. We've always been honest with each other." His knuckles were white, his grip on the leather reins tight. She yearned to put a hand on his, but she did not. She only sat high on her horse and listened as he vented his emotion. "I don't understand. What have I done to deserve this?"

"James, I never meant to hurt you. I told you before I left that this was not your fault." Her voice quivered despite her attempts at composure. "Please believe me when I tell you I am saving you from more pain and heartache, only of a different sort. If I told you, it'd fix nothing. It can't be changed away or willed away or even forgiven away. Let it be. I never meant to hurt you."

"Whether you meant to or not, you did hurt me and you're hurting me still." They were close to the town now. James clicked his tongue at his horse and rode off. Clumps of grass shot into the air as the horse ran full speed away from her.

She wanted to ride after him, wanted to do many things. Ever so badly she wanted to take his hand and erase the pain by telling him they could be what they'd once been—but they could not. If she were free to and a little bolder, she'd do more than hold his hand—she'd pull him close and press her lips to his. She'd embrace and hold him like they'd held each other so often before. But nothing had changed, not really. Chasing after him would do nothing except tease their already hurting hearts, so she watched as he rode away.

Once in town, she slid off her horse and led it toward the livery. A tingling sensation ran through her legs as she switched from riding to walking. Rarely did she spend this much time in a saddle, and her backside and legs were painfully sore. She was so focused on getting her stiff legs to loosen that she did not hear the approaching sounds of a man.

"How was your ride?"

Her head flung to the side as she peered into the dusk. She wasn't sure who she had heard, only that the voice did not belong to James.

"Sam, you scared me," she said when, at last, she discerned his face. "I wasn't expecting you."

"Sorry about that. I was finishing over at the schoolhouse. I saw you walk by and thought I'd say hello." Sam reached for the horse. "May I?"

"Of course."

He took the reins, leading the horse toward its waiting stall.

"I took the liberty of fixing the leg on your desk. I know it wasn't on the list, but I thought it might be easier writing on a desk that doesn't wobble."

"You have no idea how wonderful that will be." Agnes hadn't expected much from this man, this logger, when she'd hired him. He'd simply been the man recommended to her when she needed a repairman. Joshua had declared him a good man, but until now she'd not bothered to see it. "That was kind of you."

"How are the visits going?" he asked as the two continued to walk toward the stables. With his free hand, he pushed his sandy-colored hair from his face. The scruff on his jaw was darker but not by much.

"They're going well. Everyone seems to be taking to James once they get to know him." Agnes looked around, searching for any sign of him.

"Glad to hear it. It'll be good having a doctor around."

Then neither of them spoke. Unlike the comfortable silences between longtime friends, the quiet made her more aware of him.

"Thank you again for fixing my desk and for walking my horse back," she said when the silence stretched on.

Sam stayed beside her, matching his stride to hers.

"I've been thinking," he said before clearing his throat. "What would you say to spending a little more time with me? I'd be honored if you'd let me escort you to supper or—"

"I wouldn't do it." James's voice joined the conversation. Where had he come from? His sudden nearness made her head spin as she struggled to make sense of it all. "I wouldn't waste your time courting Miss Aggie. She seems like the sort who would reel you in just to let you go."

"James!" Agnes shouted.

"It's all right, Aggie. The doctor's just having a little fun." Sam smiled in her direction, his blue eyes void of the anger she'd expected to see. "We can talk another time. I'll take your horse the rest of the way. You all right getting home?"

"I'll be fine. Thank you again."

Sam left them, leading the horse as he went. Agnes turned toward James, knowing her emotions were evident on her face but not caring. "How dare you," she said, her voice venomous.

"Aggie."

"That was horrid."

He glared at her. "And what you did to me. It wasn't?" James threw his hands out to his sides. "You left me. I spoke the truth to Sam. You did reel me in, and you did let me go."

She started walking away, only to have him catch up.

"Can we forget it?" James ran his hands through his hair. "I'm not thinking clearly. I'd planned to handle this better, to be patient."

"What do you mean?" She stopped walking and stared, her eyes holding his, challenging him. "What do you mean? You'd planned, planned what?"

He grimaced. "That came out wrong. All this did."

"I don't believe you. Tell me what you meant."

She waited while he struggled for the right words. "I knew you were here." His voice lost its edge.

"How?" Like a flash flood, emotion swept over her. He'd known she was here. Had he come all this way for her? "How did you know I was here? I told no one. My parents were the only ones."

"Before your mother died, she let me know where you were. She never told me why you left. Only that you were here."

She'd been betrayed. Her whole life she'd believed her mother cared about her best interests. How could she have done this? Agnes pressed a hand to her thumping heart. "She didn't."

"She said for me to come if I wished. For me to make up my own mind about whatever it was that drove you away."

"No." Agnes nearly tripped. Her legs felt weak. "She told you to come?"

"She did."

"Well, she shouldn't have."

"Aggie, I—"

"If you want to live in this town as total strangers, I'll respect that. If you want to be my friend, I'll consider myself lucky." She looked off into the distance. "I can't live in the same town with you if you're going to humiliate me in front of men like Sam. I want a life of my own and I can't have it if I have to stand guard at all times. Don't badger me for answers, please don't. I'm sorry you were hurt but . . . it doesn't give you a right to behave however you wish or make demands of me." Agnes's brown eyes held his. "You'll have to find a way to be civil."

"I'm sorry, Aggie." James blew a large breath out. "I don't know what's gotten into me. Everything's different than I'd imagined."

"Life has a way of changing plans. Like McHenry says, change is the only thing we can count on." She knew she should feel some pity for him—after all, he'd showed up here only to find things so altered from what he'd wanted—but she couldn't let herself. He'd have to accept his lot just as she'd learned to accept hers. "Just forget the past if you must. It was a long time ago. It's over."

"Can we start anew? Pretend the last few days never happened? Tomorrow I'll show up, and we'll both be surprised to see each other. We'll be friends, we'll ask questions about the last six years. But only the right questions. I'll be civil. I'm committed to Penance for the time being. Let me try again." James's downcast face looked truly penitent. "I am sorry, Ag. Can you give me a chance to make it right?"

His request seemed doable and was likely the best solution to the bind they were in. There had to be a way for them to live in the same town without hurting each other.

"All right. We'll start over tomorrow." Agnes nudged him with her elbow. "We'll be friends."

"I'll try not to mess things up between you and Sam," he said.

Agnes laughed, knowing despite his pride, James wanted more answers. Relentless man. "You ought to be jealous of Sam. He fixed my desk, and I've had to live with that wobble since the day I arrived. A gift like that might help him find a way to my heart," she teased. "It wasn't right what you did. But I imagine Sam will forget it all."

"You got anything else that needs fixing?" James kicked at the dry ground before looking up. He brought his strong hands together and rubbed them as though he were ready to go to work that very moment. "I'd be happy to stop by and make some repairs. Maybe something that's been broken longer than your desk?"

"You're a carpenter now? I had no idea. You've arrived with so many new skills." She looked him over, one brow raised as she inspected him. "What other tricks have you that I don't know about?"

"Well, the truth is, I'm not too good with a hammer, but you already know that. Blame my parents. Seems they didn't teach me the skills a man needs out West." He shrugged. "I'm starting to wish they had."

"I felt that same way when I arrived. I struggled a lot in the beginning. Burnt food, smoky fires, and bigger things too. I didn't know how to fit in with these people. It gets easier."

"Or I won't last. Clint says not everyone has what it takes to make it in Penance. I could go running home with my tail between my legs. I guess that'd solve some of your problems. You could go on with life how it was before I showed up."

Was that what she wanted? Everything that had once been so clear seemed fuzzy now. Stepping onto her porch, she ran her hand along the railing. Smooth, worn wood testified of years of use. She gripped it tightly.

She knew she could throw words at him that would help him on his way. Words that would cut at him and send him scurrying back to the comforts of his fancy home and servants. Back to the world he'd loved so dearly. But that was not who she was. She'd always believed in him, in his potential. Her heart even now pleaded with her to build him up and urge him onward.

"I think you'll make it here." He stood below her, on the ground, his face looking up into hers. "James, if you want to make it in the West, you will. I know you will."

His Adam's apple moved up and down as he swallowed.

James put his hand over hers on the rail and pressed his fingers against hers. "Thank you, Aggie."

"It's the truth," she whispered, her fingers warm from his touch.

"I suppose it's time for me to say good night then. I've got to surprise a girl by showing up in her town tomorrow," he said, his voice happier. Good-natured James had returned. "I plan to be on my best behavior. Proper and respectable."

"Good night, James," she said, suddenly wishing he didn't have to go. Tomorrow they were going to be friends. What did that make them tonight?

He seemed just as reluctant to leave. "Good night, Ag."

She took a step toward her door before quietly saying, "It is good to see you. I don't think I ever said that."

James flashed his brilliant smile, his dimple showing and his teeth shining in the moonlight. "It's good to see you too. Better than good. And since I don't have to say the right things tonight, I'll say one last wrong thing."

She eyed him suspiciously but waited.

He climbed the steps and stood beside her. Inches were between them. He placed a hand on her cheek and gently moved his thumb along her cheekbone, stealing her breath as he did so. "You look just as perfect as I remember. No, you look better. You're the most beautiful, infuriating woman I've ever laid eyes on. There's not another woman like you."

"James," Agnes said, knowing she ought to be shocked by his comment, but in truth the flutter that rushed through her warmed her in an all-too-familiar way. She'd missed his touch. She'd missed him.

"It's true," he said, still so close that she struggled to

breathe. "You're breathtaking. You're every bit as perfect as I remember. Bolder, stronger, but it suits you."

Swallowing hard, she managed to say, "Why now?"

He stared long and hard into her eyes before saying, "I've never believed in coincidences. The advertisement, your mother, the timing of it all. We were meant to find each other again."

Working at the school all day had been an easy enough way for Sam to spend his day. The work was easy but fulfilling, the quiet calming and serene. Being in the school allowed him to get to know Aggie . . . in a way. Little things around the room told him more about her heart.

On the board were the words *Have a Joyous Summer.* Not a good summer or a happy summer but a joyous one. He liked that. He longed to find joy. Growing up, he always worked hard. At the end of each day, he came home to his family. There were moments of joy in that. And then there was Ruth—he always hoped to share joy with her. It had been years since he'd believed joy could again enter his life.

Aggie's desk had a little stack of books on it. Primers and a book of sermons, but there was also a book of poetry. He'd flipped through it, stopping when he saw a passage marked.

> Footsteps run across the floor
> The sound of joy worth living for
> In laughter, crying songs all heard
> The voice of a child like the song of a bird

He had no pretty words for how he felt, but these words felt like his own thoughts. For a moment he could hear his sisters' footsteps pitter-pattering across the floor of his family's home. He paused his reading, closed his eyes, and tried to picture his family members. It'd been so long since he'd been back. Did they still run after one another, laughing as they went?

Throughout the day, he found himself going back to the poetry book and thumbing through it until he found a page she'd marked. Some of the poems he read and couldn't guess why she liked them. Plenty of them, though, rang true, stirring something within him.

The longer he spent in the schoolroom, the more convinced he became that he'd like to know Aggie Pratt better. Maybe she could fill this void he felt. It didn't seem right that Ruth had a family and he had no one. Alone in the small schoolroom, he realized he had the power to change that.

CHAPTER NINE

Was Agnes truly as pretty at twenty-four as she had been at eighteen? She'd been told she was attractive many times since moving to Penance, but the words of the loggers and miners had never affected her. James's inappropriate comment had kept her up late into the night. Repeatedly, she played his words in her mind, sometimes fighting the delightful feeling they brought, other times embracing the feelings of youth and hope they evoked.

The heart she'd so carefully cut off from the world felt alive, beating again. Wildly, ferociously beating. It both scared and excited her.

As she readied for the new day, she took extra care with her hair as she pinned it loosely, allowing a few curls to fall free. She wore a freshly pressed dress that lacked both a bustle and lace, but it fit well and complemented her features.

She took one last peek in the mirror and headed to meet James at the schoolhouse for another day of visiting. Smiling into the fresh morning air, she tried to remain calm and composed. She'd insisted he leave the past alone. Flirting with him, no matter how appealing, would be wrong. After all, she'd made her decisions in order to respect propriety, hadn't she?

"Miss Aggie!" Charlotte called as she walked toward the schoolhouse, where Agnes stood brushing her giant horse's mane. "I'm so glad you're—" Charlotte stopped and stared. "What are you all dressed up for?"

"Hello, Charlotte. I'm not really dressed up." Agnes felt heat rise to her cheeks as though she'd been caught doing something naughty. Charlotte, at fourteen, admired Agnes, so she'd hate to lose credibility in her eyes. "I hadn't worn this dress in some time and decided this was the perfect way to air it."

"You look mighty fancy to me." Charlotte walked close and continued to gape, then she touched the fabric. "Sure a fine-lookin' dress."

"It's just a dress." Agnes took a small step back and picked nervously at her cuff. "Can I help you with something?"

Charlotte snapped out of her trance. "Yes, ma'am. Doctor Harris sent me. He said to tell you he can't meet you today because he's needed at the mine. Someone hurt their leg or arm. I can't remember that part for sure." She scrunched up her nose. "I think arm. Yes, it was their arm. Well . . . maybe it was their leg."

Arm or leg, it made no difference to Agnes. All she heard was that he wasn't coming. "Was there anything else?"

"Well, he said something about how your meeting each other really would be a surprise because he don't know when he'll be back." Charlotte shrugged. "I don't know what he meant by that last part. But I told him I'd send his message along."

"I'm sure that last part was not important. Thank you for telling me." Agnes sighed. "Tell me how your days off from school have been."

Charlotte explained about working in the family garden and taking lunch to her father at the mine. She told about her brothers and the mischief they got into when they let the pigs out and had to spend an entire day tracking them down. And she told about baking with her mama.

"I have to head back now. My mother is expecting me," Charlotte said after running out of news. "I promised to help her all day."

"Tell your mother and brothers hello," Agnes said before they parted ways.

"I will. I hope I grow up and look like you. I'd give anything to have a dress like that," Charlotte said over her shoulder.

Looking at her green dress, Agnes suddenly wished she could tear it off, wad it into a ball, and go back to being just a spinster teacher. James wasn't coming, and even if he had, this was childish. For a moment she'd forgotten herself and her resolve. Dressing up, hoping to be followed by his eyes was foolish. Careless. It was flirting with temptation, and she knew better.

Tucking the loose curls behind her ears, she pulled the big horse close to the schoolhouse porch and used the step to climb into the saddle, then she headed for Hannah's.

"Hannah," she said when her friend's door opened. "I thought I would stop in and say hello."

Hannah stood in the doorway, an old apron pulled over her work dress. "Come in. I'm always glad to see you."

She obeyed, although already she was regretting her choice to visit her friend. She had hoped to escape the confusion she felt. But perhaps being alone would have been better. Putting words to her inner turmoil seemed too daunting to face.

Hannah walked back to the kitchen and her bread dough. "What brings you out here today? I thought you were making visits with the doctor."

"He was called to the mine. There's been some sort of an accident. Someone hurt a hand or a leg."

Hannah didn't look up from her bread. "I'm glad it's not serious. Were you wearing your fancy green dress for the doctor?"

Agnes looked again at her dress but didn't speak.

"Sometimes two friends are close enough that even when one is too confused to talk, the other still manages to listen. I know something is weighing on you."

Pacing back and forth on the wood floor, Agnes looked down at the dress's perfect pleats and smooth fabric. "I don't know why I'm wearing it. I suppose I forgot myself for a moment. The doctor seems to have stolen my senses."

"Dreams can change." Hannah smiled gently. "There's no shame in it. You came out here with plans to be a teacher, and you've done that. No one would fault you for embracing a new season of life. Perhaps you're meant to do something else now. There's nothing wrong with giving your heart and dreams to a man."

"My dreams have nothing to do with it. I'll never marry." Agnes rolled up her sleeves.

"Marry or not, that's your choice. Just don't let your stubborn pride be the decision-maker. Listen to your heart—and to God." Hannah picked at the dough that clung to her fingers.

Agnes groaned. "I'm not stubborn."

"Course you are. Only us stubborn folks can make it out here. Joshua says we all have to be a little stubborn or this land will lick us. It's good you're stubborn. Just so long as you're stubborn about the right things." Hannah's voice was soft and kind. She was right. Penance was filled with a stubborn sort. "Let the other parts of you lead occasionally. The part that feels and yearns for beauty and happiness."

"I'm sure you speak the truth." Agnes smiled weakly. "Let me help you today, otherwise I'll have to listen to my own thoughts, and I'll go mad."

"I'll gladly take your help. Ruby is out back, but once she realizes you're here, she'll be dancing around and begging for attention," Hannah said as she handed her a broom.

"The doctor's here," someone shouted when James broke through the trees.

"Get him off his horse. These men need help," a big man with shaggy hair and a crooked nose yelled.

James felt his heart skip a beat. He'd expected to find one injured man. Were others hurt too? He flew off his horse and ran toward the crowd. "Get out of the way, let me through."

The waters of men parted at his command.

"What happened?" James fought to keep the quaver from his voice. Lying on the ground were four dirty men. Some moaned in pain, a sign of life, others he feared were dead. He bent over the nearest man and started checking his vitals. A faint pulse and shallow breaths told him the man lived. For now. Fear seized James. *"You can do this."* Aggie's words from long ago raced to his memory, motivating him, strengthening him.

"We pulled Matthew out and sent for you. These other three got stuck in a second collapse." A large man knelt beside him. "You gotta save them."

James worked quickly, assessing all four. He felt a powerful force guiding him. He functioned liked he'd been doing this on his own for years despite his relative inexperience.

Pointing to the men who stood nearby, James told them what he needed them to do, his voice strong and commanding. With each word, his confidence grew. God willing, he'd find a way to save these men, no matter what it required of him.

"Hold this wrap here," he said to the man closest to him. He told another to find water and additional bandages. The men obeyed, everyone jumping at his command.

James felt certain the first man would live. His injuries, though painful, were relatively minor—a broken arm and deep scratches. The second man suffered a puncture wound in his abdomen. The third had broken both his legs, but if set properly, they would heal. The fourth was unconscious, but alive. A head injury, possibly worse.

He focused on the second man, working to stop the bleeding as quickly as he could. "Give him this to drink," he said as he handed a man a vial of laudanum. "I'm going to have to stitch his artery first. And then the opening."

A large miner standing beside him collapsed at the sight of so much blood. "Someone take his spot. I'm going to need men who can stay in control. Come and help hold him down,"

James said without even looking at the man who'd fallen beside him.

A hefty redheaded miner took over, and James set to work. He lamented the conditions he worked under, the poor lighting, the dirt and filth, and his limited supplies.

For six hours James worked tirelessly over the injured men. Bouncing from one to another. His clothes and hands were soaked in blood, red and sticky. The pungent smell of wounded bodies sent many of the miners walking into the woods for fresh air, but he worked on, never slowing.

When at last he stood and looked at the four stable patients, he knew why he had become a doctor. Life was precious and worth fighting for. Those men still might not make it, but by putting his education and skills to work, he was giving them at least a chance at survival, at life. Never had he felt such a sense of accomplishment, never had he felt so useful. Looking at his hands, he saw the blood and dirt smeared across them, the grime penetrated deep into the creases of his skin.

Once back in town, he cleaned up, carefully scrubbing his hands and arms and changing the color of the water in the basin from clear to a murky red. He put on clean clothes and sat on his bed. But he couldn't hold still. Adrenaline pumped through him. Suppressing it was impossible. Instead, he walked out his door and toward Aggie's.

He banged on her door and waited. When she opened it, she stood staring at him, her mouth open in surprise.

"What are you doing in this town?" she asked, pressing her hand over her mouth dramatically. "I thought I'd never see you again."

He'd forgotten his promise to start over and surprise her.

He had rushed to her place to celebrate the lives that had been saved. It'd been impulsive, instinctive. And there was no one else he'd rather celebrate with.

"Well, this town needs a doctor, and I've come from the East to use my hands for good," he said, holding them out to her and marveling once again at what they had done.

"But why here?" She cocked her head to the side as she questioned him. "Why Penance? You could save lives anywhere."

"Cause I'm needed here." He grinned big, letting the act die. "Ag, I treated four people today. Four people who matter to someone. They are somebody's brother, somebody's son. And they're alive." His voice cracked as he spoke. "They're alive."

Aggie no longer had a playful look. "You saved them?"

"I did. They've a long road ahead, but they get another chance."

A smile like the ones from the past lit her face. "I knew you'd do important things. I always knew it. I just didn't know it'd be here."

"You did always believe in me." He wanted to pick her up and spin her around the room. What he wouldn't give to celebrate the day in a more familiar fashion. He held back and grinned at her instead. "There is no feeling like it. It's frightening and exhilarating all at once. Aggie, I saved them. With the help of God, I saved them."

"Why don't you come in? I fixed supper and made too much. I want to hear all about it."

"You want me to come in?" He took one step, then stopped. "I'm not sure I should."

"We've eaten together often. There's nothing scandalous

in it. Leave the door open if you want. I've long since given up chaperones and front parlors." She waved him inside. "Penance operates on survival, not etiquette." She leaned in closer. "I suppose there are a few souls with their noses in the air, but I'm past caring what they think. Come in."

He nodded before taking a step inside. "You cooked?"

"I wouldn't write your mother about it. It wouldn't impress a soul."

James didn't care what she cooked. He'd eat anything if it meant sitting beside her. "I haven't eaten all day."

Seated at her primitive table, he looked around her modest home. It was small and comfortable, nothing like her grand home in Buffalo. Just the essentials, but she'd managed to give it her personal touch. A doily under a vase of spring flowers, a blanket laid over the arm of a chair, a painting on the wall. A portrait of her parents hung on the opposite wall in a simple wooden frame.

"It looks like your swing," he said, pointing to a framed painting of a tree with a swing dangling from its branches.

"I made that shortly after I arrived. I was so afraid I'd forget it all. I look at it sometimes and wonder if my swing is still there blowing empty in the breeze. I've thought of asking in a letter, but . . . well, I'm not sure I want to hear it's been taken down."

"Wonder no more. It looks lonely, but it's still there." James pointed at the small shelf in the corner. "You have your poetry."

"Of course. And there is the box you gave me on my fifteenth birthday. You had it engraved. Do you remember?"

She walked across the room and picked up the small silver box.

"I do." He followed, took it from her, and opened the lid. Inside, the words were still easy to read. "For Aggie, the girl who makes me smile." He closed the lid. "I was not nearly as eloquent then, but the meaning still rings true."

"The words were perfect. I couldn't leave it behind." She took it from him and put it back on her little shelf. Then she squealed and dashed across the room. Her skirts in her hands, she crossed the floor in large leaps. "My biscuits!"

She grabbed a towel to protect her hand and pulled them out of the oven. She poked one with her finger and sighed. "I suppose they'll do. They're not as dark as the last batch."

"They smell good," James said.

"You're being kind. I made biscuits and stew." Aggie set a bowl in front of him, then sat across from him with her own bowl. "I don't think they'll kill you, but I can't guarantee it. Hannah showed me how to make them, but I can't seem to get mine to taste like hers."

"I always thought the cook's biscuits were a little too fluffy. These are probably just right."

She took a bite of hers and then spent several seconds struggling to chew. When, at last, she swallowed, she said, "You may want to put it in your stew. Let it soak up some of the broth and soften."

"I doubt they need that." He took a bite. Amending his statement, he said, "Maybe they do."

They both put the hard biscuits in with their stew and slowly ate. He didn't ask her why she'd left him or why she never wrote. They merely sat together, sharing the meal in her simple home like two people who shared a history.

Before leaving, he stood in the doorway and leaned against

the doorframe. "Thanks for supper. It was the perfect meal to end this long day with."

Chewing on her bottom lip, she hid her smile. "I'm glad you liked it. Someday I hope to improve."

"Don't be too hard on yourself. To be honest, I'm a bit in awe. You were reserved so often before, and it seems in Penance you've become a new woman. You're bold and connected. You've got true friends and the respect of this whole town, and you can bake a biscuit." He sighed, holding back the bulk of the compliments he wished to give. "But you are still you. I want to thank you for being there for me today. I was afraid, but then I heard your voice."

"Don't be silly, I wasn't there. I was at Hannah's, and then here doing laundry and slaving over the stove so I could make that masterpiece of a meal."

"You were there. Whenever things are hard, I can hear your voice. I know it sounds foolish, but it's true. It's always been that way. When I was so uncertain what to do with my time, I could hear you telling me I was meant to do good. It led me to medical school, and school was an excellent excuse to give my mother when she inquired after my bachelor ways."

"Oh dear." Aggie laughed. "Was she terribly ruthless?"

"The worst. She was forever arranging outings for me with women from fine families. Ladies with no backbones who could talk of nothing but the weather and socials. I quite liked being able to tell her I was occupied with my studies." He stopped laughing then and said, "At medical school, I was told I was incompetent and that I'd never make the cut. I could push away all the harsh words by listening for you. I'd hear your voice telling me I'd do great things. Today I heard you telling me these men mattered and that I could manage." Suddenly worried he had said too much, he shoved his hands into his pockets and moved to go. "I better be off. I just wanted you to know you've made a difference. I don't think I would have amounted to much without you. I would have been nothing but old money, no substance."

She put a hand on his arm, stopping him from leaving. "I hear your voice too."

"What?"

Aggie stepped a half step closer. Her chest rose and fell. "I hear you often. All these years, your voice has never left me. When I came here and didn't know how to live like this, I'd hear your laugh in my head and your telling me I'd get the hang of it. When I doubted myself in front of my classroom of students, I'd think of you and how you made children smile. In a way, you came with me."

"I don't want to live in this town as strangers. Let me be your friend. I've missed the girl who made me smile."

Swallowing hard, she nodded. "I've missed my friend."

His eyes lingered on hers before he stepped off the porch. "Good night, sweet friend."

CHAPTER TEN

Word spread faster than a Dakota wind, and soon everyone in all of Penance knew of Doctor Harris and his fine work at the mines. Introductory visits ceased due to the increased demand for James's services. Time marched on, days became weeks. Agnes spent her mornings at the schoolhouse making lesson plans for the coming term or riding into the hills to help McHenry keep his place running or visiting with Hannah or Minnie.

Sam waved and stopped for a quick hello if he saw her about town, but he never mentioned their spending more time together. He'd just stop for a minute or two and ask her about what she was reading or tell her about his work. Simple, pleasant small talk. Despite her full days, she couldn't keep her mind from wandering to her childhood friend who everyone in Penance knew as the doctor.

"They say he comes from a wealthy family back East. What do you think they thought of his decision to leave it all behind?" Minnie asked Agnes one afternoon. "I imagine they were proud to have their son rushing off to the frontier to serve the poor citizens of Penance. It makes a rather romantic picture, don't you think? A wealthy, handsome man riding into the setting sun."

Agnes pictured James's father—the crotchety Mr. Harris, with his thick spectacles, wide girth, expensive clothes, and demanding demeanor. He was arrogant and too good for anything that didn't cost a hefty sum or anyone who crossed his path without connections or title. She could imagine him storming around, yelling as he went, fuming mad that his son was leaving. He'd probably shouted about their family being old money and having a reputation to uphold.

"I know when I left the city, my parents were concerned but supportive," she deflected. "Perhaps his parents were the same."

"I bet they were proud. Perhaps the papers back there will even do a story on him. I can see the headline now. *Doctor from the Esteemed Harris Family Leaves Home and Hearth for the Frontier. There He Sweeps an Unsuspecting Maiden off Her Feet, and Together They Confess Their Love and Live Happily Ever After.*" Minnie exhaled. "If only I were younger and unmarried, it could be me." She smoothed butter into a mold, laughing while she did it.

Agnes rolled her eyes. "I think all this heat is going to your head. You have Lem and all these children. You don't want some young doctor."

"Course I'd never really trade in my Lem or young'uns. Heaven knows there isn't a more patient man than my Lem. Besides, I heard from Rose Clint that he has no plans of staying here long-term. It's an adventure for him before he settles down." She shook her head and sighed. "I'd so hoped he'd be the one for you. I'm surprised the two of you didn't know each other back in Buffalo. I suppose, though, the cities back there are bigger than here."

Agnes had never actually said they were strangers, but she didn't bother correcting Minnie either. She kept her eyes down and voice level. "When's he leaving?"

"I don't know. Rose says the mayor's made up his mind to marry him off to someone here so he'll be tempted to stay. But this is Penance. You've refused to marry, and there aren't many single women to tempt him. Besides, if he had wanted to marry, I bet there were slews of girls in Buffalo who would have wanted him." She cocked her head to one side. "Maybe he even has a girl. Maybe she's too young and he's biding his time waiting for her to grow up. Maybe they write long, passionate love letters to one another." Minnie moved her finished mold to the side. "When he leaves, we'll be back to relying on McHenry. That's an unromantic thought."

"James Harris can run back to his young bride if he wishes." She fought to keep the irritation she felt to herself. "McHenry's a good man. He may not know all the doctor does, but he comes when called and has saved a lot of lives over the years."

Minnie grunted as she scraped a knife across the next mold, smoothing it out. "McHenry's getting older and sicker. He won't do, and you know it. But if you won't have the doctor, there aren't too many choices, unless he takes a saloon gal, but I think that's unlikely."

"Poor things are forever being mocked and belittled. When I pass them, I often wonder how they became what they are. Do you remember Lila?"

"Lila?"

"She had the black hair and lived here a year or two. She was a lot friendlier than most of the saloon girls."

"I think I saw her around." Minnie wiped her hand across her apron. "Pretty thing but tainted. I don't mix with them."

"She tried to work other places. No one would hire her anywhere, all because she'd had a baby and wasn't married." Agnes pressed a hand to her stomach. It twisted within her as she recollected. "I'd been teaching her to read. I thought perhaps with a few skills she could go somewhere and start over. She told me once it hadn't been her fault that she got pregnant. And her baby didn't even survive, but still people held it against her. I felt sorry for her. I wish she hadn't gone."

"Probably for the best that the baby died. Maybe in some other town—"

"How could you say that?" Instantly, Agnes's hands clenched into fists at her sides. If Minnie knew her story, would she think it'd be better if she'd died too? "Babies should never die."

"It's a harsh world for an illegitimate child."

"Then those of us who've been in the world longer ought to change that. It's time the world stops punishing the innocent for crimes they did not commit." She brushed her hands on her apron. "Let's talk of other things. I don't even remember how we came to talking of saloon girls and babies."

"We were talking about the doctor, and I was about to tell you that I don't see why you're so against him. Besides, I see you with your students. You care for them. Seems you ought to have a baby of your own someday. And just think what a baby with the doctor would look like. Your skin and his dark hair and—"

"I'm not having a baby with the doctor." Agnes set down the bowl she was stirring with a bit too much force. "Honestly, Minnie. You say the most preposterous things."

"Why do you insist on staying single?" Minnie leaned in closer. "It doesn't make any sense and seems downright selfish in a place like this, where so many men are aching for a bride."

"The truth is, Minnie, I had someone once. He was as handsome as the doctor." Agnes's voice rose as her confession spilled from her. "Just as handsome and kind and good. You'd be swooning." She tried to stop herself but could not. "We were contemplating marriage."

Minnie shook her head. "I've been around longer than you, and I've never seen a man as handsome as Doctor James Harris. But you go on and tell me your tale, even if you are embellishing a bit. What happened?"

"Truly, he was a handsome man." Agnes folded her arms across her chest. "I left him behind when I came here. It couldn't work. Some things are not meant to be."

"Teaching is a fine thing, but so is marriage and family." Minnie rubbed her swollen belly. "Why couldn't it work? Or are you telling me tales so I'll stop hassling you about getting hitched?"

"He was real. Just as real as you or me. I had to leave him. I can't explain it, but it *was* the noble choice." She looked away. "At least I believe it was."

"And none of our men have ever measured up?"

"I can't teach when I'm married. It's in my contract. I've chosen my students. I'm content with my choice." Agnes pursed her lips, knowing that ever since James had come, she'd been anything but content. *Unsettled* better described it.

"What happened to him?" Minnie asked after licking the butter knife clean.

"To who?"

"To the man you loved. Your perfect, handsome man. A man you claim was as dashing as the doctor. What became of him?"

Agnes looked away. "I never wrote him. I just went away. I imagine he's gone on with his life."

"You left without telling him? That poor man is probably tortured by dreams of Agnes Pratt and her auburn curls." Minnie's brow furrowed together.

The look sent a wave of guilt through her. Suddenly on the defensive, she said, "He's not."

"I think you ought to spend a little time with the doctor. It couldn't hurt, and maybe it would help you forget your promise to never love again. I bet your man's forgotten all about any promises he made to you. Although the idea of him sitting around brooding over his broken heart is tragic and romantic in its own way."

Agnes shook her head. "There's no changing my mind. He can forget me or brood all he wants. I'm happy with how things have ended up. But I do feel like I need something. I don't know what. Just something else."

"Feeling restless?"

"I suppose." Agnes's shoulders slumped.

"You haven't been back home since you came to Penance. Maybe you need a change of scenery." Minnie patted Agnes's hand. "I shouldn't say that though. The truth is, I'd miss you."

"I'd miss you too. But . . . maybe."

Go back.

She could if she wanted to. James knew her location now, so going back wouldn't make a difference. Not really. And her father was there.

"Maybe I will."

Sitting at her little desk that night, Agnes put ink to paper. Three attempts later, she hoped her words conveyed what she felt.

Dear Father,

For six years, life in Penance has been relatively predictable—until a month ago, when a big surprise arrived. James Harris walked into my town. He's the new doctor. He claims Mother told him where I was. If she were present, I'd accuse her of being a traitor. As it is, I'll assume her actions were benevolent in some misguided way.

My past and my present are all tangled together now. James is much the same, yet it's different between us. He is busy caring for patients, and he does a fine job of it. Everyone is taken with him. All over town, I hear conversations about the fine new doctor. We rarely see each other, and when we do, I feel confused, not at ease like I did when we were young. Even not seeing him much has changed things. Questions about life that I've been avoiding all these years suddenly surround me.

I wonder if now is the right time to come back home. I've longed to see you, ached for it. I've missed you so very much. I admit I'm apprehensive about being back among the circles we associated with. I don't think I'd be at ease there knowing how they'd feel about me if they knew where I came from.

I do want to be there with you so I might ask you for advice and so we might make memories and laugh together once again. Tell me what I ought to do.

Your girl,
Aggie

CHAPTER ELEVEN

"I'll come back for you," Sam had yelled to Ruth as he boarded the train bound for the end of line. "I'll come back, and I'll marry you."

At seventeen, he'd believed in happy endings. He signed on with a railway company and worked for nearly two years. The pennies piled up, clinking against the glass of his savings jar. While the other men were spending their pay at saloons, he pocketed his. When he'd left, he'd told Ruth there'd be enough money to marry in two years. A month shy of two years, he sent her a letter full of romantic notions and promises of marriage. His big dreams felt so close—Ruth, land, and a roof to keep them dry.

When her return letter came, he waved it in the air for all the fellas to see. "I'm heading off."

They hooted and cheered. "Read it!" they chanted. "Read it!"

Foolishly, he complied.

Dear Sam,

Normally she addressed the letters "Dear Sweetheart" or "Dear Love." His eyes rushed to the next part, worry and dread inching their way into his mind. His stomach clenched, and his eyes stung. His welcome-home letter shouldn't sound like this.

I don't know exactly how to tell you this, but with your being gone so long, I've been spending more time with Richard. You remember him, I'm sure. He was a year ahead of us in school. He has his own land now and finished a little cabin on it. He even bought a real stove for the kitchen. He's asked me to marry him. I've been thinking hard on it, and I've decided to give him my word. I'm done waiting for you to come back. I hope you'll understand.

All the best,
Ruth

A few snickers from the crowd, some sympathetic looks. He went to his barracks, packed his few belongings, and left. He wandered directionless until coming to Penance and signing on as a logger.

At twenty-six, his pockets were heavy with coins. But he often felt just as lost as he had when he read the letter. Someday there'd be a new dream, and when it came, he'd be ready for it. At least that's what he told himself when the days dragged on.

Sam lathered his face. With the same razor he'd left home

with, he shaved the stubble from his chin, leaving nothing but smooth skin. All the while, he thought about Ruth and the years she'd been married to another man and the baby they now expected. He set the razor down and stared at his reflection. If things had worked out differently, would he be a father now? Married with a baby. He slammed his hand against the wall. Why did the thought of Ruth with a baby rile him up? It wasn't fair. Maybe he shouldn't wait for a new dream. Maybe he should go find one.

Recent rains had left the already-bumpy road filled with even deeper ruts. Exposed roots twisted across the path, threatening to trip Agnes as she made her way to Hannah's. Slowly, she meandered toward her friend's house, observing all the changes the storm had brought. The rain had been heavy, pounding down on the town, washing over the hills, and flooding the lowlands.

Agnes thought of the summer rains in Buffalo, which were so different from the ones here. The sky would be beautiful blue, the air hot and humid. In an instant, it would change as clouds came from out of nowhere, hiding the bright sun. Just as quickly, they would empty their heavy burden in fat drops and then rush away, leaving the wet grass as the only evidence. And even that did not stay for long under the summer heat.

The last rainstorm before she'd run to Penance had been memorable not just for its large droplets but because she'd been with James. He'd knocked on her door in the early afternoon, looking dashing in his dark suit. His hair was parted, and Agnes had smiled at seeing the same old spot in the back sticking up.

"The Durrants' apple tree is brimming with ripe apples. I know they won't mind if we pick a few," he said from the door, a bucket in his hand.

Agreeing, she dashed through the door after him.

"I wish the weather could stay warm like this," she said.

"Winters aren't all bad. Besides," he teased, "when it's cold, I get to scoot next to you when we ride and put my arm around you."

"James!" she said, but suddenly winter didn't seem so abysmal.

They walked to the Durrants' arm in arm. Once there, they slowly picked a few apples.

"Look at the clouds," Agnes said as she pointed toward the sky. "I don't know how they move so quickly. A moment ago, it was nothing but blue. I hate how fast things can change."

"Some things won't change," he said, planting a kiss on her cheek. "Let it rain. It can't hurt us. The clouds, the seasons, they come and go, but we won't change."

Heavy drops ambushed them, driving them toward the shelter of the branches. Mere moments later and already their clothes, hair, and faces were soaked. It made no difference how fast they ran, they couldn't outrun the storm.

"What will Mother think of me, soaked like this?" Agnes said as she squeezed water from her hair. "You are always getting me into scrapes."

"Nonsense. This is hardly a scrape." He put an arm around her waist and pulled her toward him. He held her there a moment. "You're my favorite person to get stuck in the rain with."

"Do you often get stuck in the rain with other girls?"

He smirked. "All the time."

"James!" She elbowed him. "You do not."

"All right, I concede. You are the only person I get stuck in the rain with, and the only one I ever want to with."

And then, under her favorite tree, he had kissed her. The rain had been forgotten as they stood in each other's arms beneath the canopy of leaves. His fingers had traced the curve of her cheek, then he had kissed her again. A tender, perfect kiss.

Pressing a hand to her lips now, Agnes wished she could feel it all again. Just for a moment, just once more—to have the shiver run through her when he kissed her. She shook her head. This last week it had rained buckets, and she'd stayed out of it as much as possible. There'd been no stolen kisses, just loneliness. Eager to forgo the solitude, she quickened her step.

"Sorry I'm late," she said when Hannah opened the door. "I lost track of the time. I was looking at all the changes from the storm. Can you believe all that rain?"

"I was worried the trail would wash clear away." Hannah pushed a chair under the table, clearing the way for her. "Come in."

Agnes walked through the doorway, then stopped. There at the table sat Joshua and James. He stood when she entered. "Miss Aggie."

"Doctor Harris," she said before looking at Hannah.

"Doctor Harris came by earlier, and we asked him to stay for supper. Did you know the two of you are both from Buffalo? How strange to think that you didn't know each other." Hannah walked to the cupboard and pulled out a tin plate and fork. When their eyes met, Agnes couldn't help but wonder what she was thinking.

"It is a big place." Agnes did not dare meet James's eye. "Where's Ruby?"

"She spent the afternoon with Osa. Joshua will fetch her after supper. She had not spent time with any children for weeks, so we thought it'd do her good." Hannah brought a bowl of potatoes to the table. "Sit down."

Once she was settled in her seat, Joshua offered grace. Agnes couldn't help but steal a quick glance at James while everyone's heads were bowed. His eyes were closed, but he smiled, large enough that his dimple showed. Did he find their unexpected encounter humorous? She closed her eyes again quickly as Joshua ended the blessing.

"Will school be starting again soon?" James asked once he'd opened his eyes.

"We've a few weeks yet."

"I'm sure your students are eager to get back." James scraped his fork across his plate.

"Summer always goes by too quickly. But I do love the children." Agnes busied herself by choosing a piece of meat and cutting it on her plate. She thought of mentioning her letter to her father but chose not to. Going home was still a dream, at least until she heard back from her father. "I haven't seen much of you this summer," she said without looking up.

"I've been busy. For a small place, there seems to always be a call for a doctor. Mayor Clint says you'll have more students this year than last. You'll be busy too."

Agnes, searching for signs of how he fared, watched James serve himself. He looked well, comfortable, and at ease. It could be a show though. He might be enjoying his adventure but longing for the comforts of home. "Several families have moved in. Soon we will outgrow our little schoolhouse."

Joshua joined the conversation. "I never thought I'd see the day when people would flock to Penance. It's good though. I like the idea of Ruby growing up with friends."

"There's nothing like growing up with a good friend." James set his fork down and leaned back in his chair. "It's one of the best things in life."

"I'm sure in Buffalo you had many friends. There must have been a great many people your own age," Hannah said.

"There was no shortage of peers. But I only really had one close friend. I was lucky enough to live right next door to my dearest friend. We spent nearly every day together." James looked around the table. His eyes stopped on hers for a second, and he held her gaze. "Best friend I ever had."

"Agnes had a good friend growing up too. Their houses were right next door to each other. Seems awfully strange to me. I've only ever lived in places where I couldn't see the nearest house." Hannah picked up a basket of rolls and held it out for anyone who might want more. "I'm not sure if I'd like it or not. Being so close to others."

Agnes shoveled bites into her mouth. "This is an excellent meal, Hannah."

"You grew up with a friend right next door?" James asked in what appeared to be innocence. "What was your friend like?"

Agnes struggled to swallow. Her throat turned dry. When at last the food went down, she wiped her mouth and set the napkin in her lap. When her eyes found his, she saw the twinkle of humor she'd grown to expect as a child. "Well, we were close in age and had many common interests. We knew each other very well."

"And what has become of your friend?" James asked from across the table. "Did you grow apart as you got older?"

"No, not exactly. In fact, if we were to sit in the same room today, we would still know the things to say to each other to bring a laugh or a smile." She cocked her head. "Or to get each other flustered . . . But some things have changed."

When no one looked, James winked in her direction, making his enjoyment evident.

"I bet you miss your friend terribly." James pulled his face into a deep frown. "I know I miss my friend. I'd love to go back to seeing her every day." He sighed. "If only there were a way."

Joshua set down his fork and smiled at Hannah. "That's the nice thing 'bout marriage. You get to have your friend right beside you. No property markers between you. No growing up and moving on."

"I think someday I'll have to track down my old friend and tell her to marry up with me so we don't have to be apart. I'm not sure I could convince her. She possesses a stubborn streak." He reached for another roll. "These rolls are as fine as anything I had back in Buffalo."

Agnes scooted her food back and forth on her plate, afraid to look up.

"Thank you. It's my mama's recipe." Hannah spoke in her quiet, easy way. "Eat them up—they're best fresh."

With a shake of her head, Agnes declined more food and instead watched James from the corner of her eye, on guard in case he said something shocking again.

During the post-meal cleanup, Agnes stood beside Hannah as they washed dishes. "Why'd you have the doctor over?" she said softly to her friend so no one else could hear.

"Last time I was in town, I stopped by his office to see if I could ask a few questions. He was called away and said he'd stop by as soon as he had a chance. He just showed up this afternoon."

"Does he know what happened to Grace?" Agnes asked.

"I told him all about her. He doesn't know what was wrong. He's going to write to some of his colleagues and see if he can learn more. He said he can't think of any reason why we can't have another baby. But he did say sometimes these unusual things run in families. Ruby is unaffected, but even that's no guarantee." Hannah took a deep breath. "I worry about going through that again, and it took so long to even have Grace I don't know if we'll be so blessed again or if we're strong enough to endure that again."

"I hope the doctor is able to find some answers."

"Things have always worked out for us, and I have Ruby and Joshua. But I do dream of more little feet running through my house." Hannah handed her another dish.

"I'm sorry." She knew how badly her friends wanted answers. Her little Grace had been perfect and healthy at birth and for months after. Then she stopped growing and seemed to forget all the things she had learned. Soon she stopped following them with her eyes or responding to noises. Everything left her. Hannah did all she could for the little girl, spoon-feeding her drop after drop, trying to keep her alive. But Grace succumbed to the illness.

"The doctor is kind. My hands were shaking when he showed up, I was so nervous. He sat right down and said,

'I'm a doctor, and that means people talk to me about all sorts of things. Sometimes they cry when they tell me their stories, and that's all right.' And I did cry. I cried through the whole telling. I'm not sure I'll ever be able to speak of Grace without tears."

"You don't have to." Agnes felt her own eyes stinging with threatening tears. "I hope his friends can tell him something else."

"I hope so, but even then, it won't bring her back. I think I want answers so badly because I want her to return to my arms. But nothing will bring her back. She's gone, and I believe she has been saved—only not by me. I console myself by remembering she is in the Lord's arms." She smiled sadly. "But mine are empty. I feel both happy and sad when I think of where she is."

"I do not think it is a sin to ache for someone we love. I believe it is the natural result of loving and yearning for someone we cared deeply for."

"It meant a lot to me, hearing the doctor say it wasn't my fault and that the way I cared for her was the right way. Just knowing I didn't bring any of that harm to her. It eased my burden. He spoke to Joshua too. I think it helped. I think, well, I hope we'll be able to find more peace now."

"I've been praying for it." Agnes set down her dishcloth.

The dishes were clean, but neither woman made a move to leave the little washstand. Their backs to the men, they kept talking.

"The doctor is more than a mere acquaintance, is he not? I saw how shy you were at supper. You were not yourself." Hannah's voice was low. "You knew him before, didn't you?"

Agnes shrugged in surrender. "I knew him before. But no one here knows, and I prefer it stay that way."

Hannah raised a skeptical brow.

"I never thought our paths would cross again," she said, being honest. "I'm not sure what to make of it all." She wished they were alone. In that moment, she'd have liked nothing more than to pour out her locked-up secrets to her dear friend. If she could have, she'd have told her how she'd once loved James more than any man in the world. But they were not alone.

"Well, if you want to know what I think, I think he's a very good man." Hannah leaned in closer. "I think he cares for you. More than once I caught him watching you from across the table. He looked at you the way Joshua often looks at me when I catch him staring for no reason."

"I can't tell you what the looks meant. We may have shared pieces of our past together, but we've not seen much of each other this summer."

"You ought to make time to see him a little more. And sometime soon you ought to come over and tell me exactly what sort of a friendship the two of you shared."

Agnes glanced over her shoulder at James, who was talking to Joshua. "He was my neighbor. I'll come by soon. I promise."

Hannah gasped, covered her mouth, and nodded.

James and Joshua both stood when the women left the washstand and joined them.

"I've got to pick up Ruby. Why don't you walk Miss Aggie back into town?" Joshua suggested, nudging James with his elbow.

"I'd be glad to." James held out his arm to Aggie. "May I walk you home?"

She nodded and intertwined her arm with his. Together they said their goodbyes to Hannah and Joshua.

James had spent the last weeks trying to stay away from Aggie, doing all he could to give her room to adjust to his being there. Trying to follow the advice to be patient. Tonight Providence had intervened and thrown them together.

"I've been thinking how there were probably hundreds, maybe thousands, of families like Hannah and Joshua's back in Buffalo that I never knew. Good, hard-working people. We hardly mixed." James walked slowly. His brows pulled tight as he thought. "It doesn't seem right to me now. My parents kept me from so many people, not because they were dangerous or cruel but because they were poor. Even in medical school there was an air of importance given to the wealthy patients."

"I had similar thoughts when I first came. It felt odd living all together like we do here. Everyone's families go to the school regardless of where their parents come from. The church welcomes everyone. The longer I've lived here, the more I like it." She slowed her step, her eyes wandering to the setting sun. "I do miss my father."

"Do you think you would ever return home to Buffalo again?" James looked out at the magnificent display of colors before him. Orange and pink lit the horizon as the sun left for its own journey elsewhere.

"I would like to see my father. I'd avoided going back, but I might now." Aggie stopped and picked a summer flower. She twirled it between her fingers. "I hear you have plans of returning."

That had been his plan. Come to Penance. Find Aggie. Return to civilization.

"My parents expect me to return, and I told them I would." James swatted a fly on his neck. "The people here have been good to me in a way I hadn't expected. My time has been well spent. However, I had hoped I'd see you more."

"I haven't had much call for a doctor this summer." She smiled innocently at him. "I've had a long run of good health. Must be all this fresh air."

"I hate to wish an illness upon you, but I did look up often enough hoping you'd come in through my door." He smirked, then said, "You could have faked a cold. I know you know how to."

"Are you talking about Charles? I can't believe you remember that. If you'd been forced to picnic with Charles, you would understand. He was always getting really close and . . ." Aggie shuddered. "I can't explain it. But he was a snake, and it was the only way to get out of it."

"I still can't believe your parents believed you."

"I was very convincing." Aggie coughed a few times into her hand. "I haven't lost my talent. If I recall correctly, you weren't keen on me going. You liked that I played sick. I believe you told me I was a beautiful invalid."

"Exactly. And I could have used a beautiful invalid in desperate need of my care this summer. I would have enjoyed it. You should have seen some of the patients I cared for."

"Maybe I'll come down with something one of these days." Aggie started walking a little faster. "I've been wondering about your skills. I guess that'd be one way to find out."

"Haven't you heard good things about me?"

"There has been plenty of talk. But mostly the women

talk about your dashing good looks and how long they think you'll stay a bachelor."

James rubbed his chin. "How long are they figuring?"

"Most of them can't understand why you aren't married off already," Agnes said while picking petals off the flower she held. "I can't either. Why didn't you ever marry?"

"I keep my promises. That's why. Course none of Penance would understand that. But I think you do." He tucked her arm around his. "There was this neighbor girl once who I promised to love always. And now she's threatened to run off if I mention it, so I'm bound to be a bachelor all my days."

"James."

"Yes?"

"Those promises were made a long time ago. I expected you to move on with your life. I thought you'd be married by now. I thought you'd have a wife and a baby or two." Agnes used her free hand to brush at the hair that'd come loose and was whipping about in the wind. "I confess, I wondered from time to time what your wife was like and if you loved her."

"Well, my mother certainly tried hard to find someone for me." He stopped walking and faced her. With a tentative hand, he tucked a loose strand of auburn hair behind her ear. "I'm still hoping to find my answers. I suppose it's hard to grasp for the future when the past is unsettled."

"James, I think"—she looked away—"I think you should forget our promises. If it's honor that holds you back, know that I release you. You're free from those promises."

"No thank you. I'll decide for myself when to let my word go, and right now I think I'll keep my promises."

"Why're you always heading into town these days?" Pete hollered at Sam from the other side of the tree. "They got a new gal at the saloon?"

Sam, trying not to let the man's words steal his rhythm, pulled hard on his side of the saw. *Push-pull-push-pull.*

"You know I don't visit the saloon. I've been making some repairs on the schoolhouse. Just a side job. Something to pass the time." Sam's body moved to the beat of the saw. "Plus, I get tired of spending all my time with this lot."

Pete spit a long string of tobacco. "I never went to school. But I'd go here if I could, just to stare at the teach." He kept talking, rambling on about Aggie's fine looks. But not about her brown eyes or soft curls—instead, he talked about the curves of her body.

Ever since coming to Penance, Sam had heard men talk about Aggie Pratt. He'd never joined in, but it hadn't bothered him too much. Just men spouting off, he'd rationalized. Today the words didn't sit well with him. Aggie had become a friend.

"That's enough, Pete."

"I'm just having a little fun. I gotta take my mind off all this work somehow," Pete said. "Besides, I know you've noticed the way her skirts sway when she walks down the street."

"Just cut it out," Sam said, letting go of his side of the saw and walking away.

"What's wrong with you?" Pete rushed after him. "You know it's all talk. We all do it. We all know we ain't got a chance."

"I don't think it's right. Talking about her like that—or anyone else." Sam's voice rose as he spoke. "She's not cattle at auction, she's a woman. I know her now, and I don't think she'd like it. That's all."

Pete spit again, then moved the tobacco around in his mouth while he stared Sam down. "You pining after her?"

"Let's just get back to work." Sam, anxious for the sound of the whistle, walked back to the tree.

When the high-pitched squeal sounded, he walked past the other men and straight for the mess shack, where he grabbed his gear and headed for town.

He wasn't sure what he hoped to find there. Perhaps he just needed friendly company or a change of scenery. Lately, the logging camp and bunkhouse held no appeal.

James called through the open door of the clinic as he walked by. "Sam, I'm glad I've run into you."

"Can I do something for you?"

"I need to have some more shelves built in the clinic. I've made some large orders and am hoping they'll be delivered soon. I saw what you did with the school and figured you were the man to ask. I hope you'll take the job." James closed a thick book and stepped away from his desk. "I know I didn't make the best first impression. I'm sorry for that. The job's yours if you want it."

"I figure you had your reasons for saying what you did." He looked around the inside of the simple office. Crates were stacked into makeshift cupboards, but they were overflowing with goods. "I'd be glad to make the shelves for you. Can I take some measurements?"

The two walked around the clinic, and James described what he had in mind for the space. "I want to use the vertical height for storage, free up floor space so I can treat more patients if I ever need to. These crates aren't enough."

"I can do that. It's no problem. I'll come in after work and on Saturdays. My boss let me off for the school repairs, but I don't expect he'll give me the time for this."

"I can accommodate your schedule."

James excused himself to answer a knock at the door, leaving Sam to measure and make notes. Behind him he heard James.

"Hi, Aggie, you feeling sick?"

Why did he sound like he was teasing her? Sam felt his muscles tense. Was she sick? James should take her health seriously.

"No, I'm not sick. I feel perfectly well." She laughed. "I stopped by to bring you— Oh, Sam. How are you?"

Sam turned and walked over to the pair of them. "Well enough. I'm just taking measurements for some shelves. It's good to see you."

"I've brought James a biscuit to try. I made Hannah's recipe, and for the first time they don't taste like rocks. Here, try one." She handed one to him.

Sam took a bite and smiled at her. "It's excellent. I have what I need, James. I'll be by with some lumber and get your shelves up as quick as I can."

James thanked him, and Aggie insisted he take another biscuit with him. Walking away, biscuit in hand, he wondered if there could be more to the doctor and the teacher than they were sharing.

Back at the old bunkhouse, the summer heat combined with the smell of hardworking men created a foul odor. On nights like this, the old itch to settle down resurfaced. How nice it would be to live in a home that smelled like hot cooking or lilacs or just about anything other than men.

With the sun still giving him enough light to write, he pulled out a sheet of paper and composed a letter to his sister Rhoda. She'd married only two months ago, and although he had wanted to be there, he'd missed it. They'd married at the same church he'd attended as a boy. Rhoda had worn their mother's old dress, redone to fit her. He pictured the details from his mother's letter, but still, he knew he should have been there, living the details.

She'd married a new man in town. He wished he knew him. It would be easier picturing his sister a married woman if he knew more about the groom. As it was, his mother's assessment was all the information he had.

> *He is a good man who does not have much by way of worldly wealth. But he will give her all she could have ever hoped for by way of happiness. Never have I seen your sister smile so much as she has since meeting David. Even when they're apart, I see her smiling. A new gleam is in her eyes. It is the look I hope to see on your face someday when you settle down and marry.*

Her letter had gone on and on about the wedding, the family, and how they missed Sam and prayed for him daily.

As he wrote Rhoda, inquiring after her happiness, Sam wondered about his own.

CHAPTER TWELVE

"Fire! Fire at the saloon! Fire!"

James woke to the sound of yelling just outside his door. He pulled himself from his bed and yanked on his trousers and shirt. Medical bag in hand, he rushed into the streets. The same tightness he'd known so often filled his chest. Fires meant patients with burns, and burns were scary to treat. In medical school, he'd helped treat the victims of a factory fire. The night still haunted his dreams. He could hear the agonizing cries of the victims and smell the scent of burnt flesh.

He forced away the fears and ran toward the crackling sound, the smell of thick smoke greeting him.

Dozens of men and women were fighting the flames that surged from the saloon. Old and young were both there. Even Old McHenry, who'd been staying in town so James could monitor his persistent cough, bucketed water, hollering commands and swearing as he went. Perhaps someday this night would make its way into his tales.

If it hadn't been so dangerous, it might have been a breathtaking scene. The colors of the fire and the smoke, the men and women toiling together for a united purpose. But the daunting nature of the ravenous fire overshadowed any beauty that could have existed. The hungry flames could destroy the town and the people in it. Where was Aggie? He searched for her as he ran around the side of the building looking for anyone in need of his service. His eyes left the saloon and its luminous flames when he heard Aggie's voice.

"I hear crying in there!" Aggie shouted as she waved her arms around, trying to get someone's attention. "I hear crying!" She yelled louder, pointing at the upper windows of the saloon. "Someone's in there."

"Everyone's out. Calm down, girl. It's the fire you hear," McHenry hollered back at her. Then, in an almost fatherly way, he tried to comfort her. But she only pushed the man's arms away and became more frantic. From person to person she went, yelling and screaming about what she'd heard.

She grasped Mayor Clint by the shoulders and yelled again, only inches from his face. James couldn't hear his reply, but he didn't have to. His frown and her downcast face told him the mayor felt no call to action.

Aggie ran to the next person and pleaded again. Still, no one would listen. Their eyes met then, and she ran to him. James took a step forward. He'd never seen such desperation.

"James, I hear someone crying. Someone's still in there. I need a ladder. I've got to go in and get them." Aggie grabbed his arm and pulled him toward the back side of the saloon, all the while yelling about how someone was trapped and would die without her.

Gripping her elbow, he stopped her. "Look at me, Ag. You

can't go inside. It's crumbling on top of itself." He had to yell above the raging fire and noisy crowd.

"I know I heard something. Don't let them die. Please, James. Help me find a ladder."

He looked at the building. Flames were quickly overtaking the right side. He tried to listen, wanting to hear what she had heard, but he couldn't make out anything above the din.

"I don't hear it." He put a hand over hers, trying to sooth her. "No one's in there. It's just the wood. It makes strange noises when it burns."

"James, whoever it is will die." She no longer screamed. She squared her shoulders and grasped the front of her skirts. "I don't care if you doubt me. I'm going." She moved for the building.

He wouldn't let her do that. Her skirts would catch fire and she'd die. He'd never let her die, not while blood still pulsed in his veins. Instead, he took her firmly in his arms. Looking her straight in the eye, he asked, "Are you sure you heard something? Are you absolutely certain?"

"I know I did. Someone is in there. There was crying from that room." She pointed toward a second-story window on the left side of the building. "The fire wasn't so loud when I heard the cry. But no one has come out. Not since the women who were on fire."

"Women on fire?" His looked around. "Where?"

"They died. James, they died. But this person might live."

"I'll go." A new urgency filled him. Adrenaline pumped through him. Finding strength and speed he'd not known before, he ran to the shed at the side of the building, only to find it locked. He kicked at the door. He needed a ladder, and time was running out.

Racing around the building, he searched the edge of the road for something, anything he could use to break the lock from the door. He sensed Aggie near him, but there was no time to talk. He had to act.

"James, what are you doing?" Lem stood with a bucket in hand. "Help us with the flames."

"I need a rock. Grab that one!" he shouted back.

Lem, confused, picked a large stone from the ground and handed it to him. "What are you doing?"

"I'm going in." James ran back to the shed, Lem on his heels.

"Don't do it." Lem put a firm hand on his shoulder. "You'll die in there."

James tried to push him away, but Lem grabbed hold tighter, trying to stop him. There was no time to debate. He let the rock he held fall to the ground, then swung his now-empty fist with as much force as he could muster at Lem. His knuckles connected with Lem's jaw, and Lem staggered away.

James picked the rock back up and ran for the shed. Moments later, he emerged with a ladder and the rock still in his hand.

"It came from there." Aggie pointed again toward the upper window. "I heard sounds from there. I know it was that one."

James raced up the ladder until he reached the window Aggie had pointed to. One smash with the rock, and it shattered. He heaved himself over the jagged edges of the glass and into the smoke-filled room. A dense cloud of smoke surrounded him, reaching into his lungs and stealing his air. He pulled his shirt over his face to keep the smoke from his lungs and crawled along the floor where the air seemed slightly better. Still, he worried he would lose consciousness if he did not hurry.

He could see little, only enough to know an upstairs girl lived in the room. He had never visited the saloon, never even had the desire to, but every man in town had heard the miners and loggers talk of silks and satins.

His hand brushed against the slick silk bedding, but the oft-used bed stood vacant. Crawling to the far wall, he felt a dresser and a washstand. He made his way to the corner, where he felt a hanging curtain. Reaching behind it, he felt a small room. A closet? Wood ran across the front like a gate. He sat up on his knees and reached over the wood.

At first, he felt only bare floor, but then his hands felt the softness of skin. A person. A baby. A small and motionless baby. Aggie had been right. For one moment, he froze in amazement, but then the urgency returned. He heaved the child over the gate and into his arms. The need to get air for himself and the little one pushed him onward.

With the weak but living body flopped over his shoulder, he forced his legs to carry him back across the room to the window, back to the air they both needed so badly. Using all his strength, he held the baby with one arm and used his other one to steady himself as he climbed over the jagged glass and onto the ladder. His shirt caught on the glass, ripping as he went over, but he didn't care. Getting out was his only focus. He looked back into the room and saw hungry flames eating at the door. Soon the room, with its wooden gate, would be nothing but a pile of rubble. He pressed the child tighter to his chest, aware that—if not for Aggie—the child would have been among the ashes.

He hurried down the ladder, careful of the limp child in

his arms. His body savored every gulp of fresh air, but pain shot through his lungs and throat. Raw from the smoke, they felt hot and tight.

Aggie stood below him, offering words of encouragement. Others joined her. A small cluster of townspeople now stood at the back of the building. They clapped and shouted as he made his way to the ground. With burning eyes, he searched for Aggie. No one else mattered. Only her.

"You're almost there." Her voice reached him. "Just a few more steps."

And then his foot hit the ground. His body wanted to collapse, to lie down and rest, but he fought against it and took a few clumsy steps toward the crowd.

Aggie's voice embraced him. Her arm went around his back, and with her touch he felt stronger. "It's a baby!" she said. "You found him!"

James's head spun and he feared he'd lose his grip on the boy, so he handed him to Aggie before falling to the ground. Lying there, he felt darkness close in around him one moment, and the next, bouts of painful coughing racked through him as his lungs struggled to expel the extra fluids they'd rushed to make to protect him from the suffocating flames.

"You saved him," he heard Aggie say, but he could say nothing in return. Wrestling with his own body, he struggled to gain any sort of control over himself. He submitted to the exhaustion, praying somehow his lungs would fill with air again.

When, at last, he pulled himself up to sitting, he put his head between his knees and forced the air to continue entering his sore throat and lungs. His textbook knowledge told him what was happening to his body, but he had not been prepared for the pain and confusion that came with smoke inhalation.

A hand came against his back moving gently up and down.

"James. Can you hear me?" Aggie's voice crept in from behind his ear. "How can I help you?"

He nodded his head, feeling too short of breath to speak. He lifted his upper body and laid his head on her lap. The touch of her hand pulled him from the cloud he felt trapped in.

"I'm here." She continued to rub his back. "I'm right here." Her words soothed him, and slowly his breathing found a rhythm, his pulse slowed, and the fog cleared. Silently, he sat under her touch. And then he remembered his charge, and his own suffering became unimportant. *The baby.*

"Aggie." He swallowed, trying to moisten his dry throat. "Ag, where's the baby?"

"McHenry has him. For being an old bachelor, he somehow has a touch with babies. He's rocking him and doing what he can, but he told me the baby needs you when you are well enough."

"I'll go to him now." He rose on shaky legs. "I need to help him."

She stepped beside him and steadied him. "Lean on me."

"I have to take care of him. And anyone else who needs me." He stumbled forward. "Someone died."

"You couldn't have saved them," she said, wedging herself under his arm like a crutch.

"Thank you," he whispered, his voice hoarse but the words genuine.

Tears filled her eyes. "Thank you for believing me."

"I never should have doubted you. Not for a second."

McHenry hobbled quickly toward them with the baby

in his arms. The boy's little body shook, his small frame thrashing. "I need you. You know more than I do."

James took another deep breath. "Carry him to the clinic. Aggie, can you come?"

"Of course." The three walked as quickly as they could.

James turned to McHenry as they entered the clinic. "Do what you can for the others, but if you need me, send for me or send them to the clinic."

"I will. I've seen a few minor burns, and the women we lost." He placed the shaking baby on the exam table. Then the man looked at them with his aged and weary face. "Blast it all. I'm turning into a blubbering fool, but, well . . . you're a good doctor. This town's in fine hands."

Aggie walked to the older man and put her hand on his arm. "I'm glad you're both here. Penance needs James, *and* it needs you."

"Nonsense," McHenry grumbled, but he patted her hand before leaving. "I'll send people your way."

The baby coughed, and when he did, his whole body trembled. "What's happening to him?" Aggie held the baby's hand in her own.

"It's the smoke. His body was fighting it off the best it could. His throat is swelling, but his body is trying to expel the extra fluid he's produced." Quickly, James tipped the baby's head back, trying to open the airway the best he could.

Aggie bent low and cooed at the baby. Her hand stroked the boy's head as she spoke. "James will take care of you. He'll fix you all up." She turned then and looked at him. "Will he recover? You can save him, right?"

"I think he'll be all right." James paused long enough to get a good look at the child. He was small and stocky. Golden curls famed his round face. He'd guess the boy was under a year but not by much. "Looks like a little cherub."

"I thought the same thing," she said. "He's beautiful. Why do you think he was there?"

"I could guess, but the truth is that I don't know." He rotated the baby to his side, trying to find a position that would ease the coughing.

"Shhh, shhh," she whispered. "We're here now. We're going to take care of you."

James had to pause his work on the child when a storm of coughing overtook him. Aggie fetched water for him to drink and to wipe the baby's face with.

"You always seem to know what I need." James drank the cup of water slowly, savoring the feel of it as it soothed his throat. "I could use you around more often."

"I'm glad I can help. I wish I could do more."

"You've more than helped him, you've saved him. No one else heard his cries." He felt a new sensation in his throat, different from the pain caused by the smoke. Now out of danger, he felt the severity of it all. "You were his angel, Aggie."

Their eyes locked across the table, holding each other without so much as a touch, until the baby between them cried out. A hoarse, painful cry. His eyes fluttered open, and a look of fear and anguish filled them.

"Can I hold him? Will that hurt him?" she asked James.

He picked up the boy and put him into Aggie's waiting arms. She ran her hands up and down his back, rocking him slightly as she did so. Soon the little one quieted, and his head rested against her chest. His eyes grew heavy and shut once again, and then his body relaxed. "He's asleep," she whispered.

James went across the room and brought her a chair. She sat slowly, continuing her gentle bouncing rhythm as she lowered herself into it.

"I'm going to check on everyone else. The coughing is good for him. It'll help clear his lungs, so don't let it frighten you." He put a hand on her shoulder. "Will you be all right?"

"I will. Try to find out whose he is. Someone must be desperately looking for him."

James watched her rocking with the baby on her chest. "I'll ask around. He looks content."

Back outside, James rushed as quickly as he could to the burning saloon. Weaving through the chaos, he looked for anyone needing his assistance and spotted Paul Clint.

"Mayor, who needs my help?"

"McHenry cleaned and bandaged a few minor burns from folks getting too close. The two we lost are around the corner. Their rooms were upstairs on the backside of the building, above the kitchen." He pointed in the direction of the bodies. "Both caught fire trying to get down the stairs, or so I'm told. One of them lived a few moments before passing. The other a little longer. We put out the flames, but there was nothing else we could do for them. It all happened before you were here."

James didn't need to hear any more. He walked in the direction Clint had pointed. Two blankets lay atop the deceased. Lifting the edge, he looked at their faces. He could tell they were women, but the flames had left little else discernable. He eased his conscience by telling himself there would have been nothing he could have done for them even if he had been there earlier. Reverently, he pulled the blankets back over their faces and backed away.

He returned to the mayor and asked, "Has anyone been looking for the boy?"

"No. I plan to check around once the fire is out. I'm sure by morning we'll know whose he is. My guess is he's the son of one of the upstairs gals who died." Mayor Clint shook his head. "This one shouldn't have happened."

"What started it?"

"I can't say for sure. But I've heard a few men talking about a brawl and lanterns being overturned." The mayor's eyes were watching the still-rising smoke. "They all feel like they're my fault. Every death. I'm trying to keep this town safe, and I've failed."

"I know the feeling. I never like losing a patient. Even in school when they weren't really my patients, if they were under my care, I wanted them to survive. It feels personal."

The mayor finally pulled his eyes away from the mesmerizing scene and put a hand on James's shoulder. "You saved a life tonight. There'd be one more body under those blankets if it weren't for you."

Uncomfortable with the praise, James shifted under the mayor's hand. "I did what anyone would do."

"No, you didn't. You were the only one who believed Aggie. And you don't even know her like we do."

James tapped his toe as he mulled the statement over. He'd never lied about knowing Aggie. He'd just kept the fact to himself. Something about the sober night loosened his tongue. "I know Aggie. I know her well. Better perhaps than anyone here."

Mayor Clint raised a brow. "You know her?"

"We grew up together. I've known her since we were children." James covered his mouth and fought a painful cough. When it passed, he said, "I knew Aggie was telling the truth. I knew it, and if that baby had died, it would have been my fault. I had to climb in, because if she knew someone was in there, it was the same as if I'd heard the cries myself."

The mayor listened but said nothing.

Finally, James stepped away. "I need to check on the child."

CHAPTER THIRTEEN

Agnes shifted the baby in arms weary from a long night of comforting the boy. Pressing a kiss to his smoke-scented head, she savored the feeling of someone needing her. At the touch of her lips, he squirmed, sinking deeper into her arms, then let out a little sigh as he relaxed. She whispered the words of Brahms's "Lullaby" as she rocked back and forth like a calm wave upon the sand.

James was sleeping in a chair beside her. He'd come back from the scene of the fire and sat quietly. With a far-off look on his face, he'd shaken his head and whispered his regrets from the night. Then, without another word, he'd put a hand on the baby's back and listened to him breathe. For a long moment he'd watched the baby sleeping before tipping his own head back and drifting off. For a moment she'd thought of waking him and sending him to his own room. But then she'd looked at the child in her arms and thought it might be best for James to be nearby if the baby needed him.

And the truth was, she wanted him nearby. His presence soothed her racing heart. This tumultuous night was a new memory to go with all the memories of the past. Tonight, they shared the smell of fire, the innocence of a baby, and the burden of making sense of it all. She watched him sleep and thanked the Lord that he had been there tonight and that he had believed her when no one else had. James, good and faithful James. He'd always been there when she'd needed him.

When she was seventeen, her parents had planned a party in her honor. Agnes had rushed to James's house the moment she heard.

"I can't dance in front of a room full of strangers, not when the party is for me," she had said to him. "I hate the thought of it. I don't want to be the one everyone's eyes are on. I'll forget all the steps and embarrass my parents."

"You're a fine dancer. You've nothing to worry about." James grabbed her hands. "Let's dance now and pretend like the room is full of people."

"How generous of you." She laughed as she stepped into his arms. The familiar tingle raced up her spine when he touched her.

He pulled her close. "I have a confession."

"You do?"

"This is not a completely selfless act." He kissed her cheek.

"Oh?"

Then he spun her much faster than any musician would ever play the steps. "This will never do. Just think of the horrified looks on everyone's faces if I laugh through the whole dance. They'll think me flippant."

"Maybe if I spin you fast enough, you'll even do one of your adorable little snorts. Then everyone will think you are a perfect heathen, and I won't have any competition for your hand." James pulled her closer and kissed her forehead. Agnes melted into his arms. "You know these dances don't mean a thing. In the end, it'll be you and me. And I've already heard you snort, so you don't have to worry about me leaving."

"If you promise to stay near, I might be able to get through the night." Agnes looked into his eyes and held his gaze. She was grateful for steady, unwavering James. "But don't you dare make me snort."

"I'll be a perfect gentleman. I won't leave your side." James had planted another tender kiss on her cheek. "Whenever you need me and even when you don't, I'll be here."

He had kept his word and stayed near her the entire dance.

In the end, she was the one who ran away. Just a year after that dance, she fled, and she'd not been in his arms like that since.

Looking over at James now, she wondered what sort of life they would have shared if she'd been free to marry. Would they have the house they had always dreamed of? The one with an attic bedroom and nursery. They'd promised to never consider a house if it did not have a tree that could hold a swing or a porch they could sit on together.

The baby wiggled, then smiled in his sleep. A big, open-mouthed smile. A row of little teeth showed.

A quiet thumping at the door caught her attention. Agnes tapped James with her foot, hoping he would stand and answer the door. He roused himself, wiping a hand over his bleary eyes.

"Someone is here," she whispered when he shot her a questioning look. "At the door."

He stumbled across the floor and opened the door to Rose Clint.

"I thought you might need breakfast," she said from the other side of the threshold, a tray in hand.

"Come in," James said.

"How's the baby?" she asked as she eyed the sleeping bundle in Agnes's arms. "I've brought him milk."

"He coughed through the night and was restless, but he seems to be improving." Agnes smiled at the peaceful baby. "He's strong."

"I'm glad to hear it." Rose walked over and looked at the boy's little face. "Did you hold him all night?"

She nodded.

"I can take him. I'm sure we could arrange a few women to shuffle him around until we decide what to do with him."

"I didn't mind holding him." She pulled him a little closer, and the movement woke him. His eyes fluttered open. "Hello, little one," she said to the baby before lifting her gaze back to Rose. "There's no need to shuffle him about. I've time, and I'd like to care for him."

"We've been asking around about him." Rose touched the baby's cheek.

"What have you learned?"

"His mother died in the fire last night."

"And his father?" James asked.

Rose lowered her gaze. "He hasn't one. The boy, well, he's . . ."

James said the word Rose had avoided. "Illegitimate? I'd guessed as much."

"Yes. It would appear that way. And in this case, it would be impossible to know who his father is. There are too many possibilities." Rose blushed. "I wish it weren't so. Once he's well, we'll see if we can find someone willing to take him in, or we'll send him to the nearest orphanage. He may fare better in a town where no one knows his past."

Agnes stood and paced the room, bouncing the baby as she went. "We ought to have compassion on him. What difference does it make who his parents are? He needs us now." Her voice quavered as she spoke. "It shouldn't matter. No one should care about something like that."

James stared at her a moment before walking to her side and calmly saying, "You know it matters to a good many people. It's an unfortunate reality, but this little one is the son of one of the upstairs girls, a tainted woman, and he has no father. We can't change that."

"What difference does it make?" Tears sprang from her eyes and rolled down her cheeks, dropping onto the boy's head. "It's where he comes from, but it has no bearing on where he's going, what he can become. He needs love like any other orphan." She pressed her lips to the baby's head. Her heart rebelled against the label and ached for this dear boy who would suffer all because of a title. *Illegitimate*. "Why do you judge him? He had no choice about how he came into this world."

"Aggie, calm down." James put a hand on her shoulder. "You're making too much of this."

"I'm not. It's unfair." An exasperated sob shook her. "You're deciding his future based on one fact. One thing that doesn't matter. It's cruel and hateful."

"I'm not deciding anything," James shot back. "But it's a fact. He *is* illegitimate. I didn't make the rules, so don't go assuming I did. I'm just telling you how it's going to be for him. As long as people know, they'll care. I'm not saying I won't help him. You know I will. I'll treat him, and we'll find a home that's suitable. But when I record my notes for the day in my log, I'll put no surname as I've been taught. All of us have to make note of it."

Rose spoke up, her small bird-like voice chirping above the others. "No one is deciding anything. For now, we need to make sure he's well. And you're doing a fine job of that. Just look at him in your arms—he seems to be taken with you."

Agnes ran her hand over the baby's cheek. "What's his name?"

Rose smiled. "Fred. One of the girls said she thinks he was born ten or eleven months ago, but she couldn't remember for sure. He slept in a little box in the closet. Only a couple of the girls even knew he existed. I'm afraid he wasn't always well cared for."

"No one is going to hide you ever again," Agnes whispered in the child's ear. "Don't you worry, baby Fred." His curls tickled her cheek. "None of that matters to me. You're safe now."

Agnes could feel James and Rose watching her. Did they see the injustice of it all?

Let them think what they wished. She bent over Fred and busied herself by coaxing the milk into his waiting mouth, all the while her resolve to help him deepening.

CHAPTER FOURTEEN

Once the fire was fully out and Fred's coughing had calmed, Agnes had taken him home with her. She was ill equipped to house a baby but had chosen not to mention that fact, afraid someone might suggest the baby go elsewhere. In the oasis of her home, she made do with the provisions she had. With an eager heart, she threw herself into caring for Fred.

The first day he coughed and fussed. His cry hoarse and sad. She soothed him with baths and nourishing food. Whenever he so much as whimpered, she picked him up and walked him back and forth, singing to him as she went. Each time she bent over him to cradle and comfort him, she smelled his sweet baby scent, which she found more intoxicating than the finest spring flowers. With each passing hour, his condition improved and his energy increased.

Although the days spent with Fred were long and demanding, she never tired of the sight of him, not even a little. At night, despite the pull for sleep, she would creep to his side and watch his even breathing as he slumbered. She wasn't sure how it'd happened, but something had begun to change within her. This watching over Fred was not merely charity. It was more than compassion or a call to help. She pressed her palm to her racing heart.

The lullabies, the smell, the little fingers wrapped around her own, all of it had awakened something in her, a part of her that wanted to be more than a frontierswoman and teacher. Her suppressed mothering heart had stirred within her. It did not matter that this child shared no blood with her or that his mother was a prostitute and his father was unknown. If anything, it only endeared him further. They were not so different. A desperate need to shelter and protect him had grown within her heart.

A seed of love had sprouted with each motherly act she'd shown him.

Her very soul seemed to connect with him. His strength was returning. Now, watching him play in her home, she felt content.

Freddie sat on the floor clanging two spoons together while babbling to her in his high baby voice. She spoke to him as though he understood, and then she tickled his chubby thighs. Soon he broke out in a bout of laughter that lit up the room.

"I love you," she whispered, knowing her words were true—unplanned but true all the same. She loved his soft feet, his button nose. She loved his bright eyes, his dimpled arms. She loved him, all of him. It made no sense, and reason could not explain the wild awakening of her heart, nor could she deny what was happening.

She stood and walked to the window and looked out at

the endless hills. "Why?" she whispered, knowing the Lord could make sense of all she felt. No words came rushing back to her, but the warmth in her heart grew as though she were being told she had no reason to fear the blossoming feelings within her.

Moments passed by as she stood transfixed by the power of it all. Then the thumping of his spoons brought her attention away from the window, and she stooped down in front of the little boy and whispered again to him.

"Will you be my family, Freddie? Will you let me love you and care for you and share your life?" He blew bubbles with his spit as he continued clanging the spoons together. "Will you? Will you be mine and I'll be yours?" More baby noises. And a beautiful baby grin. She grinned back. "I think that means yes."

Could it be that simple? Taking him in her arms, she spun him around the room, earning her more precious baby noises. This moment would live in her mind and heart always. She knew her life would be forever altered. Deciding she was Fred's and he was hers was a crossroads. Kissing his soft cheek, she told him again how she loved him. The perfect moment lasted until Freddie squirmed for his freedom and crawled toward Tiger. He giggled as he reached for the cat's tail.

"Now that that is decided, we need to get ourselves a little better set up for a baby." She stood with her hands on her hips and looked about the house, wondering where to start. The last few days she'd made do with very little, but it wouldn't do to live so meagerly forever. "I think perhaps we need some advice."

"It's my wish to keep him," Agnes said when she and Minnie were settled in the main room of Minnie's house. She knew her busybody friend would have lots to say about raising babies. "I decided it today."

"You can't just keep a baby," Minnie said. "He's not a stray puppy."

"I know he's not a puppy, but do you see anyone else trying to get him? No one wants him. Not a soul has asked after him. The only things I've heard have been whispered remarks about his birth. Rose mentioned an orphanage as a possibility, but I won't have it. Why send him to a heartless institution when I'm here to love him?"

Minnie shook her head. "I know you want to keep him. Of course you do. You're good and kind, and he's a darling little fellow. But you can't. Don't you remember a few years back when Winnie and Thomas both died? Their little ones were all taken away. Ended up on some farm or who knows where."

"That's because there were so few families here at the time. Just a bunch of single men, and there were too many of them for me or you to take in. This doesn't have to be like that."

"That may be, but it doesn't change the facts." She raised an eyebrow at Agnes. "Aren't you forgetting something?"

Agnes waited.

"You're the schoolteacher. You showed me your contract. You'd have to give up teaching. Then, as a single woman, you tell me how you plan to support him. You couldn't stay in the teacher's house. Someone else would live there. If you keep him, you either have to run home to your father and hope he'll let you in or marry and hope there's a man willing to take on a wife and a baby he didn't father. It'd be better for you to petition the town to see if someone would take him." She shook her head. "It'd be better to send him away. Somewhere new where he won't be haunted by his birth and talk of his bad blood."

"Bad blood." Agnes sucked in her lip, trying to keep herself calm. "That's nonsense, and we both know it."

"Look, I know you can see past all that, but some folks can't. I didn't mean I think he has bad blood, only that some folks will believe he does. I'm sure even in your civilized Buffalo those things mattered."

"They *shouldn't* have mattered there, and they *shouldn't* matter here. No one should have to run away their whole life just because of how they entered the world." She pulled Freddie tighter against her and scowled, not really at Minnie but at the horrible predicament. "Too many people run." *I ran*, she nearly said aloud. "They run when they should be taken in and helped. He lived in a gated-off closet. Do you realize this poor baby lived in hiding? He needs to touch the grass and chase the birds. I can give him those things. I'm sure I can find a way." She nuzzled her head against his soft scalp. "I love him. Call me foolish if you must, but I feel a deep and real love for him."

"You can't love him. You've only had him at your place for three days." Minnie clicked her tongue in a dismissive way. "You're just playing house."

"How long does it take you to love your babies when you meet them?" Agnes stood. "If you don't want to teach me about babies, so be it. But you can't say whether I love him or not. You're not in my heart. You don't know what it does when I see him or hear him. You don't feel any of it. You're using your own logic to judge my experience. But I have lived it, and I have felt the love that races through me. It's real."

"I never said I didn't want to help you. I just don't want to see you getting your heart broken over somebody else's baby."

"His name is Freddie. His mother died, and until I'm told he's to go to some other mother, I'm stepping up and filling that role."

"Fine. I'll see it your way if that'll make you settle back down." Minnie wiped a bead of sweat off her brow. "Summer's twice as hot when I'm expecting. Makes me grouchy. Sit yourself back down and tell me what I can do."

"Thank you, Minnie. I don't mean to be so irate about it all, but I look at him and see his need for love. I suppose it's clouded my ability to see much else."

"Being blinded with love isn't the worst thing." Minnie patted the seat and, reluctantly, Agnes sat. "Tell me what you need."

"I need to buy or make some things for Freddie. I made do with the rags I had around, but it's not ideal. I need real baby things. But I don't know where to get started."

"That's something I can help you with. I'll tell you exactly what you need." Minnie laughed. "You can stop your scowling. I'll help you. Just know that I didn't say anything you aren't going to hear time and time again." She nudged Agnes. "I thought you had a thicker skin than that."

"With Freddie, it's different. The injustice of it all infuriates me."

"He doesn't know anyone's judging him," Minnie said before gathering a few baby things to loan Agnes. Then she told her what else she needed to buy and what to expect from a baby Freddie's age.

Before Agnes left, she turned to her friend. "Thank you for helping me. I'm sorry I lost my temper."

"Think nothing of it. You're a good soul, Agnes Pratt. He's blessed to have you for as long as he can." She smiled and Agnes felt true warmth coming from her. "I always said you'd make a fine mother one day. Just never guessed it'd happen this way."

"I am the blessed one. I heard him that night, and I can't help but think God wanted me to love this child."

Minnie stroked Freddies's round cheek. "I can see the love you have for him shining in your whole countenance. Love's a beautiful thing. Though it might be a little harder for you to claim that fine-looking doctor with a baby in your arms."

When James had seen the advertisement for the job in Penance, he'd known divine Providence had intervened on his behalf. The advertisement had landed in his hands not long after he'd received a letter from Aggie's mother urging him to go to Penance. The time had come to fetch his girl, bring her back to Buffalo, and pick up where they'd left off. It had all made sense and seemed so simple and perfect. Perhaps not exactly simple or perfect, seeing as he'd ruffled his parents' feathers coming out here, but they'd believed him when he'd said adventure was his goal. He'd left them with promises of returning, and in his heart, he'd meant them. What he'd failed to mention was his desire to bring Aggie back with him.

Baby Fred, or Freddie as Aggie called him, changed James's plans. He cringed at his thought, rationalizing that his thinking didn't reflect anything personal against Freddie. Still, he worried over Aggie's growing attachment. Every time she looked at Fred, her eyes gleamed with fondness for the boy. How could he return to Buffalo with Agnes *and* a child? An *illegitimate* child. The son of a tainted woman.

He knew what happened to illegitimate people if they tried to mix with his class. Not only were there laws that kept them from inheriting, but they could never marry without it becoming public. The shame alone would be an impossible weight to shoulder. Convincing anyone that Freddie belonged to them would be impossible. They weren't married, and even if he could convince Aggie to marry him quickly, the baby's age could not be masked. Agnes Pratt, the daughter of Howard and Catherine Pratt, couldn't be Fred's mother. And certainly he, James Harris, could not ever be his father. His family was one of the oldest and wealthiest in the city. Finding a different home for Freddie would be best for everyone.

As he walked to the mayor's house, he pictured his mother's face. She would never welcome Aggie and a baby into her family. Always a lady, she would smile, but she'd also let him know that there would be no mixing with heathens under her roof. She'd politely tell him the child was an abomination, and then she'd find a charity home for Freddie to live in. To save face, she might even donate to the home. His father would not even pretend to be civil about such things. Somehow it would sort itself out, or so he hoped.

Today he and Mayor Clint needed to come up with a plan to keep the streams cleaner. He'd begun treating a man he suspected had cholera, and he didn't want an outbreak of sickness. With the recent heavy rains, James suspected human waste had washed into the streams used for drinking water. Education and changes in privy locations could save lives.

Luckily, Mayor Clint cared about more than power. He cared about this town and its people. James believed he would have the man's support.

After explaining the problem to Clint, James took a long drink from the glass Rose had brought him while he waited to hear Clint's thoughts.

"You tell us what the people need to be doing, and I'll get some volunteers. We'll all take a different section of the map and spread the word. We'll teach them how to keep the water clean," Mayor Clint said. "I don't want anyone getting sick on my watch. Some of these men just haven't ever thought twice about what water they're drinking or where they place their privies. I'm sure they'll listen."

"I figured that. I think if we take a little time and spread the word, we will prevent sickness in the future." James stood to leave, grateful for the man's cooperation. "Prevention is sure easier than trying to tackle a problem when it's out of control."

"I agree. That's why we wanted a trained doctor. We needed someone like you. You're doing good things for these people."

"I can't keep everything away. As much as I would like to. But this one is easy enough. Thanks for meeting with me."

"Sit back down. I've been wanting to talk to you since the night of the fire."

James shifted uneasily, then sighed and sat. "About that night." James took the lead. "I'd like to keep that conversation between the two of us. I don't see any reason anyone needs to know. Agnes and I both feel going about our lives here with no one speculating about our pasts is better."

"We'll keep this one between the two of us too." Mayor Clint nodded.

"Thank you, sir."

"I was here the day Miss Aggie arrived," Mayor Clint began. "I saw her, and I knew there was more to her story than she was telling. One look, and I knew she was running from something. Most people in Penance are, and that's all right with me. But Aggie was out of place. She looked like a kitten trying to survive in the wilderness. It took her time and effort to fit in. She had no skills, but she had backbone. I was sure she'd pack her bags and head for home, but she didn't. She's made herself a home here—and a life. This town needs her, and we can't have her running off."

"Sir?" James said, uncertain what his response should be.

"She managed to scare off women-hungry men and weasel her way into the hearts of not only the children but the rest of us too. I don't know what your connection is to her, but I think you ought to think long and hard before you do anything that might hurt her."

"I didn't come here to hurt Aggie," James said. "I came here to be a doctor, and I've done that. Don't assume the worst of me."

"I'm not accusing you of malicious intent. You don't seem like the type who'd hurt anyone on purpose. That doesn't mean accidents won't happen." Mayor Clint drummed his fingers on the arm of his chair. "Although you did let Lem have it pretty good the other night."

James stifled a laugh. "I hadn't meant to leave that kind of color on him. I'm glad he's forgiven me."

"Not merely forgiven. He's glad you saved the baby." Mayor Clint leaned forward.

"I know you all care for Aggie. I do too. I'll look out for her."

"She needs a good man in her life," the mayor said. "My guess is you broke her heart before and that's what she's been running from. Don't you go breaking it again. I saw the tears she shed when she thought no one was looking. She's been free of those tears a long time now."

James decided to let the accusation stand, as refuting it would serve no purpose. Instead, he shook his head and said, "I've got to ride out and check on a couple injured loggers. I'll meet you when you have volunteers ready, and we can talk about spreading the word on clean water."

"All right. But remember what I said."

"Don't you worry." James moved to leave. "I won't break any hearts."

CHAPTER FIFTEEN

"I thought your little man might be able to use this." Sam stood in the doorway of Agnes's house.

Agnes looked at the handcrafted high chair he held in his arms. "You made this?"

He nodded. "I build furniture to pass the time. Nothing fancy, of course. Just useful pieces. I heard you were looking for baby things."

"It's perfect. I've been feeding him on my lap, and he spits his food everywhere. By the end of a meal, I'm covered in it. I've never had so much laundry to do in all my life."

Sam chuckled as he set down the chair. "I guess that's all part of the fun of babies. My sisters weren't so different when they ate."

"How many siblings do you have?"

"Well, my ma was married and had me and one of my sisters. Our pa died when we were small. She remarried and had eight more." He ran his hand along the back of the high chair. "How 'bout yourself?"

"It was just me. I didn't have any brothers or sisters."

"Sounds like you and I came from different worlds." He tickled Fred under his chin. "An only child and a city girl." He whistled low. "I wonder how you ended up in a place like this."

"I wonder how any of us did."

"I suppose it could be luck." He looked away. "Or it was just what was at the end of the road."

"Is this the end of your road?" she asked.

Sam stood on the doorstep slowly rubbing his hands together. "I guess you could say I've been wandering, and this is where I ended up. It's just a place to work while I decide what's next."

"I think we all wander at times."

"I been thinking about my sisters and family and seems everyone is working toward something. I don't want to wander forever."

The temptation to ask more crept in, but she did not honor it.

He lifted the high chair back into his arms. "Can I put this somewhere for you?"

"By the table." Agnes smiled as she admired her table with the perfect high chair beside it. "I can pay you."

"No need. I wanted to do it, and the wood was easy enough to come by. The scraps at the camp are fair game." He patted the back of the chair. "I'm heading into the hills to do a little hunting. I often catch more than I can eat. Would you like a cut?"

Freddie fussed in her arms, squirming uncomfortably.

"That's very kind of you. I'm not sure I should. I probably shouldn't even accept the chair."

"Keep it. It was good of you to take Freddie in. I wanted to help."

She nodded, grateful. "Thank you."

Sam patted Freddie's head. "Glad to do it." He tipped his hat before leaving the house.

Agnes laid Freddie down and unpinned him. "What do you think of Sam?" she said as she changed the baby. "He's not so coarse as the other loggers. I'd say he's friendly, wouldn't you?"

Shaking her head, she looked down at Freddie and watched him gurgle and blow bubbles. "He made you a fine chair. You'll look like a prince sitting in it.

"When you grow up, I hope you find a sweet girl who loves you," she said in the special voice she used for her baby. "I hope she's less confused than I am. It seems I am doomed to never understand men."

James walked up to Aggie's house, but before he knocked, he listened. She was inside talking to someone.

"Oh, look at your cute little toes. I'm going to tickle those toes." Her voice was high and singsongy. "Look at that belly. I'm going to get it too."

The sweet ringing of baby laughter made its way to his ears. Without even seeing her, he knew she was smiling. Proud of herself for eliciting such joy from the boy.

More baby talk, more giggles. He stood with his hand in the air about to knock, but he hated to disturb their fun. At last, he knocked and waited.

"James, how are you?" She leaned against the doorframe after greeting him, her hands busily smoothing her hair.

He'd seen her a few times since she'd taken Freddie in. Their visits had been brief and focused purely on Fred's recovering health. Today he hoped to discover where he stood with her.

"I've been busy warning people about the water and telling them to keep it clean. Cholera is preventable, and I'd like to keep it from the town. I don't think there's anything to worry about." He cleared his throat. "I've been wanting to say that I'm sorry I upset you when you first took Freddie." He gave his best "I'm sorry" face. "You aren't too mad, are you?"

Aggie walked into the house, inviting him to do the same. "I was mad. But I've never been able to stay mad for very long. Stop making that face and come in. I heard you were traveling around. I had hoped to join you and help spread the word. I think it's wonderful you're teaching people."

"We ended up with lots of volunteers. More than I'd expected. I think people listened." James leaned around her so he could see the baby on the floor. "I see our little patient is doing well."

"He still coughs, especially at night. But he improves every day. He has so much energy now."

James set down his bag. He pulled out his stethoscope and approached the baby. "Hey there, Mr. Fred. Can I listen to your lungs?" The baby answered him with a toothy grin. "What a fine patient you are."

"You still have your touch," Aggie said. "I have to work a lot harder to get that smile. You should see some of the tricks and faces I make so I can hear him laugh."

James listened to Fred's chest through the stethoscope.

His lungs were certainly improving. "I'd like to see those tricks. Maybe they'd make me smile too."

"Very funny." Then, in her same singsong voice, she said, "Those tricks are just for my sweet little baby Fred."

James did laugh. She looked adorable—her nose scrunched up, her voice so high. Fear crept in. She looked too adorable, too content. Aggie cared deeply for Fred, there was no denying it. Would she pick the baby over him? Would she find some way to keep him over everything else in her life?

A heaviness settled in his chest, and it took great effort to force a smile. "Looks like your place is all set up for a baby."

"Minnie helped me decide what I needed. She loaned me a few things, and I bought most everything they had at the mercantile." Aggie's eyes wandered to the high chair.

"And the chair?" he asked, figuring it must have a story.

"Sam made it. He brought it by earlier." Aggie turned her attention back to Fred. "It's funny, because I've always loved babies and children, but suddenly having one to look after, I find I am doubting myself. I'm wondering if I'm doing it right."

James wanted to ask about her and Sam, but he didn't. Suddenly, it seemed the world was against him. That Fred and Sam and all of Penance were in his way and he'd never be able to call Aggie his own. His dreams of riding back into Buffalo with her by his side seemed nearly out of reach. He took a deep breath and let it out slowly—a vain attempt at calming the storm that raged inside of himself.

"He looks like you're taking good care of him," James managed to say as he watched the baby climb onto Aggie and settle in her lap. "I was hoping I could help you decide what to do with him. I want to help him find a good home."

"I plan to keep him. I'm not sure how I'll do it, but I want to." She tousled Fred's hair. "It might sound strange to you, but I think I was the one who heard him for a reason. I feel something for him every time he's in my arms. Why would I put him in the arms of someone who does not?"

She embraced him then, enveloping the little boy in her loving arms. "I watch him all day and don't get tired of it. I stare at his face, loving every expression he makes. Every sound and new thing he does captivates me." She looked away and with a quieter voice said, "No one understands. They all think I've lost my mind. They tell me there's no way to keep him, but there must be."

"Ag, I know you love babies," James began cautiously, unable to meet her eyes. "You always have, but this one is going to make things hard for you. I think we could find him a better place. There are other people who won't care about his past and that he's illegitimate. Back home in Buffalo, in our society, it'll matter."

He braced himself, knowing he might have ignited her anger. But when he looked at her, he saw tears in her eyes.

"Aggie, I wasn't trying to hurt you. I want to protect you—and Freddie too. Out here in the West, it won't matter so much. The right farmer or miner won't care. And Freddie won't be kept from inheriting like he would in Buffalo. The shame won't be as harsh. You know as well as I do what people like our parents think of all this." He scratched the back of his neck. "My mother would be appalled."

Still looking at the baby, she said softly, "People like you and your parents can think what they want. I'm past caring what they think or what they might say. You don't know me if you think I'd give up on someone because it'd make my life easier. You go and live your easy life. Enjoy your status and ease. Roll in your money and inheritance. I choose this. I choose Freddie and every hard thing that comes from choosing him. I choose him, no matter what it entails."

"You're wrong." He shook his head, unsure if her words were wrong or if he was the one in the dark. "Look, I know it sounds callous. I think he's a sweet baby. I just don't understand why *you* have to be the one to raise him." James wanted her to understand. He wanted her to choose him and the dreams they'd made together. "You're going to give up so much for him."

"I gave up Buffalo long ago. I don't want Buffalo or its pomp. I may visit someday, but it's not my home. I admit that Freddie changes my plans." She ran her fingers across Fred's arm. "We see Fred differently. I see what I'm gaining, not what I'm giving up. It's not just about helping Fred, because anyone could feed or change him. But I want to be his mother and build a world for him. I want to fight beside him whenever someone tells him he's worth less because of where he came from. I want to love him."

Leaning forward, James put his elbows on his knees and rested his head in his hands. The weight of it all pressed against him as he let out a long sigh. How could he make any of it right?

"You think he has to become what his parents were? That because he was born in a saloon, he'll lead a tainted life." Aggie's voice remained serious but calm. "He doesn't have to. Just like you don't have to be the haughty, arrogant man your father is. If you are destined to be the same as the blood that runs through your veins, then I suppose that is your lot. It's a shame, though, because I think you could be so much more than that. You can choose to be kind and good despite who he is, even if it costs you an inheritance. I suppose we all must decide what matters." Freddie gurgled happily, and her eyes went to him. "Freddie can choose too. If everyone would let him, he could be whatever he wants to be. I'm going to help him become something wonderful."

She brought the little boy closer to him. "Look at him, James. He has a future ahead of him, if we will only give it to him."

James hadn't thought of it that way. He'd never liked the way his father treated others. He hadn't even liked the way his father treated him. As a young child, he'd thought he had to be like his father, but then as he grew, he'd decided he would be a kinder man. He'd promised himself he would be different. Could Fred be different from the woman who gave birth to him? The man who fathered him? James wasn't sure. Worried he would dig a deeper hole for himself, he stood, bag in hand. His shoulders slumped from shame and uncertainty.

"I'm sorry, Ag." He moved for the door without meeting her gaze. "His lungs sound fine, and he looks happy. I wouldn't doubt yourself. You're taking good care of him."

"James?"

"Yes."

"Won't you try to know him? I think you'd see him differently. I think you could understand why I care so much." Aggie's rich brown eyes pleaded with him. "Stay and play with him like you would any other baby. Show him one of your tricks and make him laugh."

He hesitated but set his bag back down. "I'll stay. I've always had a soft spot for babies."

"I know you have. And I think you could love him too."

Scooping him out of Aggie's arms and into his own, he held the baby high in the air. "Does Freddie want to fly like a bird?" he asked the little boy before racing around the room with him. Though he played with Freddie, his eyes wandered back to Aggie, searching hers to see if he'd found any sort of approval.

For half an hour, he used all his tricks on Freddie, earning him giggle after giggle. But more important, he saw Aggie's eyes soften toward him. Deep inside he knew this path led to danger.

"I have to get going." James put a finger on the tip of Freddie's nose and made a funny noise.

Aggie walked him to the door. "Come and play with him again?"

"I will."

If James could love Freddie, maybe he could love her despite her secret. The thought of telling him made her queasy with excitement and fear. If she dared to speak the words aloud, what would he do? What would he think of her? The memory felt raw and fresh despite the six years that had passed since her life had changed.

She'd rushed inside one beautiful afternoon and flung her arms around her mother.

"I'm going to marry James! I've always known it, but he's asked me. Not officially, of course, because he still has to ask Father, but I've said yes all the same." She danced around the room. The world had never felt so right. "It's the most perfect day. Oh, don't you just think it is the most wonderful of all days?"

Her mother smiled at her, but not the vibrant, excited smile Agnes had expected. Then she took Agnes's hand in her own. "There is not a more perfect man in this world for you. James is so good. He's so constant and thoughtful. He's the type of man you deserve. But it might be more complicated than that."

Agnes stilled and looked at her mother. A tangible feeling of dread washed over her. "What do you mean? More complicated?"

"Wait here. I want to fetch your father, and then we can all sit and have a talk. I'd feel so much better with him here."

"Tell me now," she said. "Tell me so I can stop worrying and enjoy this day. Tell me."

Her mother muttered under her breath, "We should have told you years ago, before it ever got this far." She put a hand on her daughter's shoulder. "I'll hurry back. I can't have this conversation without your father. But it can't wait any longer. Stay here. I know it's difficult, but I'll hurry."

Agnes's heart pounded faster while she waited. What could possibly be complicated? James loved her, she loved him. They knew everything about each other. Didn't they? Did her parents know something about James that she didn't? It couldn't be so. She treaded back and forth across the room, nervously wringing her hands together, trying to believe nothing could keep her and James apart.

At last, her parents returned. They were holding hands when they entered the room.

"Talk to her, Howard," her mother said, after they all sat down.

"Aggie, I heard young James wants to make things official,"

her father said with a gentle smile. "I should have guessed that boy would be eager to make you his own."

"Yes," she said, the excitement gone from her voice. "He asked me today. He hopes to speak with you this evening. But something is wrong, and I don't know what."

"Well . . . we've been debating for years about when we should tell you about your past. It never felt right, but I guess some things never do. I wish we could go on as we are, nothing changing." Her dear father fidgeted as he tried to pull words together. "Just the three of us in this home. It'd sure be easier that way. It's always been so happy like this."

"Tell your secret," she said in a dry whisper. "What are you trying so hard to tell me?"

"Sit, Aggie. Let me start at the beginning."

Agnes sat and tapped her foot on the ground in worry.

"My sister was ten years younger than me. We'd not seen her in years, then one day she arrived on our doorstep. We were living in New York City at the time." Her father paused a moment, rubbing the stubble on his face. "My sister's name was Nora. She was young, and she'd fallen in love. He'd made her promises that he never kept."

Agnes glanced between her mother and father, their faces solemn.

"When Nora showed up, she had a brand-new baby in her arms," he said softly, his eyes refusing to meet her own. Why wouldn't he look at her? She needed his fatherly assurance as the pieces of this story swirled around her, stealing her breath. "A little girl."

"A girl," Agnes whispered.

"With curly hair and rich brown eyes." He spoke quietly, slowly. The words hovered above them. She fought against them, not wanting them to soak in. Despite her resistance, they assaulted her.

"No," Agnes said softly as she shook her head.

"The most beautiful baby," her mother added. "I'd never seen one so perfect. We loved you right away."

Agnes fingered her own curls. "You're not my parents?"

It couldn't be so. They were family. A perfectly happy, respectable, loving family. More than respectable, they were practically Buffalo nobility.

"You were that baby, Aggie." Her father's voice was full of pain. "But we are your parents. Our family back in New York City, many of them know. Your birth is recorded in the church's birth records and you're listed as Nora's daughter, with no father listed. When we moved here to Buffalo, we didn't tell anyone. No one questioned if you were ours."

"No father?" She rubbed her throbbing temple. "I'm . . . I'm." The word wouldn't come out. She'd heard it mentioned in hushed conversations, but now in reference to herself it didn't seem plausible. It couldn't be.

"You're illegitimate. Nora left you with us," her father said, his gaze averted.

"What became of her?" Agnes asked. It was all too much for her to absorb. "Was she run off in shame?"

Her father cleared his throat. "Years later she went West with a good man who agreed to give her a fresh start. She did what she believed was best for you."

"And you hid my history." Agnes could no longer sit, so on shaky legs, she rose and walked back and forth.

"We saw no reason to dwell on the darker side of your past." Her father took his wife's hand.

"But we can't pretend any longer," her mother said, wiping

her eyes. "If you marry James, it'll be on the front page of the papers, and the world is not so small that those who know your story won't speak up. The headlines will tell the world that James Harris's bride-to-be is illegitimate. I wish it weren't so."

Illegitimate. Agnes's stomach twisted. Illegitimate children were a class of their own. They were shunned, they were despised.

Her mother stood and crossed the room. She put a hand on Agnes's shoulder. "We've always been against such shaming, but there was nothing we could do about it and your best chance of fitting in was to pretend it wasn't so."

"But they won't pretend. It will matter to them—to James and his family." Aggie groaned in sheer agony. Sick at heart, she wished she could escape it all. "They won't let us marry. I've heard his father talk. He cares so much about what others think." Swallowing hard, she fought back the flood of emotion that raged inside. She brought her palms to her forehead, pressing against the pounding within. "They'll keep us apart. Ruining everything all because of how I came into this world. All to save face."

Her mother wiped at her eyes with a handkerchief. "I don't think they'll approve. James is a good man, but I can't say how he'll feel. He could lose his inheritance if they don't accept you. He's a Harris. His way of life depends on impressing others." Her mother wiped again at her eyes. "I'm sorry, Aggie. We shouldn't have let you become so attached. We should have told you when you were younger. But the two of you just happened. You were jumping rope together one moment and the next you were dancing partners and now you want to marry. Oh, Aggie. I wish I could tell you it would all work out and that you could have your James. I wish we could throw a party and shout it from the rooftops. As it is, I don't know what to do."

She wasn't listening any longer. Her mind was too busy trying to make sense of it all. "It could hurt you too. If anyone finds out. They might turn their backs on you, call you a traitor for keeping a secret from them."

Her father frowned. "They may call us all sorts of names, but it doesn't matter. Now that you know you must do whatever is best for you. We'll stand by you."

Running her fingers through her tangle of curls, she struggled to stay in control. Asking them to move was not fair. Her mother's doctors and her father's business investments were in Buffalo. She paused, her eyes roaming the comfortable home she'd spent her life in. She'd been happy here.

Her gaze stopped on the window, on the world outside of her own. Nora had fled and began a new life. Agnes could flee too. "He'll never know. Promise me you won't tell him. No one can know. It will only hurt him—and all of you." She folded her arms across her chest. "I can't put any of you through that. I'll find my own way."

"We don't have to decide anything right now." Her father stood and stepped near her.

"There's nothing to decide. I must leave. And I have to tell James I can't marry him." Saying the words aloud made it all too real. Not marry James, was there a worse sentence to carry? Her heart broke, and she could feel the pieces crumbling inside of herself. "I have to tell him before he spreads the word about our plans to marry. I won't put him in a position where he has to decide between his family or a future with me. I won't do it."

Agnes fled to her room. Sobbing, she flung the door closed and fell into a heap on the floor. James was the only man she'd ever loved and the only man she would ever love. She would leave and go somewhere far away, somewhere he couldn't find her. Someday he would marry. He'd make his family proud and never have to forsake a single thing because of his wife. Knowing it would break her further to watch him live a life without her, she deepened her resolve to go. Staying in Buffalo would not do. She loved him too much to stay.

That night and the days that followed were dark and miserable. Sad and brokenhearted, she moved forward with her plans, the whole time trying to understand how this curse had befallen her.

Now, sitting here with Freddie in her arms, she wondered if James could ever see past the baby's origins. If he could, maybe he could see past hers as well. A delightful shiver ran through her at the thought of being James Harris's girl again. Oh, how she longed to be the one he turned to, the one he held, the one he laughed with. To be in his arms again. To kiss his lips again.

No, she fought the rush of euphoria that ran through her. It wasn't an option. If he decided to have a future with her, he could lose everything back home. That hadn't changed. His inheritance, his standing, and his parents. She wouldn't ask that of him. She couldn't.

"Freddie Boy, we'll find a way," she said, pressing a kiss into his hair.

CHAPTER SIXTEEN

"You've brought the baby to the picnic," Sarah Merts said. Sarah arrived in Penance two years ago from just east of the Mississippi and believed it her moral duty to correct the ruffians of Penance. "How lovely."

"I couldn't very well leave him home. Besides, he loves being outside." Agnes adjusted Fred's little hat.

"What will you do with him when school begins?" Sarah asked. "I hear there are orphanages that will take foundlings, or perhaps there's a couple in town who don't mind who his mother was."

Agnes clenched her teeth. "I'm raising him."

"But you can't."

Hadn't she done a fine enough job thus far? Freddie was healthy and growing and happy. "I already am."

"The teachers I've known have all signed contracts. Haven't you?"

Agnes fought the urge to lie, but too many people knew the truth. She nodded. "I have."

"Well, the ones I've seen have all mentioned proper behavior, forfeiting the position if marrying, things like that." Sarah put a hand on Fred's back. "I don't think raising the son of a tainted woman around all the children is wise. They respect their teacher, and you'll be showing them by example that you have no respect for morals."

"No respect for morals? You're wrong." She took a step forward, only to feel a hand on her shoulder.

"Sarah," Minnie said from behind Agnes. "Milo's looking for you."

"Oh, I best run along. You all enjoy the picnic."

Agnes didn't bother saying goodbye and turned to Minnie. "How dare she!"

"You're going to have to accept that loving Freddie comes at a cost. You can't let everything folks say get you riled up. Sarah's not all bad. She's just spewing back what she's been taught." Minnie linked arms with her and nodded toward Freddie. "He doesn't know what people are saying."

"He will though. He'll know someday, and it will hurt him." She stepped away with Freddie in her arms. "I never want him to shed a single tear because of hateful people."

"Knowing you, you'll find a way to change these people's minds about him. Just give it time. Let's visit. Not everyone feels the way Sarah does." Minnie led her around the yard.

Hannah came racing across the lawn, her arms outstretched. "Hello, Mr. Fred." She took Freddie and snuggled him close. Hannah had been supportive from the start, coming over when she could to help Agnes settle into her caretaking role. "I've missed you. Oh, Aggie, look at him. He's so darling. I think he's grown since I saw him last, and it's only been two days."

"I think that every time I look at him."

Hannah leaned in and spoke quietly. "Let's walk over to the trees. I want to talk to you."

Agnes willingly agreed, following Hannah with Freddie in her arms away from the crowd.

"The doctor heard back from some of his medical friends. He said they looked at old case notes and found some that sounded similar to Grace. They don't know much, but it does seem to have happened before. The case they found was of a brother and sister. Both babies were thriving—they were starting to crawl and could eat soft foods. Then they regressed. They could no longer crawl or walk, just like Grace. It wasn't long, and they couldn't swallow. They were Grace's age when they died. I fear that it must run in families. The doctor says Ruby seems perfectly healthy. He doesn't understand it all, but he says it seems to be able to jump around in families."

"What do you make of it?"

"One part of me feels a deep ache knowing another mother out there has endured the agony of watching her child suffer in the slow, cruel way Grace did. The other part of me is comforted knowing I am not alone. Is it wrong to feel that way?"

"No." Agnes connected to Freddie, knowing they shared similar histories. That they were both fighting the same hateful prejudice. "Likely she'd feel the same knowing you were out here, walking the same path she's trod. Finding solace in another does not equate to wishing it upon them."

"I asked James to find her address. I think I'll write her."

Hannah smiled at Freddie. "I'll tell her I am sorry she had to endure so much. That I know how horrible it is to lose a child. I'll tell her I know the ache can be so strong and powerful that the very idea of rising in the morning seems too much to bear."

Tears rose to Aggie's eyes as she remembered sweet Grace and the many hours that Hannah held her, crying and praying over her. "Those words will bring her comfort. I think it's a good thing finding each other."

"Look at you and your tears. I didn't mean to ruin your picnic."

"You haven't ruined anything. It's only . . . now that I have Freddie, I understand in a small way what you felt for Grace." She wiped a stray tear. "Even yesterday, when he reached a fat little finger out and touched the cooling stove, I hurt for him. I don't know how you endured watching Grace suffer so greatly. I'm sorry I didn't understand better before."

"You were what I needed then. And just what I need now." She squeezed Agnes's hand. "It's horrible watching a child you love suffer. Poor Freddie touching the stove." She took Freddie's finger and planted a kiss on the red fingertip. "You are a lucky boy to have found such a wonderful home."

Freddie smiled, openmouthed, at Hannah. She smiled back.

"Miss Aggie!" Agnes turned to see Goldy running toward her. "Miss Aggie, I learned a magic trick. I want to show the doctor and you."

"He's not here, but I'd love to watch." Agnes smiled at her young friend. "Show me."

Goldy held up a rock. "See this rock?"

Agnes and Hannah nodded.

"I'll make it disappear." Goldy clapped her hands and slid the rock into her dress sleeve. She tried to do it quickly, but she lacked the sleight of hand a true magician possesses. "It's gone."

Agnes clapped, then tried not to laugh when the rock slid out and fell to the ground. "Keep practicing, Goldy, and you'll be as clever as the doctor before long."

Goldy promised to come back and try again, then went off to practice.

Agnes sighed and looked out at the crowded meadow.

"I heard Sam made you a high chair," Hannah said. "It's not every day you find a logger who knows about babies. Of course, I think the doctor does too. How will you ever decide?"

"Hannah," Agnes whispered. "You sound like Minnie."

"You blush more when the doctor is around, but who am I to say."

"I don't blush around the doctor." Agnes put her hand on her cheek. "None of that talk."

"Nothing wrong with having rosy cheeks," Hannah said, then waved at Ruby. "Let's go back. Ruby's been wanting to play with Freddie."

Sam meandered through the clusters of townsfolk, looking for Aggie. He'd hoped to muster the courage to ask her to stroll with him. He spotted her, but she was engaged in conversation with someone, so he shied away from approaching her. Minnie waved at him and he waved back.

"Sam, I was going to say hello to the mayor. Join me."

He looked around, wondering if there was some other

Sam nearby, but there wasn't. Minnie wasn't an easy woman to dismiss, so he followed her to where Mayor Clint and his wife stood.

"I'm not sure how to handle this. I've had complaints, and there is the contract," Mayor Clint was saying when they walked up. "I'll have to talk to her."

"About what?" Minnie butted her way into the conversation. Sam took a few steps back, unsure if the mayor's words were intended for his ears. Minnie shared none of his reservations. "What complaints?"

Rose answered her query. "It's about Freddie and Agnes. Two separate people have complained. They say it's not right, her having the baby when she isn't married. Then there's the matter of her contract, which specifically states she's to give up teaching if she chooses to marry and have a family."

"She's taught for a long time and she loves it. But she'd give up her position to keep Freddie. I've never seen her look so fondly at a child as she does that baby." Minnie put her hands on her hips. "But if she gives up her job, she'll be homeless."

"Yes, we've discussed that too. The home she lives in was built specifically for the teacher. It's a predicament. It'd be easier if we sent the boy somewhere else."

"You can't take him from her. She loves him." Minnie shook her head. "I was a skeptic too, but she loves the boy."

"We're looking for solutions." Rose put a hand on Clint's arm. "It's all very unfortunate."

Sam stepped even farther away and picked up a stick. He took his knife from his pocket and whittled. His hands were busy, but his ears were still alert and listening.

"We know she cares. And we don't want to move him. But

the teacher's contract can't be dismissed so easily." Mayor Clint wiped his brow. "My hope is that she'll marry. I'd have to find another teacher, but the town wouldn't lose her. She'd get to keep the baby, and with a man's support, she wouldn't be destitute." He looked toward the crowd. His brow furrowed. "I'm afraid her heart was broken so badly before that she won't ever consider marrying. Wish she would though. I'm not sure it's wise to leave the boy with her if she's penniless and without a home."

Minnie laughed. "I don't know her whole story, but I happen to know she was the one who did the jilting. She never did tell me the reason or his name, but I know it wasn't for lack of loving him."

"*She* left *him*?" Mayor Clint sounded almost excited by Minnie's statement. "You're saying she was the one who left him?"

"I don't know who *him* is, but I know she's the one who ran off. She told me once he was as handsome and good as the doctor."

Clint grinned. He smacked his leg and let out a whoop. "I think I might know a way to help the two of them."

"The two of them?" Minnie asked. "Aggie and Fred? What have you got planned?"

"Don't you start playing matchmaker," Rose said to her husband. "Agnes is a grown woman. She's smart. She'll find a way."

"I know she's grown. Don't mean she doesn't need a little help occasionally." Mayor Clint winked at his wife.

Sam glanced up from his stick in time to see Minnie pacing around like an angry hen. "Who are the two people you are trying to help? Who are you trying to put together?"

Neither the mayor nor Rose paid any attention to her.

Clint smirked at the women. "I'll be right back."

"What is he up to?" Minnie asked when the mayor had gotten several strides away. Sam inched closer, his curiosity getting the better of him.

Rose watched her husband's back as he walked away. "I can't say for certain."

"I don't understand." Minnie's voice sounded almost desperate. "What's he planning?"

"With time, I'm certain we'll know." Rose started walking toward the baskets of food. "Let's get something to eat."

Sam, unsure of what he'd heard, stood all alone then. He shook his head and went back to whittling. There were reasons he stayed out of other people's business. Life was simpler that way.

"Agnes, might I have a word with you?"

"Of course, Mayor." She adjusted Freddie on her hip.

"I've got a problem, and I think I might have found a solution." Clint looked as though he were suppressing a grin. Clearly the man had a motive. What could such a look mean? She braced herself for the worst.

He continued. "Truth is, Aggie, we're in a predicament. I've had two complaints from citizens about you raising this baby and teaching school. Your contract is specific in terms of expectations."

"I know." She looked down at her feet. "I can't give him up."

"You'd pick him over teaching?"

She inhaled deeply. "Yes. I'll always love this town's children, but Freddie needs me in a different way."

"You know what that means?"

"I do. I'll have to leave." She jerked her head away. The composure she'd fought to keep felt ready to crumple. "I need time to make a plan."

"I have a plan." Mayor Clint leaned in.

"You do?" She held her breath, hoping that whatever he'd thought up was better than what she'd managed to conjure on her own.

"Well, summer's turning to fall. School is set to begin soon, and I won't be able to find a teacher before the term begins. I'll buy you some time. I'll convince the town to allow you to teach and live in the teacher's housing until your replacement is found. But . . ."

"Yes?"

"While I'm looking for a teacher, you ought to be looking for a husband or a new situation. You could go back home if you've relations who will support you, but this town would feel the loss if you went."

She swallowed. He was right. Her choices were limited.

"I think I can get the town's council to agree to let Freddie stay in your care until the teacher situation is sorted out. I'm doing what I can to give you a few months, but my suggestion is that you pick a man and you marry him."

"You want me to marry someone? That's your plan? That's what you are grinning about?"

"Yep."

"I wasn't going to marry," she whispered. "I'd planned to teach . . . but for Freddie . . ."

"You've done a fine job teaching. Now you have Freddie, and you're doing a great job with him. But you might have to change your plans. And you might want to change them quickly. I believe there are men who'd be willing."

Agnes couldn't deny that her closed-off heart had opened to Freddie. She'd promised him she'd do anything for him. Would she do this thing? Marry a man she didn't love? Taking a deep breath, she weighed it quickly in her mind. She pressed her sweaty palm to her chest and fought to steady her breathing. Freddie's sweet face became her anchor. She nodded.

"I don't want to see you lose the baby. Besides, marrying would give the boy a stable family. It's for the best."

"I don't like it." She steadied her breathing. "But I'll do it. I'll marry. Don't spread the word. I like to think I could make a match on my own." Agnes offered Mayor Clint her hand, knowing when he took it that her life again would be on a course she'd not picked. "Promise me you won't take Freddie away before a new teacher comes."

He nodded and shook her hand. "I'll get the council to approve his staying and your teaching for the time being. Find a good man, Aggie."

He spun around and walked off, heading toward Rose and Minnie. She thought she heard him laughing as he went. Did he find this humorous? This horrible predicament?

Fate had a funny way of changing. "I'll never marry" had been her mantra, and now she had a few months to convince someone to marry her. Going back to Buffalo wasn't an option. She'd never subject Freddie to the pomp and prejudice. Needing to clear her head, she walked with Freddie to the wild blackberries that grew at the edge of the field and distracted herself by picking them.

Sam shoved the wooden spoon he'd carved into his pocket. He took a step away from the tree, only to pivot and return.

Minnie, Rose, and the mayor were not far off, and he couldn't help but wonder what they were up to now.

"I've let her know we'll be looking for a replacement teacher. She's agreed to teach until one arrives. Then she'll have to move from the teacher's house," Mayor Clint explained to Rose and Minnie. Arms folded across his chest, he looked pleased with himself despite announcing that Aggie would be homeless.

"The poor girl." Minnie's brows knit together.

"It'll work out for the best."

Rose gave him a questioning look. "But what will she do? She'll have to marry. That's not much time to find a love match."

Sam's ears perked up.

"She doesn't have to. She could give the baby up and go on teaching. But I've seen the way she looks at him. I don't think she'd take to that suggestion. It's up to us to spread the word, discreetly of course, that she's changed her stance on marriage. And if anyone says anything about the baby, tell them that for the sake of the schoolchildren, we're allowing Agnes to continue teaching until a replacement is found." He pulled on the bottom of his vest. "If I'm correct, Miss Aggie will be a married woman before long."

"How could you?" Rose sighed. "She doesn't want to be forced. There must be some other solution."

"You know me better than that. She needed a push, and this is just the thing." Mayor Clint put his arm around his wife. "Besides, I've picked up a few stray pieces of the Agnes puzzle along the way. I think this might just be the way to put it all back together." He kissed his wife's forehead. "Marriage doesn't have to be a dreaded sentence."

"This does beat all," Minnie said, interrupting their moment. "Aggie doesn't know what kind of trouble she's getting into. When word gets out, this town will be buzzing with excitement."

"I said to be discreet," Clint instructed. "She'll run off if we aren't careful."

"I'll be tactful. I can do that if I try hard."

"My, she must love that baby," Rose said. "She must really love him."

"Hannah!" Agnes called out as she approached. "Hannah!"

"Aggie, what is it?" Hannah stepped away from Joshua and Ruby.

"The most horrible thing has happened. I must talk to you about it right now." Agnes grabbed her friend's arm and pulled her away from everyone.

"What is it? Tell me what's happened."

"I'm getting married." Agnes set the squirming baby on the ground to play and leaned close to her friend as a lone tear rolled down her cheek. She wiped at it, trying to remain in control. She had to think. She had to plan. She couldn't turn into a blubbering fool right now. "It all feels unreal. I don't know how this happened. I should have expected it, but I tried to pretend it away."

"To whom? You've become engaged since the beginning of the picnic?"

"I don't know who I'm marrying." In a single breath, she explained her predicament. "Mayor Clint will let me keep teaching until a replacement comes. After that, I'll have to leave my house. Freddie needs a home. I never dreamed of marrying like this."

"A marriage of convenience." Hannah's voice was tender. "You would do that for Freddie?"

"Wouldn't you do that for Ruby?" Agnes asked, knowing her kindhearted friend would do anything for her daughter. "I can't allow him to go to a foundling home or be taken in by someone who will not love him. Babies like him deserve love." She looked down at Freddie. "Everyone like him deserves love."

"They do all deserve love." Hannah put a hand on her shoulder.

"I can give him that love. But love is not enough. He'll need a roof over his head, and without my teaching job, I can't give him that." She groaned. "I won't take him back to Buffalo, where he'd never really be welcomed. Marrying is the only option, if I can find a man willing."

"It's settled then, but who will you marry?"

"I don't know." Agnes's throat tightened. James jumped to her mind, but just as quickly, she pushed the image away. "Hannah, will you and Joshua take Fred if I can't find someone to marry me? I know you want more children, and he's a good boy—the best. I don't want him to ever live away from me. But if he must, I'd want it to be with you." A knot twisted in her stomach as she forced herself to ask, "Will you take him and love him?"

Freddie played with his feet and gurgled, oblivious to the life decisions being made around him. Hannah picked the baby up and put him in Agnes's arms. Agnes buried her head in his sweet-smelling hair. The thought of losing him pierced her heart.

"We do want more children, and we were ready to take Fred when we heard about him. But then I saw him with you. You had him in your arms, and he had a hand up by your cheek. The way you were holding him and looking at him, it's how I remember looking at Ruby and Grace when they were babies. I've thought of him as yours ever since."

Choking on her words, Agnes said, "But will you take him? If I'm not married. If I can't find a way to keep him, will you?"

"Yes, but I won't have to. We'll make sure we get you hitched to someone before a new teacher arrives." Hannah laughed. "And I thought you weren't the marrying type."

"I tried telling Mayor Clint that. It did no good. The nerve of that man, and he was smiling so wickedly the whole time we talked."

Hannah patted Fred's back. "Your mama's going to get married."

"It's all happening so fast."

Hannah turned to face the picnic. "Who will it be?"

"I can't even think about that now." She groaned as she paced back and forth. "I can't think clearly. My head feels as though it's spinning. Marrying me means being a father to Freddie. What if no one wants that?"

"They'll want you, and I believe the right man will want Freddie too. I'd say you could pretty much have your pick."

Agnes's eyes darted around the crowd. "I'd have to find someone who doesn't care about titles or surnames. It's not as simple as it seems." Sighing heavily, she planted a kiss on the baby's head. "It doesn't seem very romantic, does it? Getting married like this."

Her friend laughed.

“It’s not funny.” Agnes pouted. “It’s all rather horrible.”

“And a little exciting. Might as well let yourself have some fun with the prospect.” Hannah tickled Freddie under the chin. “You’re getting yourself a mama and a papa, Freddie Boy.”

CHAPTER SEVENTEEN

Agnes read the letter from her father twice. The middle section brought tears to her eyes. If only it'd come sooner, she'd have run to his arms.

I received your letter and have thought long and hard over your words. I know coming back would be difficult for you. You'd have to leave your schoolchildren and home in Penance. You'd have to remember the ways of the city. But if you are willing, I wish nothing more than to have you near me again. I've never been very good with my words. I know I never said some of the things I should have, but I want you to know you and your mother were my joy. The house is far too quiet with both of you gone.

Come home, Aggie.

In the six years she'd been gone, not once had he asked her to come home. He'd never once said he missed her. He'd always written about the house, the neighbors, and the city, but never did he hint at sadness. It was too late though. If the letter had come before the fire, she'd have gone. As it was, Freddie's life would be better here, or so she hoped.

She laid a fresh sheet of paper on her desk and looked at it. She wondered how to tell her father she wasn't coming home, that she had a baby, that she planned to marry someone but didn't know who. After much contemplation, she acknowledged that perfect words were not to be found. And so she wrote from her heart, hoping somehow that the story would make sense. That he would understand and not be hurt.

Dear Father,

I had planned to return to Buffalo. But life seems to be forever changing for me. I have taken in a baby. A little boy named Freddie. We have a great deal in common, as both of us entered the world in a similar fashion. When I held him in my arms, I felt something inside me come alive. I believe it was my mothering heart. It beat for the first time when I saw him and has been beating hard ever since. I love him even when he cries or when he wakes at night and I am beyond tired. In both hard and easy times, my heart adores him.

When I go to pick him up in the morning, his big brown eyes find mine, and they come alive. He puts his arms in the air and waves them about until I reach for him. He feels safe in my arms. I am his haven, and that is something I've never been before. It is a gift to be needed.

I want to call him my family always. I can hardly take my eyes off him, and I so desperately want to witness every new move he makes. I like to think you and Mother felt the same about me when you took me in. I promised him I'd take care of him. And though he does not comprehend all I say, I cannot break that vow.

My contract does not permit me to teach if I have a family. The mayor has agreed to allow me to keep my post until a replacement can be found. At that time, I'll have to leave my house. To keep Freddie, I must either marry or go back to Buffalo. I can't take him back to the same world that would not accept me. The solution is to marry quickly. I do like the idea of Freddie having a father. I can't imagine my life without you. It seems right to me that a child should have both a mother and a father if possible.

I gave up dreams of marriage long ago. Now I think a loveless marriage might not be the worst idea if it means keeping Freddie. I like to believe there are honorable men who would welcome me. I haven't sorted it all out yet. But I know I can't come home. Not now. And maybe never. I expect this letter will alarm you. Don't worry over me.

I hope you will understand. Know I want to be with you. I want it so badly it hurts writing these words, but I can't come. Pray for me. Pray I'll know the right thing to do.

Love,
Aggie

Would he understand? She hoped he would and that he would know her heart sought to do right. She fanned herself with the neatly addressed letter before slipping it into her basket. What would her next letter to him contain? Would she be telling him news of a wedding? How strange to entertain such thoughts.

She crept near Freddie's bed and watched the gentle rise and fall of his chest. His damp curls lay matted against his forehead. Amazed he slept so peacefully in this heat, she took a handkerchief and wiped his face. He stirred but slept on.

I'll find someone, she thought to herself. *I'll marry for you, Freddie. I will, and I'll honor those vows. I'll give you a roof and a family. I'll give you love.*

But who? Who could she marry?

Many a logger and miner had tried to court her, but she'd never entertained the notion long enough to see where it could lead. She thought of James. Handsome, witty James. Marrying him would be a pleasure. An impossible pleasure. There had to be someone else. Someone tolerable and safe.

Sam.

Sam had never been anything but kind. Being married to him did not excite her, but it also didn't scare her in the same way the idea of uniting with some of the rougher men did. She couldn't imagine Sam being unkind. She'd never heard an ill word spoken of him.

Sam seemed a safe, wise option. If only he seemed a romantic option. She sighed. Perhaps that could come later.

CHAPTER EIGHTEEN

Agnes held up her skirts as she crossed the muddy street. The teams of horses pulling heavy loads churned the damp ground into pits and gullies of mud. A group of strangers caught her attention. She'd heard that a new mine was opening deeper in the hills. These men must have been coming to work there. A sturdy man with red hair waved in her direction.

Startled, she turned away and hurried off as fast as she could, no longer caring if the hem of her dress became soiled.

"Look out!" someone yelled. Before she could make sense of what was happening, she was thrown to the ground. She'd been pushed, she knew that much, and her backside hurt. The air in her lungs escaped in a giant whoosh. Unsure of what had happened and struggling for breath, she lay motionless.

"Aggie." Sam, his face flushed, stood above her with his hand reached out to her. "Are you all right?"

She pushed herself to sitting, then took his hand. "What happened?"

"The lumber wagon." Sam helped her stand. "The load broke loose. I saw it happening. I jumped from my horse when I saw it coming loose but wasn't fast enough to get you out of the way without using a bit of force."

Agnes followed his finger to where two logs lay in the center of the muddy street. "You saved me."

"I was riding behind the wagon so I could help unload at Mr. Reeves's sawmill. I wish I'd been faster."

She brushed at the dirt that clung to her. "Freddie's at Hannah's. I can't imagine if I'd had him." Her hands shook as she trembled at the very thought of Freddie being hurt, perhaps worse than hurt, by the loose logs. She watched as men jumped off their horses and lifted the logs back onto the wagon. "Where did your horse go?"

"He ran off, but he never goes far." Sam took her elbow. "Let's get you out of the street. Were you headed somewhere?"

"The mercantile, but I think I'd rather go home now and clean up."

He looked her over. She didn't shudder under his eyes, as nothing about them led her to believe his intentions were anything but honorable. "I'm sorry I had to knock you over."

"Don't be. Having you rush to me . . . that meant a lot." She shook her skirts. "This is just mud. You were here exactly when I needed you."

"We all need someone to rescue us from time to time." He looked down at his shoes. "If you're willing, I'll run ahead and tell the fellas I'm walking you home."

"I'd like that." She waited for him, her mind racing from

the valiant way he'd saved her to the fact that she needed a man in her life. She brushed at her hair with her muddy fingers before groaning and accepting it'd do no good. Before she'd had time to decide how to proceed, he was back beside her.

"I'll have to catch up with them so I can help them unload. It's a big job, but my horse moves faster than the loaded wagon."

She squeezed his arm and smiled at him. "I'm so glad. I've been wanting to spend more time with you." She looked away, embarrassed to meet his gaze. Guilt crept in. Was it wrong to lead Sam on? To flirt with Sam and toy with the idea of marrying the man in order to keep Freddie?

He rubbed his free hand along the stubble of his chin. "I'd like spending more time with you. I've been thinking it might be time for me to court a woman. If I found one willing. My sister just got married. It has me thinking. Maybe . . ."

Did he say marriage? She tensed. Though marriage was her goal, she felt suddenly hesitant. She released his arm and pivoted. "I told Hannah I'd come and get Freddie. The time has gotten away from me. I wanted to walk with you, but I'd better go straight there. She won't mind the mud."

He put a hand on her forearm. "You don't have to run off. I wasn't proposing or anything. Just talking, that's all." Sam shrugged his big shoulders. "Let me walk you to get Freddie."

"You'll be late to unload. It's too far. Besides, I'll probably stay and visit. She was watching him so I could get the classroom ready for the new school term."

"All right. Be careful walking up there," he said, his voice genuine.

She dared to meet his gaze. Sam's kind eyes held hers.

For a moment they stood frozen. "Perhaps . . . we can walk another time."

"I'd like that." Sam tapped the brim of his hat and headed off toward the lumber crew.

"I heard you were almost hit by a falling log," James said as he walked toward her later that evening. Aggie took a sheet off her clothesline and folded it. "You're not hurt, are you?"

"I might be sore for a few days, but it could have been so much worse." She smiled over her shoulder.

He stepped closer, wishing he could reach out and touch her. Since hearing about the incident, he'd wanted nothing more than to rush to her side and reassure himself that she was well. "I was worried when I heard."

Aggie set the sheet in the basket, then sat on the porch step. "I've been here six years and I've managed fine. I've been safe enough. You weren't worried then."

James gritted his teeth. "I might not have known where you were or what to be afraid of, but I've been worried about you. I wanted to be near you for so many reasons. One of them being so I could keep you safe."

"I've been in a good place. People here in Penance look out for each other. Sam pushed me out of the way of the wagon."

Sam.

Blast that Sam and his uncanny ability to be in the right place at the right moment. At *his* moment. He'd gotten to know Sam a little better and couldn't think of anything wrong with the man other than the fact that he feared Aggie cared for him, or could. He was in the way. Or was he the one in Sam's way? James kicked at the dirt path. "Don't ever be afraid to tell me you need something. I'm on your side too. After all, I'm part of this town now. You can tell me *anything*."

"Anything?"

"Yes."

She patted the porch. "Sit by me?"

He sat down harder than necessary. "You could start by telling me why I'm hearing rumors about you being on the hunt for a husband." He turned toward her and tentatively reached for her hand. "I don't know what you're up to. All I've heard since coming here is your telling me you'll never marry, and now I'm not sure what to think." She eased her hand away and folded it in her lap. He struggled to contain the frustration he felt. "Seems you've changed your tune. Well, sing away, but you might want to practice a little caution. You never know who'll come knocking on your door."

"You don't know what you're talking about." Aggie's back straightened. "It's not so simple."

He raked his hands through his hair. "This all feels like asking for trouble. Is the gossip I'm hearing true?"

"The truth is, James, I don't know exactly what the gossips are saying, and I don't know what's in my future. I'm at a crossroads. To keep Freddie, I'll have to give up my position. Without my job, I can hardly raise a baby." She leaned her head against his shoulder. The feel of her melted him as his anger was replaced by the strong desire to simply comfort her. "What I know is right now I need to sit here and close my eyes and not worry about anything. Just for a moment."

"I'm sorry, Ag."

"It's all so much sometimes. I'm up at night either caring for Freddie or worrying over the future." She turned her head into his shoulder and sighed. "Life is hard. So much harder than I imagined it'd be when I was young."

He leaned his head against hers. "Those youthful days went by too quickly. I thought you'd always be there beside me. I never imagined it'd end like it did."

He felt her head turn, and he knew she looked out at the evening sky. Stars were beginning to appear. "Sometimes I close my eyes and try to imagine I'm sixteen again and swinging on my swing. I can almost feel the wind in my hair."

"I remember pushing that swing." The quiet moment of truth prompted a boldness within him. He touched her cheek with the tips of his fingers. "Just promise me you won't be afraid to ask for my help. If you need something, turn to me." He let his thumb brush across the smooth skin.

"You're a good man." She did not turn her head to look at him. With her head still facing the heavens, she whispered, "The best man I've ever known."

They sat in silence a long time. When he stood, a coldness that had not existed with her beside him crept over him. Would she ever lean her head on his shoulder again? He'd tried to be patient, but if she were to marry another, no amount of patience would be enough.

Agnes thought there would be more time for courting a man, but with school back in session, her days were filled to the brim. From the moment she woke until she retreated at night, she labored.

"Miss Aggie!" Tommy said a week into the new school term.

"Yes, Tommy?" Agnes replied.

"I heard you gone and got yourself a baby. Where's it at?"

"Mary Jones is watching him for me." The familiar pang of longing pierced her heart as she thought of Freddie and all she missed being away from him. "I'd be happy to introduce him to you sometime."

"How'd you get a baby? You ain't married. My ma told me babies grow inside of women when—"

"My baby's mama died. He needed someone to care for him."

"Why don't his pa just raise him?" Tommy asked.

"He don't got no pa, stupid," Matt, a big boy in the back, said. "Haven't you been listenin' to anything all summer? The boy's a—"

"Enough!" Agnes shouted. "I will not listen to one more word of this talk. Freddie is a sweet baby with blond curls and chubby cheeks. That is what he is. He's perfect."

She looked over her head at the clock. *Half an hour. You can do this*, she encouraged herself, rallying her tired spirits.

"Clara, come to the front and read to the primary students. Children in back, we will be reviewing our arithmetic."

No one said another word about Fred. But Agnes hated knowing the townsfolks' conversations included gossip about her boy's unfortunate upbringing. Let them whisper, let him be the talk of the town, but whisper about his golden curls and button nose. Whisper about the ruckus he made at the store while she shopped or the bobbing up and down he did while the congregation sang hymns at church.

"You may all be dismissed," she said when the long arm of the clock finally made it around. The roomful of boisterous children stood, and for a moment there was a horrible din of children clunking across the floor and shouting as they gathered their belongings. When the last child stepped through the door, she gathered her books and she, too, left the schoolhouse, grateful another day had come and gone.

When she arrived at Mary's to pick up Freddie, she felt her frustrations melt away. Freddie had that effect on her. Gone went the tension, gone went the weariness. All of it replaced with an eagerness to hold her child. "Thank you for watching him. I hope he wasn't too much trouble," she said, ready to tuck him into her arms and rush him off to her house where she could tell him about her day.

Agnes had planned to have Freddie spend his days with Hannah, but when Mary and her family moved to town, desperate for money, Aggie decided to leave him with them. It saved her the long walk each morning, and Mary seemed well skilled in caring for Freddie.

"No trouble," Mary said, waving at Freddie, "but I can't watch him tomorrow."

"You can't?" Agnes asked.

"No, ma'am. My brother's sick. He picked up something on the trail here. We all thought it would pass once we stopped pushing him so hard, but he's no better. It's worse, and now others of us are feeling poorly. Mama needs my help taking care of everyone."

Agnes looked at Mary, noticing for the first time her flushed cheeks. "You're sick too?"

"I'm worn out, that's all. Traveling and now trying to settle into a new place."

"I'm going for the doctor." She backed away with Freddie held tightly in her arms. "I'll send him over to look at you all. He'll make sure it's nothing serious."

"No. You mustn't. We don't have no money, not yet. We'll manage. We've been sick before. It'll run its course."

"The doctor won't care about money. I know he'll want to help." Freddie squirmed in her arms, but she did not let him down. She ran from the little rental home. Her legs pumped fast, and she gave no heed to the attention she was drawing.

Once at the clinic, she rapped on the door. "James!" she shouted. "James!"

Where was he? She opened and closed her sore fist, then banged again.

"Have you seen the doctor?" she asked Lem when he walked by. "I need to talk to him right away. It can't wait."

"I haven't seen him, but I know he's been checking in on an old miner most every day. I think he'll be back before long. Unless he stopped to hear one of McHenry's stories." Lem looked at Freddie. "Baby sick?"

"No," she said, hoping he wasn't and that he never would be. "He's fine. It's a new family. The ones in the Norbert place. They've brought something with them."

Lem scratched his head. "Last thing we need is a wave of sickness. Take the baby home. I'll be working for a while yet. When I see James ride in, I'll tell him."

"Thank you, Lem."

You did all you could. James tried to console himself. *He's in God's hands.*

He rode slowly back to town, hoping to avoid any curious citizens who might inquire after his patient's health. Being the bearer of bad news was never a part of the job he enjoyed.

The only way it'd ever get easier was to become calloused, and he didn't want that.

For once, he was grateful to be getting back so late. The streets had few people on them, and those he did see looked more eager to return to their homes than to ask him questions. Saying as few words as possible, he left his mare at the livery and walked toward the clinic. He needed to record the events of the day. But writing it all down would mean reliving it. Instead of pulling out his record books, he pulled out an old journal.

Unsure what he hoped to find, he flipped through it with no true purpose. Maybe a happy memory to cover the dismal feelings that were crowding around him.

June 10, 1871

All my plans for the day changed when Aggie showed up with a tiny kitten in her hands. It was orange and white, and its little eyes were still shut tight. She found it, all alone, under the front porch of her house. Together we took it inside and tried to figure out how we were going to feed it. We cleaned an ink quill and carefully dropped milk into its mouth. At first it didn't know what to do, but with time, it learned. One drop at a time, we fed it. Ag fussed over that kitten all day long. Holding it and talking to it. Someday she'll probably coddle our babies just the same way.

The kitten is weak but seemed better by the night. She has named him Tiger. Ag says a strong name will inspire him to survive. I didn't admit it to her, but spending the whole day watching her nurse that little Tiger was as fun as going to the races would have been. There is something about Aggie that just feels right. It always has.

Tomorrow I'll have to catch up on everything I should have done today. Unless, of course, Ag talks me into spending the day with Tiger.

James closed the journal and rested his head in his hands. Aggie *did* talk him into helping her with the kitten the next day and for many days after. They took turns feeding him at night and during the day.

When Tiger's eyes finally opened, they both celebrated. In fact, everything the kitten did was celebrated. Whenever they were in the yard, Tiger would walk to them, jumping over the clumps of grass. They loved seeing who he would go to first.

"He must love me more," she'd say, her voice high and almost musical, whenever Tiger walked to her. "It's because I'm his mama."

If by chance the kitten went to him, she'd say, "Poor Tiger. I think something is wrong with his eyesight."

The two of them were always vying for the kitten's affection.

When she left, Tiger went too. He hadn't thought about their shared cat in many years.

Did she still have him? He'd been to her home but never noticed a cat. He scratched his chin. There may have been a cat there. He couldn't remember.

Leaving his report unwritten, he stepped away from the clinic, bound for Aggie's house. He knew he'd find a balm for his weary soul in her friendship.

Two steps away from the clinic, he heard his name.

"James." Lem approached. "I've been watching for you all afternoon."

"Is everything all right? Minnie's baby isn't coming yet, is it?" It was much too early for the baby. It'd be too small to make it in the world. The thought gave him a chill, as losing babies was worse than losing old men who'd worked hard their whole lives.

"No, Minnie's fine. Well, as fine as an expecting woman can be. It's Aggie who needs you. She told me the new family that's renting the Norbert place is sick. I told her I'd let you know. She seemed awfully worried about them."

Exhausted from his emotional day and a lack of sleep, he struggled to embrace the idea of more doctoring. But he'd promised to answer the call of the weak and invalid, so he would put off going to Aggie's and instead visit the Norbert house and check on the newcomers. "How did Aggie know they were sick?"

"The oldest daughter's been watching Fred during the days while Aggie's at school. She didn't say it, but I think she's worried he might get sick too." Lem shrugged. "Hopefully just a little trail fever."

"Aggie, open up," James whispered loudly through the door. He knew it was late, too late to be paying a personal call, but he had just gone to Mary's and needed to talk to her, so he knocked.

Long moments later, the door opened, and his weary eyes became alert again with the sight of her. Her hair hung loose around her shoulders, the curls he loved so dearly freed from their pins.

"Your hair," he said without thinking.

She touched her curls. "I wasn't expecting anyone."

Effortlessly, her fingers parted the hair and began weaving it into a loose braid.

Putting a hand over hers, he stopped her. "Leave it. It's beautiful." His hand remained on hers, and then he put his other arm on her shoulder and pulled her close. Patience gone, rules set aside, he held her. "Ag, I don't know if I can do it." Swallowing back the emotion that rose with his words, he held her tighter. "It's too much. Being the doctor, the one responsible for helping everyone."

She pulled away but held his hand with her trembling fingers as she led him onto the porch steps and sat down. "Sit down and tell me everything. I want to hear about your day and about Mary's family. What has you doubting yourself?"

He sat beside her, their knees knocking together, reminding him he wasn't alone—not entirely. There'd been a time when every fear, every worry, had driven them to each other.

"I lost a patient. An old miner who was thrown from a horse. His leg was cut deep about a week ago. I've been checking on him regularly, doing all I could. But it's dirty up there. I told them to use clean bandages, and they put soiled rags on him. The wound started festering days ago. I tried removing the infected skin." James put his head in his hands. "I debated amputating his leg, but he was old and against the idea. I lost him today. I lost him, and I don't know if I could have avoided it. What if I could have given him a few more years?"

Aggie put a hand on his back. "I'm sorry," she said. "I'm sorry for it all. But, James, you put too much on yourself."

"I want to help them all."

"You've done good things for this town in the time you've been here. You've saved lives, stitched countless wounds, and who knows how many you saved when you rode from house to house teaching about the water. Remember those things."

Crickets chirped at their feet, and in the distance a far-off coyote yipped. But to James, it felt like they were alone in the world. Just him and his Aggie. She'd always been there when he doubted himself. Her voice buoyed him up and onward.

"Ag, do you ever wonder where we would be if . . ."

"I hadn't left?" Aggie finished his thought. "I try not to, but sometimes I do."

James reached for her, wanting to go back. Back to before. He put his hands in her hair, the familiar curls swallowing his fingers. "I don't know why you ran. Won't you give me a chance? If you're thinking marriage, think about me. Let me be an option. Your mother said be patient, and I have, but now—"

"James, don't. My mother was sick. Her health was poor. I'm sure she was worried about me, but she didn't always know what was best."

"If there's another man—"

"James."

"Aggie, I need to know. If there's someone else, I'll get out of your way. I might kick and scream as I go, but I'd do it for you."

Freddie whimpered from inside the house. She stood and stepped away, putting more space between them. "Freddie needs me."

Before she stepped inside, she said over her shoulder. "Let's talk of other things. Tell me about the rest of your day. I was so frantic earlier. I was afraid Freddie was sick, but he went to sleep peacefully. He seems well enough. Did you check on Mary's family?"

"I did." He shifted on the porch. "I'm hoping it's nothing, but keep an eye on Freddie just in case." James didn't want to tell her how bad it might be. Not yet—not ever, if he could help it. Spreading panic when there may not be a need to do so was foolish. "I'll keep checking on them. I'm not ready to make a diagnosis. I'll let you know how they fare in the morning."

He waited on the porch, uncertain if Aggie planned to return. A cat meowed from somewhere nearby.

"Ag, what happened to Tiger?" He asked when she returned with Fred in her arms.

"Tiger! You remember him?"

"Of course. I remember you saying he was my cat too. I think I spent as many nights up with him as you did." He smiled at her and for a moment they were just a boy and a girl sharing a moment.

"Those were long nights." She chuckled at the memory. "Remember how small he was? How long it would take to feed him, one drop at a time?"

Freddie squirmed, so she shifted him onto her other hip. It did little to soothe him. James took the baby and tucked him into his own arms. Soon the boy's little head relaxed, and his breathing found a peaceful rhythm. James smiled down at him. So small and helpless, not so unlike the kitten he'd raised with Aggie. When he shifted his gaze to Aggie, he was surprised to see her watching him and not Freddie.

"Tiger's here. He's as fat as ever. Turns out that if you don't feed him kitchen scraps all the time, he catches mice."

"Really? Good ole Tiger's still alive and catching mice?"

"He is. He comes and goes as he pleases. Sometimes I don't see him for a few days, but he always comes back."

"When I come by next, we'll have to see who he likes better."

"Of course, he'll love me best. Because I'm his mama," she said in the same voice she'd always used with the cat. A playful façade masked the seriousness of the night.

He laughed. "Maybe I can convince him that his papa is an all right fellow."

"He told me the other night that he missed you all these years. That he worried over you and wondered about you." Her eyes held his. He licked his dry lips, knowing they were saying so much more than they were saying.

"Did he?"

She pressed a hand to her heart. "He said he hurt inside sometimes just thinking about you."

In a shaking voice, he said, "Tell him I missed him terribly. That I'm not so proud that I can't admit I cried from the hurt of it all."

"You cried?"

James nodded, remembering the many tears he shed when she left.

"He wishes it had all worked out differently," Aggie whispered.

"As do I."

A long silence followed as they stood locked in each other's gaze. At last, he shook his head. Then he laughed under his breath. "It seems you've taught Tiger a good many things since I've been gone. He speaks now?"

She nodded slowly as though she too were struggling with the memories of the past. "Only to me, and don't tell anyone or they'll think I'm insane." She stepped closer and put a hand on the baby's back.

James felt the baby's head. It was a little warm, but he seemed peaceful. "My guess is Freddie will be Tiger's favorite before long."

As if on cue the little boy smiled in his sleep.

"Did you see that?" He asked her.

"I did. My guess is he's dreaming of pulling the cat's tail again." She leaned in and kissed the boy's round cheek. "I like to think he has beautiful dreams."

"With you in his life I am certain he'll dream peaceful, happy dreams." James eased Freddie back into Aggie's arms. Then he kissed her cheek. It seemed only right. Here they were in the twilight hours sharing memories and rocking a baby. "You're better than any dream," he whispered in her ear before stepping away from the oasis of Aggie's presence and back to the world of sickness that awaited him.

Agnes eased herself into bed, but sleep would not come. She found herself staring at the ceiling. Slowly, she breathed in and out, trying to calm the rush of feelings that raged within. She rolled to her side and looked over at the baby sleeping an arm's length away.

She buried her head in her pillow and stifled a sob. If only she could have James beside her to comfort her as she worried over Freddie. If only she could rest her head on his shoulder and breathe in the scent of him. She threw off the blanket and stepped out of the small bedroom. She wanted to scream and stomp and somehow change fate. Desperately, she wanted James. Watching him walk away repeatedly seemed more than she could bear. Telling him she wanted mere friendship tortured her to her very soul.

Someday he'd walk away for good, and she'd die inside all over once more.

She sat at the small kitchen table and buried her head in her arms. "I'm so sorry, James," she whispered to no one. "I'm sorry."

Love required sacrifice, and she loved James.

CHAPTER NINETEEN

"Minnie told me you needed help with your roof," Sam said to Agnes the next morning. "I told her you hadn't mentioned it, but she insisted."

Agnes rubbed her eyes. She'd been up most of the night with Freddie. He'd fussed whenever she tried to lay him down.

"My roof's fine. I don't know why Minnie said that." Agnes immediately regretted the irritation that had seeped into her voice. Then, remembering her husband quest, she fought off her frown and replaced it with a weak smile. In truth, it'd been generous of Sam to offer help.

Sam shifted on her porch, his head down. "I'm sorry. I'll go."

"No . . . stay . . . I'm about to feed Freddie." She motioned to the house. "We'd be happy to have you."

"Much obliged." He stepped toward her. "Maybe there's something else I can help you with."

Agnes thought a moment. "Well, I think there might be a front railing that's loose. I won't stop you from fixing it."

"I'll get right to it," he said, "I saw a quarantined sign on the old Norbert place. Hope they're all right. I haven't seen a sign like that in a few years."

"No! There can't be. I just saw James last night." Agnes put a hand to her heart.

"Sign was being nailed as I walked by this morning. I watched them hang it. Course, it could be a precaution."

She motioned for him to come inside before grabbing an apron and wrapping it around her waist. When she went to tie it, her hands were shaking so badly she couldn't get them to obey her commands. Finally, giving up, she threw it on the ground and said, "Will you excuse me? I need to check on Freddie. He's usually up by this time."

She rushed into the little back room and knelt next to her baby. She put a hand to his flushed face. Heat crept from his body. She felt the dread that came when she knew something but didn't want to know it.

No. Not Freddie. He couldn't be sick. He'd already been through so much.

"Wake up, baby," she said. "I'm making you oats. Let's sit in your big boy chair and eat. I know you love it."

Pulling him into her arms, she tried to rouse him. Freddie's eyes fluttered open, then closed again. He brought his little thumb to his mouth and sucked on it, asleep despite her efforts.

"Sam," she called. "Go find James."

Sam didn't hesitate. She heard the door shut moments after she gave the order. Alone with her little son, she fell to the ground and prayed. *Please, Lord, don't take my baby.*

Sam returned to the house with James at his heels. "Aggie, James is here," Sam said as they entered the house.

"James, something is wrong with Freddie." She had him in her arms and was rocking him back and forth. "I don't know what to do. He fussed all night, but this morning he's not making a sound and he has a fever."

James crossed the room in two giant strides. One look at Fred and he knew. "Ag, he has scarlet fever. Mary's family has it too. I confirmed it this morning. I'd been hopeful it wasn't, but they've got it."

"He can't have it." She shook all over. "James, he can't be sick. I promised him I'd take care of him. I told him I wouldn't let anything bad happen to him." Tears pooled in her eyes. "Tell me you're wrong."

"It's not your fault. These things just happen." He took the baby and laid him on the big bed. After taking Freddie's clothes off, he examined him. "See this rash?"

Aggie nodded. "It wasn't there yesterday."

James turned to Sam. "I'm going to have to quarantine this house. You're exposed and so is Aggie. It's the only way I can stop the spread."

"You don't have to quarantine me. Remember? I was sick when we were children." Aggie put her palm on her baby's flushed cheek. "I can help you."

"I'd forgotten," James said. "You were so sick. I was afraid you'd die."

Sam cleared his throat. They were not alone.

James and Aggie looked at each other, then at Sam.

"We knew each other. We grew up together. But we haven't

seen each other in years." Aggie's voice remained soft. Her eyes were on the baby. "It's all in the past. Our story is complicated, and really, it doesn't matter now. We'd rather everyone not know. The gossips in town would make such a fuss over it."

James tried not to let the sting he felt show. It *all* still mattered to him.

Sam nodded, though he had a confused look on his face. "It's your secret. I'll keep it if that's what you want. Tell me, what can I do to help?"

"Aggie's right. She's immune, and so am I."

"No, you never caught it," Aggie said. "The whole street had it, but you never did."

"I picked it up in medical school. I came down with it pretty badly. I shouldn't have to worry." Speaking to Sam, he said, "Have you had it?"

"No." Sam stood tall. "But I feel healthy."

"Makes no difference. I'll have to quarantine you. You can't leave this house." James shoved his hands in his pockets. "We can't be too cautious. It's the only way. Otherwise, there will be rows and rows of graves, and this town will never be the same."

"I have to stay here?" Sam's eyes darted around the room. "I just came by this morning."

"Yes. You can't take it back to the logging camps," Aggie spoke up. "And I'm going to help James."

"If you're willing, I'll take help. I'm hoping we have this contained, but I need to spread the word. Make sure anyone with symptoms reports to me." He feigned confidence, but inside he shook to the very core. "I have to stop its spread."

"I'll take care of Freddie. I can do that much." Sam stepped closer to the sick bed. "Just tell me what he needs, and I'll do it. I've no experience with scarlet fever, but I have nine younger siblings, so I know about babies."

James gave Sam instructions and told him what to expect.

"Aggie, I know Freddie needs you. But I need to spread the word, and I could use your help." James saw the pained look in her eyes. Even though she'd volunteered, the act of leaving her sick child required much fortitude. "You don't have to. I won't make you leave him."

"I'll help you," she said as she ran her hand along Freddie's warm skin. "It's the right thing to do."

James stepped near her. He whispered in a low voice, "I won't let him die." His stomach churned as he said the words. He'd been taught to never make such a promise. He cleared his throat. "I'll help him get well."

"Tommy, go fetch your mama," Agnes said the second the boy opened the door.

"Why?"

Tommy's questions would have to wait for another day. She needed to spread the word and get back to her baby. Putting a hand on the doorframe, she looked at him sternly.

"Get her, Tommy. Now!"

The little boy obeyed and ran through the house yelling for his mother. He returned moments later, pulling his mother by the arm.

"Miss Aggie wants to talk to you. She won't tell me what it's about. She says—"

"I've come to tell you we have scarlet fever in town. The doctor wants everyone to stay in their homes." Agnes tried to slow down. "It spreads by being in contact with someone who is sick. Keep your children away from others. There will be no school until this is over. Hang a flag outside if you become sick. There are men assigned to ride by and help if they see a flag."

"Miss Aggie, what's scarlet fever?" Tommy started in on his questioning.

"It's a sickness. A really bad one. The only way to keep it from spreading is to keep everyone away from one another until it's gone."

Tommy picked at a scab on his finger. "Does it kill you?"

His mother tried hushing him.

Agnes said softly, "It can. But not everyone."

"Will I die if I get it?"

Her heart felt too big for her chest, and fear stole her breath. "I can't answer all your questions right now. Stay with your mama and be a good boy for her. I have to go now."

"Miss Aggie?"

"Yes, Tommy," she said, fighting to keep the tears in her eyes. "What is it?"

"I'll miss you and school." He smiled at her, his round face looking up at her. "I hope the fever don't stay for too long."

"I hope for the same thing. I hope I see you real soon."

"Thank you for coming by," Tommy's mother said from the doorway. Agnes saw her bend and put her arms around Tommy.

Scarlet fever loved to take children, creeping in and snatching them away from their families. Far too many people endured each day with holes in their hearts where a precious child had been. Each time she warned one of her schoolchildren's families, she left feeling nauseated. Would the fever take them too? When this ended and school began again, would there be empty seats?

Don't let it take the children, she prayed as she mounted her horse. *Keep them safe.*

Despite her silent prayers, she knew children did die, even when loved and prayed over. The same disease had almost taken her as a child. She had always trusted God knew best. But what if Freddie succumbed to the fever? Could she live with that? Grace had died despite the many prayers said on her behalf.

She wouldn't lose faith—not now, not ever. Faith was the only way to make any sense of the pain. She clung to the unwavering belief that the good Lord had a plan so big and profound and beautiful that it could explain even the most exquisite pain. That his love could right any wrong. She grasped the reins tighter. She'd do what she could to help God's purposes along—be his instrument if he'd let her. Together with James, they'd fight the fevers. She rode faster, determined to do her part and then return to her own child.

I'm coming, Freddie. Mama's coming.

CHAPTER TWENTY

"Hannah! Joshua!" James shouted as he approached their property. He slid off the back of his horse when he spotted them in the clearing near their home. "I came by to tell you we have several cases of scarlet fever in town."

Hannah grabbed Joshua's hand.

"It came in with a new family. We're asking everyone to keep to themselves until we can control this and put it behind us."

"Mary's family?" Hannah put a hand on her heart. "They brought it?"

"Yes. There was no way they could've known. All we can do is try to contain it and pray it doesn't spread."

"Mary was watching Freddie for Aggie. Is she well?"

"Aggie's fine, but Freddie's sick." James took off his hat and crumpled it in his hands. "He doesn't look good. It's early yet. I'm holding on to my hope for him, but his body is weak." His voice caught in his throat. With a shaking hand, he rubbed at his jaw. "I can't let him die."

"What can we do?" Joshua asked. "We'd like to help. If there is a way."

"Keep yourselves away from others. It's the only way to stop the spread. Hang a flag out your window if you're sick. The mayor's busy organizing volunteers to check for flags and get me word. Take care of yourselves. Aggie needs you to all come through this." James shifted his weight, every part of him tense. "I don't want to lose anyone. Just steer clear of it."

"No one will blame you," Hannah said, seeming to sense the burden he carried.

"I'll blame myself if Freddie dies." He tried to smooth his hat back out. "I have to warn other families and get back to the sick ones."

"We'll do it. You take care of Aggie."

"She's not sick," James reminded them. "She won't get sick because she's immune. She had the fever as a child."

"But she'll still need someone to take care of her—especially if she loses Freddie. No matter what happens, she'll need you. She's been brave here on her own all these years. Fever or no fevers, she needs a bit of tenderness." Hannah put up her hand. "Wait."

She ran into the little cabin and returned with a small package wrapped in brown paper. "Give this to Aggie. Tell her I'm thinking of her. Tell her I'll miss her while we wait this out and that she'll be in my prayers."

"I will." He took the bundle from her. "And know that I'll be there for her."

"How is he?" Agnes asked before the door shut behind her.

"He's been restless all day," Sam said as he rocked the baby in his arms. "I think he's worse. He's sleeping now, but it's been a hard day for him."

Agnes had been riding hard all day, and now the sun was going down. Despite the heaviness of fatigue, she reached for Fred. "I'll take him. You rest."

Sam put Freddie in her arms. He opened his eyes and looked into Agnes's. "I'm here," she cooed. "Just go to sleep. I'm here now."

"I was wondering where you wanted me to sleep." Sam's face looked flushed as he said it. Sickness or a blush? For once, she hoped for the latter. "Your porch?"

"No, you can't do that. We've had such unpredictable weather. You need to be inside." Agnes rocked the baby. "If you get sick, being outside won't be good for you."

"I'd head to my own place if I could, but James said I shouldn't. It'd put the other loggers at risk." He rubbed the back of his neck. "I feel awful about all this."

Agnes thought for a moment. "I'll take Freddie over to the clinic at night. I like the idea of him being near James if we need him. His room is above the clinic. As long as you are well, I'll bring Freddie back during the day. That way you can stay here, and I can nurse alongside James."

"It doesn't feel right putting you out of your own home."

"I don't mind." Agnes ran her hand through Fred's damp curls. "I'm glad he had you today."

"My ma had us all help with the little ones. I can manage. I'm not sure I could handle this whole quarantine situation if I had to sit around doing nothing."

"Don't try to do it all on your own. If Freddie gets worse, be sure to let us know."

"I promise." Sam stood, fiddling with the edge of his shirt. "This may not be the time to ask you, but . . ."

"What is it? You can ask me."

"I've been thinking about how you and the doc knew each other before. I've never been one to chase after another man's girl . . . Not that I'm chasing. I'm just, well, I'm just wondering, that's all." Sam let his words hang unfinished in the air.

"You want to know if I'm James's girl?"

He nodded his head.

"Um . . ."

"If you have a mind to answer." Sam shrugged. "I'd like to know. Whatever you tell me, I'll keep it to myself. I'm not one to gossip."

"I trust you. And I'll answer. I'm too tired tonight to fight it." Agnes took a deep breath and let it out slowly, all the while trying to find the right words. "The truth is, I was once. Long ago, before I came here, we talked of marrying one day." Embarrassed and vulnerable, she kept her eyes on Fred. "Don't judge James too harshly. I left him and didn't tell him where I was. Only my parents knew. My mother was sick, and she told him where I was before she died."

"He came all this way for you?" Sam looked confused. "Why'd you leave him like that? It doesn't seem like something you'd do."

Agnes took a deep breath. "I've never talked to anyone about all that. It's something you might not understand."

"I won't go telling no one. I just need to know where I stand. Maybe the telling of it will free you." Sam walked near her and put a hand on the baby's forehead. "He looks peaceful in your arms. Calmer than he has been all day."

She smiled at her baby. "I was like this baby."

"Alone?"

"I'm illegitimate, same as him. Only I didn't know it until I was ready to marry the man I'd grown up loving. When I told my parents about James's proposal, they told me the truth about my birth. I knew I couldn't tell him. It's different in Buffalo. It's not just shameful. I didn't leave him because I was afraid people would mock me. It affects things. Laws prevent illegitimate people from inheriting anything, and his father would have disowned him."

She sighed and studied the sweet features of Freddie's face. "It'd affect James's standing, fortune, and family. His parents care deeply about such things. I knew he'd insist it didn't matter, but if I'd told him, I would have forced him to pick between me and everything else he had." She finally looked up. "I'd heard his parents talk down often about people like me. I knew they'd never accept me. I kept him from having to make an impossible choice."

It felt strange telling so much about herself. But the doors were open now, so she kept talking. "Just like I didn't pick where I was born, James didn't pick either." She kissed Freddie's cheek. "Maybe if I'd loved him less, I could have asked him to marry me and give up his world. So, the answer is no. I'm not James's girl."

She stopped and caught her breath, her secret hanging in the air.

"Does he know now?"

"No. I told him that if he pressed me for answers, I'd leave. I insisted we live as mere acquaintances. I know it seems harsh, but what other choice was there?"

Sam didn't mask his shock. "You left without telling him,

and you've still not told him? What if he wanted to choose you?"

"He feels the same way most folks do about illegitimacy. I stepped away so he could have a life. I thought he'd be married and settled by now." She felt a tear escape and race down her face. "It's a gaping canyon between us. I know he's tortured by questions, but the answers won't fix what he wants fixed. It's all so awful. He'll go back someday and move on with his life. I won't shame him." Agnes fought to rein in her emotions. "I'd like to keep things the way they are. No one knowing."

Sam moved his hand from Freddie to her shoulder. "You can trust me. James will never know, not unless you tell him. But do you still care for him?"

"It doesn't matter how I feel. It's something that can never be." She shrugged uneasily, wishing he'd move his hand and at the same time wanting it to stay. "It's decided. It's over."

"If you say so." He let out a heavy breath. "I had a girl once too. I left home planning to save up enough money so we could marry."

"You did?"

"Yep. She wrote me right before I was to head back. She told me she was getting married to someone else. I never had a chance to plead my case." He shifted. "I've always wondered why she didn't wait for me."

"And if she'd told you everything, would it have changed anything?"

Sam sighed. "I don't know. I think it might have. I was so angry and hurt for so long. Maybe I could have let all that go if I'd understood better."

"You think James needs to know. That's what you're trying to tell me."

"I don't know him well and it's not my secret. It's an unfair world we live in, but . . ." He paused. "I know wondering can make a man crazy. I'm sure you know what's best."

"I *don't* know what's best. I wish I did. But thank you. And thank you for caring for Freddie. He means so much to me." Her throat felt tight. The tiredness, the confession, the fear—all of it felt so overwhelming. "I love him. I want to keep him forever. I just have to figure out how."

"No one will take him from you," Sam said. "I'd do whatever I could to help you keep him."

She straightened. "No, I won't let anyone take him. No matter what it requires, I'll keep him."

"James, can I sleep at the clinic with Freddie?" Agnes asked, the weight of the baby heavy in her arms. "Sam's at my place. I can't stay there. Penance isn't much for rules, but I . . . I wouldn't be comfortable. I thought if I stayed here at night and brought Freddie back home during the day, that might work."

"Come in, Ag." James took the feverish child into his arms. "Let me look him over, then I'll run upstairs and get blankets."

"Have there been any new cases?"

"Two so far. I've quarantined them. I've told everyone I can think of and asked everyone to spread the word. We've riders lined up to check for flags outside of the town." James sighed. "I don't know if I can handle a full-blown epidemic. Pray, Aggie. Every chance you get, pray that we caught it early enough."

"We'll stop it." Picturing her schoolchildren's faces deepened her resolve. "We'll fight it. Together."

James nodded in agreement, but his brow did not relax. "We will fight."

"We'll win, James. We *are* going to stop it. I've watched you with your patients. You know how to help them."

James nodded as he laid Freddie on the table and reached for his stethoscope. "When children get scarlet fever, it's extra hard on them. His body has been through so much since the fire."

"Freddie's going to be fine. I know he will be." She reached for his hand and held it. Normally Freddie tightened his fingers around her own, but tonight he did not. "He has a fighting spirit."

Freddie moaned, then shook with chills. They both tried to calm him.

"Stay with him. I'll go for blankets, and we'll get him comfortable." James took Agnes's hand before leaving. Squeezing it, he said, "I promise you, I'll do everything I can for him."

"James."

"Yes?"

"I'm afraid for him." She stepped closer, wanting and needing him to touch her, to comfort her with his strength. "I know I've done you wrong. I've asked you to be patient, and you've given me that. I've no right to ask you anything else, but I need you to help him. I want him to live."

"Ag." He put his arms around her and pulled her close. She rested her tired head against his chest and closed her eyes.

Then she felt him kiss the top of her head, his lips lingering. "We need to sleep. Tomorrow will be another long day."

"You're right," she said.

He left to get blankets from his upstairs apartment, returning with an armload of bedding. Together they transformed the clinic into temporary housing for Agnes and Freddie. James checked on the baby once more before bidding her a good night and going to his apartment.

Alone in the room, she sang Freddie songs. Silly ballads and reverent hymns, anything she thought would soothe him. When, at last, he had settled into a deep sleep, Agnes laid him on one of the makeshift beds and watched the rise and fall of his small chest.

Upstairs, James lay in his bed. Eyes staring at the ceiling, he tossed on his lumpy mattress and thought of Aggie below on the hard floor. He rolled to his side, trying to will himself to sleep. But knowing she was there, so near and yet so far from him, made it impossible. Would the distance between them ever melt away? Over the last few months, Aggie had tried his patience. But he saw the hurt and the twinge of sadness in her eyes. Whatever her secret may be, it weighed on her. Was it right to demand answers? If only Catherine, Aggie's mother, had given him more than just her location.

When sleep still would not come, he picked up his journals, hoping to take his mind somewhere else, somewhere free of sickness and unrequited love.

May 17, 1874

Last night we attended Frank White's birthday celebration. Never have I seen a hall decorated like his was. Gaudy hardly explains it. But it was Aggie who held my gaze. I wasn't the only one who found her stunning. Frank asked her to dance two times.

In her own quiet way, she was the belle of the ball. Aggie doesn't throw herself at people. They flock to her—slowly but reliably. I've yet to meet a soul who does not find her utterly pleasant. The funny thing is, she has no idea. Before a party or outing, she is always whispering her fears to me.

She trusts me with her worries, and I like that. I want to always be the man she turns to when she is afraid. I can't remember a time when I didn't want to be everything to her. Watching her, I realized there is no doubt in me that she is the girl I want by my side every day. I don't think I'll wait long to ask her for her hand. I want the world to know that James and Aggie are promised. I won't make a show of it. I don't think she'd want me asking her in front of a room full of people. I'll just ask her. On a walk perhaps or while I push her on the swing. I think that is how she would want it.

Many nights he'd dreamed of her. He knew tonight he would again. If she were to visit his dreams, he hoped for sweet dreams of them together, laughing and dancing. Holding and comforting her for those brief minutes had been a balm to his own soul. Someday he hoped to hold her for no reason at all. Let him dream of that. Of them together without any sickness, without any unanswered questions.

CHAPTER TWENTY-ONE

James crept quietly into the clinic as the sun made its way up for the day. Aggie lay curled on her side with Freddie close against her, her arms protectively wrapped around his small body.

He watched her. Time had not taken the goodness out of her. If anything, it had grown. Every person he'd met since coming to town spoke fondly of her. Not only of her teaching but of her kindness and devotion to the town. She'd been there for Hannah while baby Grace slowly slipped from this world, for McHenry, and even for him when he'd needed her help meeting everyone. And now she offered her goodness and love to Freddie. Easy, natural love. It was how he had always felt about her. Never had he *tried* to love her. It was effortless. No different than breathing.

Oh, how he loved her still.

"Aggie, wake up," he whispered, gently nudging her.

"Freddie," she said, pulling herself up. She put a hand to his forehead. "He's still hot."

"He will be for a few days. Maybe longer. It's a hard sickness to fight. We'll put cold compresses on him and do our best to fight the fever."

She stood slowly and rubbed her back. "I think I'm getting old."

"Did you sleep much? I don't want you pushing yourself too hard." James brushed a cluster of curls out of her face. "You sure you're up for another day of this?"

"Freddie woke often in the night, but I'll be fine. Tell me what I can do to help."

"First, you can sit and eat some breakfast. Rose said she was going to bring breakfast every morning. It's her way of helping. She'll leave it on the doorstep around seven." He looked at his watch. "It's quarter to now, so I'd expect it any minute."

"That's good of her." Aggie kept rubbing at the knots in her back. "I don't think I stopped to eat yesterday."

"Today you will. I'll see to it. Oh, I forgot. Hannah sent this for you." He pulled the wrapped package from inside his bag.

Aggie fingered the paper. "I wish I could go to Hannah. I'd sit beside her and cry. I'd tell her how worried I am for Freddie. I'd tell her everything."

"I'm here. I'll listen."

She looked at him with bleary eyes. "But you are not a woman, and there are times when a woman needs another woman to talk to. It's not an insult, merely reality."

James forced a smile. "I can't be a woman friend for you. When this is over, Hannah will be there. But for now, you might as well enjoy her gift."

"She's always so good to me."

"She says the same thing about you. You going to open it?" James asked. If he were the one with a gift, he would tear right into it.

"Of course. It's just that I want to savor it." Slowly, she pulled on the string.

James laughed. "You have always opened presents slowly."

"I like presents, and I get to enjoy them longer this way." Very slowly she opened the package. When the string and paper finally fell open, she gasped. "Oh, look."

"What is it?" James asked, trying to see what had her smiling so brightly.

"Look." She held up a small piece of embroidery surrounded by a simple wooden frame. On it was a finely stitched tree. At the bottom of the tree it said Agnes, and up in the branches it said Freddie. "There's a note."

"Read it."

Aggie shook her head. "Later."

"Come on, you know you want to read it. We've time for that before breakfast. If you don't, your mind will be on it all day. And today could be a very long one."

"You do know me well." She held the paper near the light so she could see the words.

Reading aloud, she said,

Dear Aggie,

I wanted to make you a special gift to celebrate your little family. When you have a husband, I'll add his name beside yours. Then I'll add the names of all the brown-eyed, curly headed children you bring into this world.

I believe there is a man out there who will love you no matter your secrets. The right man will want you. All of you. Your past and your future. He'll feel honored and blessed to be at your side.

Stay strong.

Love, Hannah

He watched her without speaking. The note shook in her hand. Was it because of the names and the tree or because of secrets? There were always secrets. No, that wasn't true. Long ago he'd believed only honesty existed between them. He felt his fist clench.

"You have plans to add new names to that tree anytime soon?" James asked, unable to keep the edge out of his voice. "Anyone in mind for the husband spot?"

"I don't know," she said softly, her fingers running over the neatly stitched gift. "The world is not an easy place for a woman and a child to be alone in. But I've made no decisions at present. Today I plan to help you nurse and to hold Freddie as long as I can. Other than that, nothing is decided."

He nodded. Being a doctor meant caring for others' needs before his own. "Let me see Fred. I want to examine him."

"Tell me your plan." She rubbed her eyes. "What do we do after breakfast?"

"If I had my way, I'd take you for a walk up into the hills. We'd find a meadow that no one had been to and we'd explore it while you and I talked about the past and the future. I'd figure out whose name you are planning to put by yours on your family tree." He licked his lips. "Then once that was all behind us . . . well, we'd . . . we'd see if our older selves still enjoy kissing like our younger selves used to." He inched toward her, longing even now to reach out and touch her.

She crossed her arms. "James Harris, do you think this is the right time for all that?"

"Seems there is never a right time." He stepped back, toward their sobering reality. Today he'd cool fevers and nothing else. "After we fill up on Rose's breakfast, I thought we would start by checking in on Sam, then the other quarantined families." His voice took on a formal tone. "I'm going to pack all the supplies we have."

"I wish there were a cure."

"There's not. We'll try to keep our patients at an even temperature. Warm them if they get the chills and complain of being cold and fight to bring any fevers down." He shook his head. "Other than that, we'll adjust their diet and can try Epsom salts, but little works." He opened his bag and began putting clean rags and iodine for cleaning inside.

James stopped and looked at her. "Some of these people don't even know how to cool a high fever. They practice old methods and try to raise the temperature in hopes of burning the fever out of them somehow. We'll help them know what to do."

Aggie handed him his hat, then gently lifted Freddie into her arms. He moaned painfully, and his eyes fluttered open then closed again.

"I hate moving him." She pressed a kiss to his fevered brow. "How long will this last?"

"Days, for sure. Often, it's weeks. In medical school, they said if a patient made it to day nine, they had a chance."

"Nine days of this?" She sighed.

"It could be longer or shorter. Moving him back and forth

like this won't help any. If he gets much worse, I don't think we can continue with this plan. He's small enough, though, that he doesn't have to use his own energy to be moved." James filled a bottle with milk. "Let's try to get him to drink."

Aggie took the bottle. Propping Freddie up, she tried to get the liquid down his throat, but it only ran back out as he sputtered and coughed. Again, she tried and had the same results. "James, he won't take it. He just turns his head about or spits."

He took the boy in his arms. "Here, let me hold him. I'll tilt him back and it should go down better."

Holding Freddie in his arms, James could feel the heat coming off him. *Let him live. Please let him live*, James prayed silently. Freddie settled his head against James's chest. One dimpled hand reached out, and without thinking, James put his finger in the boy's palm. Freddie's fingers wrapped weakly around his own. Then James sat a moment, looking at the miniature fingers with their rounded fingernails and soft skin. This was why being a doctor mattered. Because these patients mattered. Freddie mattered.

For the first time, he saw Freddie for who he was and not for where he came from or what difficulties he brought with him. Everything in James wanted to cure the boy, not just for Aggie but because Freddie deserved a chance at life. A chance to have his own moments of wonder and discovery. A chance to love and be loved.

Tipping Fred's head back, he helped Aggie get the fluid in him. "We'll have to make sure he gets something in him as often as we can."

"Sam will. I believe he cares for Freddie and will give him whatever he needs."

I care too, he wanted to say but knew it would sound trite. Instead, he bent over and pressed his lips against Freddie's perspiring forehead. James did not look up. His gesture had not been for Aggie. It had been for himself and for Freddie. The little hand squeezed his tighter. Then the boy rallied and opened his eyes. "Mama," the hoarse voice mumbled. "Mama."

James found Aggie's eyes, only to see them flooded with tears.

"He wants you," he said to her. "He wants his mama."

Aggie gulped back a sob before taking him again in her arms. "Mama's here," she whispered over and over to him. "Mama's here."

James got up and stood behind her and put a hand on her shoulder, the three sharing a simple moment together. They stood reverently—James and Aggie united as they pleaded for the same cause. For the first time, James realized he did not want a future with just Aggie. He wanted a future with Aggie *and* Freddie.

Why now, when Freddie teetered near death? Why was his heart opening now, when it could so easily be hurt? And what would she think of him if he couldn't save her baby? Love was a gift, though, and he wouldn't reject it. And he'd finally found love for Freddie.

"Make sure he drinks every couple of hours." James handed the bottle to Sam after entering Agnes's house. "Even if you have to wake him. He needs fluids in him. I expect he'll also have diarrhea and possibly vomiting."

"I'll take good care of him. Don't worry."

Agnes looked at Sam. "Promise me, Sam, that you'll find a way of getting me if you need me."

"A bright flag. I'll do it. I give you my word." He reached for Fred. "Let me help you get him settled on the bed."

She nodded but carried the boy herself. Laying her child on the bed, she knelt next to him and stroked his feverish head. Then she leaned closer and whispered to him, "I'll come and check on you soon. While I'm away, I want you to sleep and have nice, peaceful dreams." The baby didn't stir. "Dream of the summer sun and the two of us walking together. We'll stop to pick flowers to put on our table, and we'll look at the clouds. We'll look for pictures in the clouds. How does that sound? Will you dream about it?"

Freddie's head rolled from side to side, then stilled.

"Good . . . good." She felt a shiver race through her. "You're going to sleep. Just like Mama wanted. Go to sleep and dream beautiful dreams. When I come back, I'll hold you again." Her voice trembled as she spoke. "I'll rock you and sing to you. I promise I will."

She pressed her tear-streaked cheek against his hair and silently sobbed. Then she traced his cheekbones and nose with her finger. She memorized the shape of him all the while silently pleading for his recovery.

"Sleep," she whispered. "Sleep, sweet boy. Mama will be back."

Sam stood beside her. Stepping closer, he put a hand on her shoulder. "I'll watch him, Aggie. I won't leave his side."

She covered his hand with her own. "Thank you, Sam. You've been so—"

"Stay with Sam and with Freddie."

Agnes looked up and saw James, whose lips were pursed and fists were clenched.

"James," she whispered as she stood and stepped away from Sam's touch. "We need to go. I meant to hurry, but I find it's so hard to leave Freddie. I'm so worried," she rambled. "I'm coming though. I want to help."

James shook his head. "I can go alone."

"No, I'm coming. I promised you I'd help." She moved toward him. "Sam will let me know if I'm needed."

"Go. I'll take care of everything here," Sam said. "Don't worry."

James searched Sam's eyes. "Are you feeling well? Your face looks flushed."

"I'm fine. I'll manage here."

The two men stared hard at each other.

"Don't leave this house," James said to Sam.

To Agnes he growled, "If you're coming, Ag, then let's go."

She looked back toward Freddie once more, then walked away. James's pace was so swift, she had to race to keep up with him.

"James, don't walk so fast," Agnes said, out of breath. "Are you worried about the fevers or is there something more? Are you angry?"

"No. I'm not angry," he snapped even though he stood with fists clenched at his sides. "Why would I be angry? You've told me enough times that I ought to get on with my life. I will and you can have your life with Sam or whoever else you want."

"That's not fair."

"I thought I knew you better," James shot back. "I thought

I could trust you. You said there was no one else. I believed you. But then I see you with Sam and—"

"What is that supposed to mean? I touched his hand. He's helping me fight for Freddie's life. These fevers have you out of your head."

"It's not just the fevers." He grimaced. "The Aggie I knew, the one I fell in love with, wouldn't keep secrets from me. She never lied to me. And now it's always secrets." James walked even faster. "But you're a big girl. A frontierswoman, an independent woman. Maybe the girl I knew doesn't exist anymore. I tried to follow your mother's advice and be patient. I really have, but I can't any longer."

She rushed toward him and grabbed his arm. "Stop and talk to me." He stopped but didn't look at her. "James, we need to work together. Can't all of this wait? It's been between us this long. It can wait another week or two. This town, *our* town, is more important than why I left. Can't it wait?"

"If you say so." He shrugged and kicked the toe of his boot at the dirt. "You always set the rules."

"I do not."

"These last six years it's been all your rules. You left without telling me, you gave me no choice in that. I show up in town and you tell me I'm allowed to be your friend, nothing more. Now you're telling me to wait to talk. It sounds like your rules to me." James started walking again. "Let's just go check on our patients."

"Stop, James." He kept walking. She shouted after him again. "James Theodore Harris, stop!"

He did, throwing his hands out to his side. "What is it, Ag? What do you want me to do? I can't seem to get it right." His Adam's apple bobbed. "I've been patient. I've tried to coax your story from you without scaring you off. I've left you alone when I thought that's what you wanted. But now I don't know what to do. So just tell me, and I'll do it."

She stepped closer to him. "I've been trying to do the right thing. I know it doesn't seem that way, but I thought all this time I'd done what was best. I thought that I was protecting you by leaving."

"You think running off was the right thing." He no longer sounded angry. Only hurt. It was worse, more painful for Agnes than the anger. "You think lying to me is the right thing. If you've given your heart to someone else, come out and tell me. Don't waste our time telling me it's all so complicated. Tell me the truth, even if you think it'll hurt me. I'd rather you stab me in the heart than continue to torture me."

"James, when this is over"—she put her hand on his arm—"when the scarlet fever is gone, when Freddie is well, I'll tell you everything. You can decide for yourself if I was wrong. It's a hard thing for me to say, and it's big enough that I think it deserves more than a few scarce minutes in between tending the sick. The fevers, the lack of sleep—it's got us thinking crazy. Let's talk when we're past it." Agnes felt the flutters of fear in her stomach, but she nodded her head. Staring into his eyes, she knew he needed this. "It scares me. Even now my heart feels like it might burst from my chest. But I'll do it. For you, I will."

"Do you promise?" He set down his bag and grasped her hands, and she sensed his urgency. "Do you promise you'll tell me why you left?"

"I promise." Agnes wiped a tear that had come out of nowhere, then she put her hand back in his. "I promise you, and I'll be true to that promise." She squeezed his hand. Since childhood she'd loved the feel of her hand in his. "But it won't be easy. And I won't like it one bit. I can't believe I even agreed—"

Shaking her hand slowly up and down, he said, "But you did agree. We've shaken on it, and I need this. I can't sleep at night. I am so consumed with wondering over it. It plagues me."

She held his gaze and kept her hand firm in his. "I will tell you why I left. I promise I will. I loved you. I ran because I loved you too much to ever hurt you. But now—now I see that there will be pain no matter what. I'll tell you. Then you'll be free to do with my confession what you want."

"Thank you, Ag. Let's go and do what we can for the sick." He pressed his fingers tighter against hers before picking up his bag. "Let's go save some lives and put scarlet fever behind us."

"Tell me what I need to know."

He told her about Mary's family and the dire circumstances they faced because they were still weak from the trail. He also briefly told her all he knew of the illness. "But there's no one way. Sometimes people you think won't make it do, and others who seem so strong are overcome by it."

"I'm worried about Sam," Agnes confided to James as they walked toward Mary's home. "He looked flushed to me. I don't think he wants me to worry, so he might act like everything is all right when it really isn't."

"I noticed a bit of color on both your and Sam's cheeks after you shared your tender touch."

She slapped his arm. "You know it wasn't like that. I'm being serious. He didn't look right this morning."

"Maybe he's blushing because he spent last night in the bed of a pretty lady." James smirked.

"James!" She smacked him again. "You're awful. You know that was the only place he could go."

"I know. I couldn't resist though." James adjusted the bag he carried. "Besides, I don't think it's fair he gets to be the only one to have fun with you."

"What is that supposed to mean?"

"Just that I've been here for months now, and I haven't spent nearly as much time with my good *friend* as I would like. When this is all behind us, you owe me an adventure." He glanced in her direction. Then, raising an eyebrow, he said, "For old times' sake?"

"When this is over and I've slept for a solid week, I'll consider it." Agnes smiled at him. "I might even look forward to it."

"Good, an outing and answers to *all* my questions. Let's hope this fever runs its course quickly. I haven't been this excited in years."

"I never agreed to answer *all* your questions," she said. "You're putting words in my mouth. I only said I'd tell you why I left."

"Shh, Aggie, we're almost to Mary's. You don't want the whole town knowing you are going to go courting with the doctor."

Agnes groaned. "I never said I would go courting."

"That's not what I heard. I heard you say you were going to go on an outing with me. I was taught that when a grown man and woman spend time together, that means courting."

James nudged her playfully. "And knowing how big some of these ladies' mouths are, maybe we can get a few rumors going about the schoolteacher and the doctor. I think I'd like that better than some of the other nonsense I've heard about you."

She looked around her. People were starting to walk the streets. She leaned in and quietly said, "I'm not courting you or anyone else."

He grinned.

"What are you smiling about?" she whispered.

"Oh, nothing," he said. "Just enjoying those familiar pink cheeks. And feeling grateful I'm the one who made them that way this time."

"You're horrible." She straightened and brushed her hands on her skirts.

"Remember when we were young, and we'd visit my sick grandmother together?"

"I remember. She liked it when I read to her."

"Someday this will be a memory too. Like all the other memories we share. We'll talk about the time we fought scarlet fever together. I'll tell everyone about the noble woman who battled beside me."

"Let's go help Mary." She stepped closer to the door. "Let's help them all so it can be a happy memory."

Moments later, footsteps were heard within the old walls. The cabin, small and primitive, was one of the original dwellings in town. It needed chinking and the roof needed patching. It offered only slightly more comfort than would be had staying out of doors. Families often rented it when they first arrived in town. Most didn't mind; they came to town hopeful, dreaming of better days ahead.

Before the door opened, he put a hand on her back. His voice was low now and void of any humor. "When I saw them yesterday, half the family was sick. It's too early to say, but it didn't look good. I can go in first if you want."

"We'll go in together."

CHAPTER TWENTY-TWO

They'd spent the first hours of the day with Mary and her family, administering to them, cleaning linens, dumping bedpans, and cooling fevered bodies. From there they checked back with Sam and Freddie. Her baby was worse—shaking with chills but covered with beads of sweat. His body hot and clammy. Reluctantly, she left to help the Johnsons, and then they got word that Goldy was sick. Her pa rode through town shouting for the doctor.

"My Goldy, my little nugget, she's sick!"

That's all it took, and they rode into the hills to check on the girl. Fear kept them going when they longed to stop. For two hours they did all they could to soothe her and help her parents know how to care for her. Agnes and James promised to return as soon as they could. Before leaving, James went to the suffering child's bedside.

"Do you want me to do a trick for you?" he asked. "I know one I think you'd like."

She nodded her weary head slowly.

"I was hoping you would say yes." He leaned in close to her. "See this shiny penny?"

Her eyes followed his hands, but she did not speak.

"Watch it closely. I will make it disappear." He clapped his hands together then. When he separated them, the penny was gone. "Where do you think it went? Do you have a guess?"

Still, she said nothing.

"Do you think it's under the blanket?" He lifted the edge. "No, it's not there."

He looked several other places. Finally, scratching his head, he said, "I think it's gone. It's nowhere to be found."

Agnes joined them. "Look one more place. It must be here somewhere."

"I think your teacher is right. I think I'll look one last place." He reached behind Goldy's ear and pulled out the penny. "There it is. You had it all this time." A weak smile formed on her face. "When you're better, I'll teach you my trick and you can show all the children at school."

James and Agnes, both weary and afraid, left and headed back to town. They picked up Freddie from the house and returned to the clinic. "Get some sleep, Aggie," he said. "If we're lucky, we will have no new cases in the night."

"I'll pray for that."

With Freddie asleep, the clinic was so quiet. She tried closing her eyes, but all she could picture were the little gravesites she'd seen back in Buffalo. The rows of them all with the same death date. Would that happen here? Would Freddie and Goldy be laid to rest together? Others too? Would she lose them all to this horrible monster?

She stumbled across the room, oil lamp in hand, and then

settled into James's chair behind his desk. She was moving a stack of papers so she could lay her head down on the desk when a sheet of old newspaper caught her eye. The front of the clipping was a postal announcement informing citizens of changes in postal policy. Agnes scanned the article but found little of interest. She'd never thought or cared much about what happened to letters that got lost in the mail, and she'd never heard of the Dead Letter Office. She flipped the clipping over and saw an advertisement for a deputy sheriff in some place called Azure Springs, Iowa. Next to that was a listing for a guard at a women's prison in New York. And then there it was, a listing for a doctor in Penance, Dakota Territory. She'd helped to fund that advertisement. She shuddered, imagining this crisis without James. He'd come just in time.

Agnes leaned her head against the back of the chair and watched the light from the oil lamp dance across the ceiling. "I always knew you'd do great things," she whispered toward the floor above.

Freddie's cry pulled her away from the desk and back to the makeshift bed. He cried again, a soft and painful cry that pulled on her heartstrings.

"Mama's here," Agnes said as she gently rubbed his back. All through the night she offered him as much comfort as she could, soothing him with cool cloths and gentle words. If he awoke, she coaxed him to drink and lulled him back to sleep with the sound of her voice. Despite her efforts, in the early morning hours, he slipped from consciousness.

She set his limp body on the blankets and then ran around the building and up the back steps to James's upstairs apartment.

"James, you have to come!"

"Freddie?"

Agnes just turned and ran back to the clinic. Grabbing Freddie in her arms, she tried to rouse him. Anxiously, she pleaded with him to come back to her. "Freddie, wake up. Come on and wake up now. James wants to see you. He wants you to get well so he can fly you around like a bird. Don't you want to fly like a bird?"

James came beside her and gently took the boy in his arms. "He's alive, Ag. He's still here." With quick hands, he stripped the baby's clothes off and soaked a rag in water. "Wipe him down. Let's try to lower his temperature."

She carefully wiped his fevered brow and worried over his flushed red skin. "He won't look at me. James, why won't he look at me?"

"Don't give up. He's fighting a hard battle, and he needs you." James put a hand on Agnes's shoulders. "Ag, you can do this. Calm down and just love him."

She couldn't stop shaking. Even as she dipped the cloth into the cool water, she shook. All over she shook. Her baby wasn't responding. She was going to lose him. Her little family tree was being torn apart before it had ever bloomed.

James talked slow and gentle. "Aggie, no matter what happens, Freddie needs you. Hold him, talk to him. Let him hear your voice. If he leaves you today, let him go feeling your love."

In a barely audible whisper, she said, "I can't lose him. I can't. I've lost everyone I love. I can't lose him."

James set Freddie back in her arms. "Hold him, Aggie. He needs his mama. Be his mama right now. The rest is in God's hands."

Her shaking stopped only when her child was in her arms. Suddenly forgetting her own fear, she thought only of Fred's. She needed to do everything and anything she could to comfort him. Wanting to take his fear and his pain, she rocked him slowly back and forth. James sat beside her, wiping the boy's perspiring body and listening to his weak but steady heartbeat.

Neither spoke as the time passed. There were no words fitting for a moment such as this. Freddie's spirit and body were battling to stay together. James and Agnes gave him what comfort they could, neither wanting to voice their fears.

When the sun was high in the sky, James stood. "Ag, I have to check on my other patients. Will you be all right?"

"I will," she said, her body bent over Freddie's. "I know to cool him and try to get nourishment in him if he wakes."

"You know more than that."

She nodded. "I know how to love him. I will give him every bit of my heart as long as I can."

James leaned against the doorframe and tried to memorize the scene. There Aggie was, rocking her baby. Light from the windows poured in and illuminated the heartbreaking scene. It was a reverent and sacred image, a mother holding her suffering child. Loving him, soothing him with no regard for her own aches. Anguish filled his soul. He felt it boiling up inside of him, about to erupt. It all seemed so unfair, so unjust. He stepped away, but even then, when he could no longer see her, he knew he'd never forget the moment.

Outside the clinic, away from Aggie's eyes, he hit the side of the building. He pounded his fist into the wood planks and kicked with his foot, not caring about the pain that shot through him. Again and again, he pounded. He wished he could knock away the hurt and pain he felt. Rid himself of all the responsibility. Most of all, he wanted to make things right for Aggie and for Freddie.

When weariness replaced the rage, he rested his forehead against the building and sobbed. He was going to lose Freddie. The baby he had never planned to care about but who had taught him so much in so little time. He wanted to see Freddie get a chance in the world. The chance he deserved. And what of Aggie? How would she survive the loss? For a long time, he stood in the shadows battling with the ache that tried to consume him.

There was no running from his calling. He was a doctor. With a heavy heart, he walked away. Head bowed, he made his way through the town and tried not to dwell on the suffering he had left behind him.

"I've come to see how you are," James said when he arrived at Aggie's house to check on Sam.

Sam did not stand as tall as the day before. He hunched and leaned against the wall. James knew the answer. He was sick, sick enough that he could no longer pretend to be well.

"Aggie didn't come back this morning."

"She's at the clinic with Freddie. He's worse, and we didn't want to move him. I'm not sure he'll make it through the day."

"No." Sam shook his head. "Not Freddie. It'll break Aggie to lose the boy."

"Scarlet fever shows little mercy. Especially with the young."

James couldn't talk about it. Not now. Other patients needed him. Being in control was imperative. "Are you bad?"

"No, it's nothing."

"Scarlet fever is never nothing. Aggie or I will be back to check on you. For now, while you're in the early stages, rest and eat and drink, even though your throat will try to convince you not to. You'll need your strength for the fight ahead." James looked around the house, noting its many supplies. "Stay in bed, and we'll be back."

"Tell Aggie I'm thinking of her." Sam rubbed his neck. James noticed again that his skin was flushed. "And tell her not to worry about me."

James nodded and walked away. He felt nothing—not anger, not pain. Numbness settled over him. He began operating on instinct, and his desire to be near Aggie again became his driving force.

All day he served his patients. He helped bury one of Mary's little sisters, a five-year-old named Caroline. She'd come down with the fever quickly and left this world with little fight. The first grave of the epidemic. He rode into the hills to check on families outside of town. Sam was the only new case for the day, which should have boosted his spirits, but it did little to help. The pit of his stomach tightened as he approached the clinic door after the long and tiring day. He stalled outside and tried to slow his racing heart. What words of comfort could he offer?

There were no words, none he could think of. Words alone would not be enough. He would find Aggie's lifeless child in her arms. Tomorrow he'd dig a hole and lay her family in it. From then onward a piece of her heart would reside in heaven. The newfound noise of a babbling baby would be gone from her life. Her plans would change, and her world would never be the same. The little hand she so loved to hold would never again reach for her.

Slowly, he pushed open the door. Peering inside, he tensed, expecting the worst. What he saw was a single lantern. A ring of light glowed from it. To his astonishment, Aggie was sitting in that light at his desk, baby in her arms.

"Ag!"

Her eyes darted up. She stood, tears streaming down her face. "James! James, I thought I was going to lose him. But look at him. His eyes are open. His fever's not as bad."

"Let me see him." He reached for Freddie. The weight of him in his arms eased the weight he'd been carrying all day. He'd been certain Fred was going to leave this life, but he had not. He was here. He was alive. James kissed the baby's forehead, his cheek, the crown of his head. "Fred," he said as he pulled him closer still. "Oh, Freddie Boy, I'm so glad."

"It's a miracle. I know it is." Aggie stood beside him, and together they cradled the baby, taking turns kissing his brow and caressing his soft skin. "All morning he was bad. He wouldn't look at me. I feared he was gone already, but I couldn't set him down. I sat on the blankets and rocked him. All morning I held him, and I sobbed, James—I've never cried like I did when I thought he was gone. My very soul screamed out in pain. I prayed too. I pleaded with the Lord to let him stay with me."

"What happened then?"

"I started singing all the songs my mother used to sing to me. It was so quiet in here. I was afraid of death and losing him. I had to fill the room with something, so I sang."

James tore his eyes from the baby and looked at Aggie, noticing for the first time the dark circles under her eyes. "I remember your singing."

"In the middle of my singing him 'Abide with Me,' I felt him flinch. It was nothing really. Just enough that I dared to hope. I sang and I rocked. I had no idea what time it was, but in the afternoon, he opened his eyes again. He moaned, and it was the most beautiful sound I've heard. Look at him, James. Doesn't he look better?"

He didn't speak right away. The image she'd painted in his mind of the painful, miraculous morning astounded him. The senses that had been numb burst back to life. "I want to promise you he'll make it. And I believe you have every reason to hope. We all do." He kissed the baby again. "You've done well, Aggie."

"You told me to love him, and you were right."

"Look at his eyes. He's so tired. I'm going to lay him in his bed. He'll need a lot of care in the coming days." When James straightened, he looked around the clinic. It didn't provide much by way of lodgings. "You haven't slept enough in days."

"But he's alive. I'd give up all my sleep if it could help."

He took one of her hands in his own and pressed his fingers tightly around it. "Your baby is alive."

She stepped closer, inching her way toward him. His breath caught in his chest. Then she stepped on the tips of her toes and kissed his cheek. Warmth spread through him.

"What was that for?" he managed to ask.

She put a hand on his arm. "James, my baby is alive, and every part of me wants to celebrate. I thought I'd lose him. I was certain I would."

"Death makes you want to kiss me?" He smiled at her.

"No. Living makes me want to." She took a step back. "I'm sorry. You're right. I've not slept enough. It seems to have affected my impulses."

"Don't be sorry. I wasn't complaining." He winked at her. "If you feel impulsive again, no need to hold back."

"James!" She nudged him. "Tell me, how do our other patients fare?"

Somberness replaced the lighthearted moment. The room fell quiet as Aggie waited for a response.

"Caroline died today. She was so weak already." James exhaled. "They're all sick. The grief won't help them fight."

"Poor Caroline." Aggie winced. "Just a child."

"Sam's sick too. The Johnsons and Goldy are sick and so is Old McHenry."

"McHenry too?"

"He's really bad. He was too weak to even tell me one of his stories. He did ask me to tell you to live in a big way, and he says he's grateful that you came to him so often." James put an arm around her. "Then he said something about wishing he was younger so he could convince you to marry up with him."

She laughed through her tears. "He begged me plenty of times. I think if he'd been younger, I might have considered him."

"He's a good man."

"I can't imagine Penance without him. He's been a dear friend."

James swallowed and sighed. "I wish I could promise you he will get well, but it doesn't look good. What I do know is that we need to sleep. We could have weeks of tending the sick ahead of us. Knock on my door if you need me. Don't ever hesitate."

James bent low and planted a tender kiss on Fred's head. "Get some rest, little one. You have a whole future full of adventures ahead. Perhaps you'll be a legend like Old McHenry."

CHAPTER TWENTY-THREE

With a racing heart, Sam ran faster through the trees, running back to Ruth. He had to stop her before she married someone else. Thick fog surrounded him, and he wasn't sure he'd be able to find his way to her. Tripping, he reached to catch himself but was unable to regain his balance. His fall brought with it shooting pain through his chest and up into his throat. He tried to swallow, but pain seared through him.

"He's been screaming off and on all afternoon. It comes out of nowhere," a woman's voice said from above him.

"He's hallucinating. All we can do is try to keep him comfortable." This time it was a man's voice.

He tried to tell them about the woods and the pain, but nothing came—only darkness. The same darkness that had swallowed him time and time again. There was no fighting it. He'd tried and always it won.

How long had it been dark? Again, he tried to open his

eyes. This time streams of light attacked him, hurting his eyes. He tried to turn from it.

"It's all right, Sam. Just rest. I'll close the curtain." Someone was there with him.

"Water." It was the first word he'd said by choice. "Water." The word felt harsh on his dry throat.

A cup touched his lips, and cool liquid ran down his throat.

"You're going to get well. I know you will," the voice said. "You look so much better today. I'm certain you'll be on your feet in no time."

Forcing his eyes open, he stared at her. It wasn't Ruth, that much he knew. Ruth had smooth, light hair and olive skin. Swallowing, he tried to work up the energy it would take to ask her who she was and what was happening.

"It's Aggie," she said before he uttered the words. "You have scarlet fever. But it's not going to beat you. You're going to get well, and then you're going to have a great life."

"How long?" he managed to ask.

"You've been in bed eight days." She pushed his shoulder into the pillow. "Don't try to get up. Just rest. Let me take care of you."

Finally, her face came into focus. Before giving in to the darkness once again, he saw her smile.

"No new cases. It's been two weeks since we've had anyone come down with it." James leaned over and kissed Agnes's cheek as they sat on the porch steps. "Don't go getting any ideas. That's just me celebrating that this town might survive scarlet fever. Sam's back on his feet and looking better every day. And Goldy sat up to greet me when I showed up to check on her today."

"She did?"

"Yes, she's thin and pale, but she's doing so well. I stopped by the mayor's place on my way back into town. We're going to have a bonfire and a dance the night of the sixth." He tickled Freddie's tummy. The baby laughed and climbed onto his lap. "Everyone's bringing their belongings that could be infected. Everyone who's been sick is scrubbing their cabins from top to bottom. I've let Sam know too."

"What of McHenry's place?"

"No one is up there. I still don't know how he caught it, as he wasn't around anyone. Usually I can track a communicable disease and put together its path." He frowned. "Before he died, he held my hand. I remember looking at it and seeing scars on his skin. He lived a lot of life."

"I've never known a gruffer, kinder man. He could be callous and coarse, yet his heart was so big."

"I wish I could have saved him and Caroline."

Agnes sighed. "If Mary's family had gotten out and met more people or if more folks had gone to welcome them, this could have been so much worse. But any loss is one too many."

"They'd been so weary from their travels that they hadn't gone to church or a social. We can praise the Lord on that account. Now we have to make sure the fever doesn't come back. We'll burn McHenry's place when the rains are heavy. I boarded it up right after he died. I'm hoping that'll be enough to keep any hunters from calling it home. I also put a sign on the door." James sat back against the step, his long legs stretched in front of him. "Want me to help you gather up what needs to be burned at your place?"

"Later. Right now, let's sit back and relax. I'm so tired."

"You haven't stopped nursing in weeks." James put a hand on her tired shoulder. "I could not have battled this without you."

"Doesn't it feel like ages since we've had an afternoon with no one needing us?" Their bodies close, they sat beside each other watching Freddie toddle around in front of them, a smile on his face. Some of the roundness in his cheeks was gone, but his skin had peeled and each day he grew stronger.

"It does, like a lifetime ago. I've never worked so hard before, not ever. I think these next few days I'll take it easy. Unless something unusual happens, all I've got to worry about is an adventure with you and peppering you with questions." He winked. "Don't give me that look. You promised. Look at Freddie. He's well and happy."

"He's doing so well. Have you heard his new word?" Agnes waved at the little boy. "Freddie, come here."

He walked toward them, his hands out at his sides to keep his balance.

"Show James how you can say kitty." Agnes smiled at him. "Come on, say kitty."

Freddie smiled at her but said nothing. James scooted off the porch and knelt in front of him. "Say kitty."

"Kitteee," Freddie said back. Tiger, who was lounging on the porch, lifted his head. "Kitteee."

"Looks like Freddie likes doing his tricks for me," James said as he picked the boy up in his arms. "What other tricks do you know? Your mama's not teaching you any of her naughty tricks, is she?"

"James!" Agnes said from behind him.

"Your mama likes keeping secrets."

She put her hands on her hips. "I told you I had my reasons."

James looked at her and smiled, and she saw the twinkle in his eyes. "It won't be long, and you'll be forgiven."

Agnes brightened.

"Now, I'm having a private discussion here if you'll kindly refrain from interrupting." Giving his attention back to Freddie, he said, "Never eavesdrop. That's also very naughty."

Agnes walked closer to them. "Come here, Freddie, let's go for a walk." She reached for him. Freddie turned from her, putting his arms tight around James.

"I see I'm not needed here." She sighed dramatically. "You two have each other, so I'll just go for a walk alone."

"Let's both take him for a walk. We'll show him the leaves that are changing and tell him what fall in Buffalo looks like." He set Freddie on the ground and took hold of one of his hands. Agnes took his other.

"Fall in Buffalo was beautiful. But don't you think Penance has its own charms?" she asked.

"More than I'd expected when I came," James confessed as he and Agnes swung Freddie in the air. He broke out in the most delightful laughter. "I don't think I ever heard a sound so charming in all of Buffalo."

They swung the boy again, their own laughter mixing with Freddie's.

Alone in his room, James pulled out his leather journal, anxious to record a good day in it for a change. One free of confusion and pain. A slow, easy, perfect day. He wrote a new entry.

October 4, 1880

Today was a perfect day. The first in a very long time. I believe scarlet fever has left Penance, taking two lives with it, a tragedy I wish I could reverse. Knowing what scarlet fever can do, I consider our town blessed. Any slight variation in circumstances and we'd have lost many more. On the sixth, we will burn anything that could contain the disease and our lives will move on. Today I got a glimpse of what moving on could feel like. The sun shone vibrant in the sky as little Freddie played in the grass. Ag was beside me, a beautiful smile of contentment across her face. If I could have any wish in the world, it would be for all my afternoons to be like this.

James closed the journal. It was all true, every word of it. He had arrived in Penance longing to take Aggie back to society, where he could relive the life they'd had before. That was no longer his dream. Something had changed. He wasn't the same man anymore. Penance was his dream now. Doctoring. Loving. Truly living. Penance with Aggie and Freddie was his dream.

CHAPTER TWENTY-FOUR

Agnes put anything that might be carrying scarlet fever on her front porch to take to the bonfire. Dresses, aprons, and quilts were all stacked high. Some people boiled their belongings, but she wasn't willing to take the risk. Not when she knew what this monster of a disease could do.

She stepped back inside, only to have Freddie toddle over to her. He leaned his head against her leg and babbled.

"It's so quiet and empty," she said to him as she looked around her small home. With so many of her belongings gone and Sam well enough to return to the logging camp, it felt different. "It's just the two of us now."

With the tumult of the fever dying, Agnes had become more aware of the weeks she'd lost. Time had passed, but in an eerie and odd way. Now she and the rest of the town were waking from the nightmare that had so deeply consumed them. She began again to think of husbands and ordinary days.

Agnes walked to the small mirror hanging on the wall and buttoned the last button on her green dress. She'd carefully ironed the dress's beautiful fabric this morning, pressing the wrinkles from it. James still hadn't seen her in it. Would he notice? Did it matter?

In her hair, she gently placed ivory combs among her curls. She'd brought them from Buffalo but had never worn them. It felt strange spending so much time on her appearance. She'd cared so little about how she looked this past month.

A knock sounded on the door just as she pushed the final pin into her hair.

"Come here, Freddie. Let's see who is here."

Sam stood on her porch in a fine suit. His hair had grown longer while he convalesced, but now it was short. And his face looked smooth, no longer the scruffy face of an invalid.

"Sam, look at you. I hadn't expected to see you until the bonfire. You look very nice."

"I started missing you both already." Sam tickled Freddie. "Besides, I . . . I thought I'd come by and offer to escort you to the bonfire, but you look ready to go to the ball."

Agnes felt a blush warm her cheeks. She'd not anticipated a reaction from Sam when she'd donned the dress. Since the fever had arrived in town, she'd spent a great deal of time with Sam, caring for his needs, reading to him, and talking with him when he had the energy for it. That'd been different though. Necessity had been the motivating factor, but tonight he'd come with no invitation, no need.

"Thank you. It's nice having a reason to dress up." Avoiding his offered arm, she put both hands around Freddie. "I'm grateful for the company."

Sam's eyes looked behind him and around. "Someone else wasn't coming for you, were they?"

"No. No, it's just me and Freddie."

He seemed to relax then, his kind and friendly smile returning.

Together they set out for the bonfire. It'd been over a month since Agnes had stopped and talked to any of her friends other than James and Sam and the other patients. Eager to see everyone, she quickened her step, fighting the urge to skip off like her schoolchildren did when she called recess.

"I'm sure your friends are eager to see you," Sam said as they approached the gathering. "No need to stay by my side. Enjoy the celebration."

"I am eager to see everyone. It's been a long time." She sighed. "Are you sure you don't mind if I go and talk to everyone?"

"Of course not." He pointed ahead. "Someone must have seen you coming. I'll let you visit and meet up with you later," he said before stepping away from her.

"Aggie! Aggie's here!" Minnie shouted, leaving her children and waddling toward her. "We haven't seen you in so long. We've all been worried about you. And a little jealous. We heard you had a man staying with you."

Agnes laughed despite herself. "You're the only person I know who would be jealous of anything that had to do with scarlet fever."

Minnie's belly had been large before, but now it looked ready to burst. She swayed as she moved toward Agnes. When she laughed, her whole body shook.

"Look at you, Minnie. Your baby will be here soon."

She rubbed her stomach. "Could still be a few weeks or more. Can't come soon enough though. My back is aching badly all day and night now. I'll be glad to have this new one here." She took a deep breath, then let out a slew of words. "I saw you walk up with Sam. Did he escort you here? Tell me everything. I want you to start at the beginning and tell me what I've missed. You've spent so much time with James—and Sam. Something must have come of it. Is Sam *the one*?"

"Slow down. I haven't chosen anyone." She looked over her shoulder and let out a sigh. "I've been so busy that I haven't had much time to think about courting. I'm hoping the mayor's had poor luck finding a replacement. I could use a bit more time."

"You must have gotten to know Sam. Was it terribly romantic wiping his fevered brow and spoon-feeding him?" Minnie waved her hand in front of her face like a fan. "Did he look up at you and stare into your eyes?"

"Minnie, you could make anything sound romantic. Honestly, I was tired the entire month and often fell asleep while I sat beside his bed." Agnes shifted Freddie in her arms. "I'm not sure I could find the idea of courting Sam romantic."

"Tonight, when you dance with him, scoot a little closer than necessary and rest your head against his chest. When you hear his beating heart, you might find yourself completely taken with him." Minnie pursed her lips. "Yes sirree! I'm sure he would have you, and he's an honorable choice. A wedding will be so exciting. It's what we need after this dreadful sickness. Besides, he's already slept in your bed. Tell him you want to have him there always."

"Shh . . . I'm not going to say that to him. It was never like that. Stop this nonsense before someone hears you."

"Hear what?" James's voice sounded from behind her, a hint of humor in his tone. "You have more secrets, Aggie? I'll never keep up with them all."

"She hasn't told you?" Minnie said. "She's planning to marry soon. Selecting the groom is the hard part."

"Minnie," Agnes snapped. "It's not funny. Go away and let me have a word with the doctor."

"Suit yourself," she said before waddling away.

Turning away from Minnie, Agnes rolled her eyes for only James to see. "Can you believe her?"

Agnes was ready to rant about her busybody friend, but instead she stopped and stared at James.

For a month he'd lived in nothing but wrinkled, disheveled clothes. But tonight he looked polished.

She put her hand on her stomach, trying to still the churning she felt. "Your hair . . ."

He reached his hand to his head. "Is it sticking up?"

"Let me get it." She stepped close to him and pushed the hairs back down, only to have them come back up.

"Leave it. No one will notice. Everyone will be looking at you tonight. You look beautiful." One side of his mouth pulled up in a half smile, his eyes never leaving hers. "You're stunning. You always are. I thought it when you were busily caring for Mary's family and especially when I saw you tending to Freddie. And tonight, tonight you ought to be called the belle of Penance."

"Thank you, James. I don't think a woman has ever been so finely complimented."

"I meant it all. Come on." He grabbed her hand and pulled her through the quickly forming crowd. "I saw Hannah earlier, and she had me promise to bring you to see her as soon as you arrived. And you know I always keep my promises."

Agnes wanted to ask which ones he was referring to, but instead she just followed him, saying hello to everyone as they passed.

"Aggie, Freddie, I've missed you," Hannah said when they broke through the crowd. "So often I've wished I could see you. I wanted to help so badly." She grabbed Agnes's hand and squeezed it. "I've been so eager to tell you something. I've heard from the other mother who lost two children to the same disease that took Grace. I've found a kindred soul in her."

"I'd hoped you would."

"She offered her comforting words. She also told me about a foundling home. She said it's full of children who need families. When I read her letter, my heart leapt. It truly did. Joshua and I are going to take in children from the home. Children like Freddie."

"This is wonderful news."

"I'd never thought of growing our family this way, but after seeing you with Freddie, it feels right. And James has agreed to help us."

"James? How are you helping?" she said loud enough for him to hear. He stepped back toward them.

James shrugged. "I'll be back in Buffalo, so if they send letters of inquiry to the foundling home with me, I can deliver them. I might even be able to meet the children. I agreed to help make arrangements if I can."

She straightened. "You're leaving. When? Why?" Her voice rose. He couldn't be leaving. Deep down she'd feared the day would come when he would go back. His home, his position in society, his parents—all of it was waiting for him. Who could give up such things? She put a hand over her mouth to hide the trembling.

"Forget it, don't worry about it right now. I'll talk to you about it all later."

"Tell me now," she begged. "I need to know. I've been with you every day. I wish you'd told me."

"I said I'll tell you all about it later. I'll keep my word."

"James," she pleaded, inching closer to him.

He pointed toward the front of the crowd. "Clint's getting ready to make some sort of speech." James reached for Freddie and took him into his arms. "Let me hold him. Your arms must be tired."

Brows knit together, she scowled at James.

He leaned in. "You know what your mother always said. You make that face long enough and it'll freeze that way. Are you sure you want to look like a shriveled potato forever?"

She tried to keep the scowl but could not. Soon the corners of her lips pulled into a smile. It was too fine a day to spend it upset. They had too much to celebrate, too much to live for. All the worries could wait.

In this moment, she chose joy.

"We had quite a scare this past month." Mayor Clint's big voice quieted the crowd. "We lost two lives that meant so much. Both Caroline Jones and Stanley McHenry will be missed. Tonight we gather to celebrate the lives they led. Caroline was new here, but she represented all of us. At one time or another we all journeyed to this town. We all were strangers until we became friends. Caroline would have become a friend, I'm sure of that. Her family already means a great deal to us."

Heads turned to the grieving Jones family. Minnie walked over to them and put her arms around the mother. The crowd watched silently as Minnie offered the comfort that they all wanted to give. James must have felt it too, the desire to reach out and hold someone. Without speaking, he put his arm around Agnes's shoulder.

"McHenry we all knew, because for many years he was the closest thing we had to a doctor. Rarely a day goes by that I don't hear a tale about Old McHenry. He was a part of this town's story. I hope we'll all keep that story alive. When the winter weather blows in and we are tucked in close by our fires, gather your little ones around you and tell them the stories of Old McHenry. Legends start that way, and we were lucky enough to have one in our midst. Let's hear it for McHenry." The crowd broke out in applause. Cheering and whooping. Hats flew in the air.

"He'd like this," Agnes said to James. "McHenry never did anything in a small way."

When the applause died down, Mayor Clint went on with his speech. "We mourn our losses, but we celebrate the many lives that were spared. Any one of us could have caught the fever had it not been for Doctor James Harris." Mayor Clint pointed toward James. "James Harris came to this town from the big city of Buffalo, New York. With him he brought his wisdom, his hard work, and his compassion. This past month, the good doctor worked tirelessly to prevent an epidemic that could have further devastated Penance. Each of us here has this man to thank."

The crowd clapped and cheered again.

"It would be unfair to recognize only the doctor. Beside him through it all and beside him now stands Miss Aggie.

This past month I have watched her walk from one home to another, a look of exhaustion on her face. She cooled fevers, cooked and cleaned for the suffering families. At the end of the day, she didn't rest. She cared for the patients who were in her own home."

Mayor Clint paused, and Rose joined him in the front of the crowd. "While the pair of you worked tirelessly to save us, the town put together a token of appreciation. Would you both come forward?"

Agnes felt a hand grasp hers. James guided her to the front. He leaned down and whispered low so only she could hear, "They love you, Aggie. Can you feel it?"

She squeezed his hand. "You too. You're one of them now."

Agnes looked at the crowd and saw all her friends smiling at her. Hannah was holding Joshua's hand. Minnie stood in the center of her cluster of children. Tommy, Osa—all her schoolchildren were there waving and smiling at her. This was her town, and these were her people. They were not perfect, but she knew their hearts, and she'd felt their goodness. A love for them swelled within her. Like a richly fertilized seed, it grew until she feared she could not contain it.

Rose, with her sweet voice, spoke then. "We all worked on patches for a new quilt. It's nothing fancy, but we hope you like it. Those of us who've been healthy have been sending our squares with the men who've ridden the routes checking on everyone. Laura collected them and pieced them all together. We quilted it at the church last night. We hope you'll cherish it."

Carefully, Rose unfolded the large gift. Agnes had never seen a more chaotic quilt. Shapes and colors of all varieties were haphazardly sewn together. Stepping closer, she ran her hand along it, admiring it. She felt the softness of the fabric beneath her fingers and the edges where seams met. Calicos and cottons that had once been shirts and dresses had been carefully salvaged. Each piece from someone in her town, each piece a part of the masterpiece. It was the most unique and exquisite quilt she had ever beheld.

Swallowing hard, she tried to speak. She wished she could find the words to say how truly lovely it was, how looking at it she saw all of them wrapped up in the tiny stitches. Just like the town, there were both bright colors and quiet ones, busy squares and calm ones. These people all together, in their variety, meant something deep and profound to her.

"Thank you," she said, still mesmerized by the gift. "It's beautiful."

Rose blushed. "We got so busy working on it that we didn't think hard enough about it and, well . . . we should have made two."

"Don't apologize. This is truly a treasure." James smiled out at the crowd. "I've never seen anything like it. Other doctors talk about prestigious awards they've received, but this is a finer gift than anything else. Thank you."

"I suppose Rose is right. Two would have been the way to go." Mayor Clint slapped James on the back. "Now we'll just have to find a way for the both of you to share it."

Agnes snapped back to reality. "Mayor!" she said, her outburst inaudible above the din of the applauding crowd.

"Time to get this bonfire going and the fiddles playing!" Mayor Clint shouted when the noise subsided. "Men, let's light this fire!"

Whooping and hollering set in as people readied themselves for the festivities.

It wasn't long before the small fire started smoking and then burst into flames. A wide burn line had been dug around the fire to help keep it under control, and buckets of water waited in case of emergency. But no one seemed worried. They watched in awe—some holding hands and others bouncing babies—but all eyes were on the flames. As they ate the mound of belongings, they also swallowed the disease that had threatened their safety and stolen two of their own.

Agnes felt a hand take her own. "We did it. We beat the fever."

Still watching the fire, Agnes could not fight the smile that spread across her face. They *had* done it. It was not a perfect memory. There had been loss, but there had also been unity and triumph. "I knew you'd do big things, James Harris." She pressed her fingers tighter against his. "I never doubted."

He quickly brought her fingers to his lips and kissed them. "I knew we'd do big things, Agnes Pratt."

"Mama," Freddie said, pointing at the fire. "Mama."

"You like that fire, Freddie Boy? I do too," James said to him. "Always appreciate its power."

The blaze ate voraciously, devouring the piles of personal belongings. Agnes watched as the faded yellow dress she'd worn so often during the last month succumbed to the flame's insatiable appetite.

For a half hour the crowd stood quietly watching, until finally Mayor Clint whistled over the roar of the fire.

"I think it's safe to say the fire's doing its job. It's not very often we are all together like this. I've assigned men to take turns manning the fire. The rest of you, come on. Let's start the music and do some celebrating."

James still held Aggie's hand, their fingers fitting together so naturally. "If I find someone to watch Freddie, will you dance with me? Say yes."

"I will. But you have to tell me why you're leaving." Agnes had tried to put it from her mind, but it plagued her. "I must know."

James nodded and went over to Hannah. Agnes saw the two exchange words and James pass the baby to her. Someone stopped him on his way back and shook his hand. Probably thanking him for his good work.

"I think I have enough energy for a dance."

She turned around at the sound of Sam's voice. "Oh, Sam, I . . . already told James I'd dance with him." Agnes smiled weakly. "Later, perhaps?"

"Of course. I'll find you later." Sam walked off, and Agnes wondered how she'd ever make it right with him. This was merely a dance, but had she led him to believe they were more than friends? Agnes cringed. She'd have to sort it all out someday soon.

"Come on, Ag," James said when he returned. "It's been a long time since we've danced. You think we'll remember how?" His eyes twinkled with mischief. His big hands came around her waist, and she felt completely at home. "Think these old legs can keep up?"

"Depends. Zeke plays the fiddle very fast. You'll have to be light on your feet. This is hardly a Buffalo ballroom. Folks out here really know how to dance."

"I'm up for the challenge."

They swirled around for an entire song. His hands on her

waist, their eyes locked on each other. When the music slowed, and her heart found its normal beat, she once again remembered the world around her.

"Tell me why you're leaving?" she asked, looking away for the first time since he'd taken her in his arms, knowing her face would be a window to the hurt she felt. "Is Penance not enough? Is there nothing here you'll miss?"

"Agnes Pratt, have you not heard me pleading with you all these months to give us a chance? You know me better than anyone in this world. Would I say those things if I didn't care? Would I say them if I didn't mean them?" James moved her about the dance floor, effortlessly weaving her between other couples. "Whenever I'm apart from you, I miss you."

Agnes pulled herself free of his arms and stood there in the middle of the crowd. Frustration raging through her, she glared at him. "But why then? Why are you leaving?"

Laughing, he reached for her again. "You know, I actually like it when you do that."

"Do what?"

"I think your face looks rosy and adorable when you're all flustered."

"Ohhh . . ." She started to pull away again.

Ever so gently, he reeled her back. "Don't run off. It's not a secret. I'll tell you my plans. My parents want me to return, but more importantly, I've been asked to present at the medical school on practicing medicine in the West. I wasn't sure if I'd be able to make the trip if we couldn't contain the fever, so I didn't bother telling you. I should be able to make it out of here before the weather gets too rough. I'll leave this week."

"You'll go back, and your parents and the people at the

school will all talk you into staying there. I know your parents. I know without even being there that they hated you coming here. Leaving your fancy house and fancy position in society, it must have made them furious. If you go back, you'll stay." She looked past him at the other dancers. It wasn't a ballroom. It was a primitive dance floor in the middle of nowhere. Did he see it the way she did? Charming, rough around the edges, beautiful.

His hands were firm on her waist. "Ag, before I showed up this summer, you never thought you'd see me again and you were fine with it. It was what you wanted. Why the anger now?"

"I wanted to marry you and build a house with you. I wanted to have children with you and love you always. I just accepted that we couldn't be together. I never wanted it." She wiped her face, angry at herself for caring so much. "I'll accept it again. Let me go. I want to get Freddie. It's too late for him to be out. I want to take him home."

"Stay right here in my arms and dance with me." He leaned closer. "Tomorrow I'm coming to get you first thing. We're going to ride out away from Penance, and we're going to answer all the questions I know are rolling around in your mind. And you're going to answer mine too. We can talk more about those babies you wanted to have with me and every other dream. But tonight, let's dance. Let's enjoy the fact that all these people we care about are alive. That Freddie is alive, and we are together."

He put a hand under her pouty chin and pushed it up. "You've tortured me all these months. Toying with me and testing my patience. You have no idea how I've wanted to throw you over my shoulder and ride off with you into the hills. I'd have refused to take you home until you told me every blasted reason you had for running and not coming back. Tomorrow we'll get to the bottom of it all."

"You wanted to throw me over your shoulder?"

He laughed. "I would never have dared. I've seen your wrath. Tomorrow?"

"Yes." She nodded. "All the mystery goes away tomorrow."

"Then tonight we dance." For two numbers, she remained in his arms. She tried with all her might to forget his impending departure and the coming day's confession. For brief moments she felt young and carefree. Like the girl she'd been in Buffalo.

Duty pulled them apart when Agnes saw Freddie squirming in Hannah's arms. "Hannah needs a chance to dance with Joshua. Let's get Freddie."

When they were close, they heard Sarah talking. "I was told she'd be giving her position up."

"She will be," Hannah said. "I just spoke with the mayor. He says they've found a new teacher, but she can't come until after Christmas."

Sarah huffed. "I suppose she'll keep teaching until then. I think it's a horrible example."

"You're being too harsh. He's just a child." Hannah defended the child in her arms.

"What will Ruby think when she hears how he came into this world?" Sarah shook her head as though the very idea sent her into a tizzy. "You have to think about her. We have—"

"What will Ruby think?" James said. "That depends on us."

Sarah pursed her lips. "You should know more than the

rest of us what it means to have bad blood. I bet your family wouldn't think twice about not letting you around someone like *him*."

James took Freddie from Hannah, smiling his thanks to her as he did so. "You're right. My parents do feel that way. But they're wrong, and so are you for condemning him when he had no say in the matter. I used to be like you. I couldn't see past it. I'd been trained to see the wrong things. But once I got to know Freddie, I learned pretty quick that defining him by where he comes from isn't a good way to know him. Now when I see him, I see all he can do and become." He lifted the boy a little higher. "Freddie's going to change the world."

"Well," Sarah said, still trying to win the argument, "Aggie can't keep him. She's not married. Even the mayor said he'd have to intervene if the new teacher arrives and Aggie hasn't made new housing arrangements." Hands on hips, she gloated at him.

"She'll keep him," James said, turning his back on her. "This is her son."

Agnes followed him away from the crowd. She'd stood as a spectator to the exchange, but her heart and soul had been actively involved.

"James, you do care for Freddie?" she asked when they were out of earshot of the others. "You care about him even though he's illegitimate?"

"Course I do. You were right. I'd been spending too much time looking at his past and thinking about him the wrong way. But I don't see him that way anymore." James pulled Freddie tight against his chest and hugged the boy. "You done with this bonfire?"

"Yes . . . I mean, no. I promised Sam I'd dance with him. I'll go find him and tell him I'm leaving." Looking back at the crowd, she spotted Sam. "If you wait for me, I'd let you walk me home."

"I like the sound of that. Freddie and I will go find ourselves something to eat."

Reluctantly, she walked to Sam. Holding a cup in one hand, he stood talking to a fellow logger.

"Aggie." Sam set down his cup.

"I promised you a dance. I'd like to get Freddie home soon. So, if you're free . . ."

Sam excused himself from his conversation and walked with Agnes to the edge of the crowd. "Aggie, I think you need to tell James everything."

"You do?" She'd never understand this man. He was good and kind and noble. If only he were coarse and mean, it would be easier to ignore the pain she feared she had caused him.

"I do. I'll be honest with you. I've been itching to settle down. I've been looking for someone who might want that too." She felt her cheeks turn warm. "I thought maybe you and I . . . but it's James you want, and I see it. I saw you with him when you danced." He looked over at James and Freddie. "I thought I was all right with just marrying a beautiful, kind woman, even if it wasn't a love match. I've seen plenty of marriages work that started with less. But I think I'd like to make whoever I marry feel something."

"I'm sorry, Sam."

He smiled, but she couldn't help but see disappointment in it. "Don't worry over me. Just go on and tell James. He needs to know. If he wants to give up his money and his position in society for you, let him. It means he's choosing love. You're not the kind of woman he'll ever regret."

"I don't want him to settle for me."

"Marrying Agnes Pratt is not settling." He smiled at her. "It's marrying up. No matter the cost."

Agnes bit her bottom lip, letting his words sink in. "I'm going to talk to him tomorrow. We've already planned it. I'll tell him everything, but then he's leaving, and I don't know if he'll come back. He's going East. It's a world of luxury compared to all this." Agnes paused. "I want you to know I never meant to hurt you."

"I know. I don't have any hard feelings. If he doesn't come back, what then?"

"I'm afraid the new teacher will come while he's away. I've promised to leave my house then." She shook her head. "I won't have many options. I don't want to take Freddie to Buffalo. It's a harsh world for a boy like him. It'd be unfair." She shrugged. "I'll figure something out. Somehow I'll give Freddie a good life."

"You'll be able to keep him. There'll be a way," Sam said. "If James won't have you, I will."

"But you said—"

"I know. But maybe, with time, you could feel something for me. I've money saved. I could give a wife and a child a roof over their heads. I'd do it for Freddie and for you." Sam looked off toward the still blazing fire. "If James doesn't realize what he has before him, then he's missing out. Don't fret over it now. I think he'll come back. But know I'm here. You were there for me when I was sick, and you were a friend to me before then. I know enough about you to know you're a fine woman. One I'd be proud to have by my side."

His gesture was not lost on her. She stood speechless for a moment. Such generosity, such kindness. "Thank you, Sam. It means a great deal. More than you'll ever know."

CHAPTER TWENTY-FIVE

"Here," James said when he arrived the next morning. He held a letter in his hand. "Your mother sent this to me. It's how she told me you were here."

Agnes reached for it. "Can I open it now?"

"Bring it with us. Rose packed us a meal so we could spend the whole day getting to the bottom of everything." He picked up Freddie. "Can I hold him while we ride?"

Freddie put his arms around James's neck.

"Of course. He loves being with you."

They rode out of town, stopping only when they came to the banks of a small creek. A brilliant blue sky, not a cloud in sight, filled the space above them. The perfect weather for an outing.

James spread the quilt from the townspeople on the ground, and Freddie immediately crawled on it. "Since we must share it, I thought I'd bring it along. A picnic seemed like an acceptable time for the both of us to use it." He winked. "Most of my ideas for how we could share it didn't seem *appropriate*. At least not right now."

"James!"

"I'm only playing. Sit beside me." He patted the mosaic quilt. "I'll remember my manners. Though I wouldn't mind sharing it more often if our circumstances ever change."

"You're a regular rake."

"Ag, you can't be a rake if you've only ever loved one woman."

She laughed despite herself. "Can I open the letter now?" Agnes settled on the blanket beside him. Freddie crawled over and sat beside her.

"You haven't been able to think of much else since I handed it to you, have you?" he asked. "Read away."

She looked at him. "You seem awfully happy today."

"Today is over six years in the making. It's been a long time coming. Go ahead and read it," James said, leaning back on one elbow. "Read it aloud."

She unfolded the paper. "It's dated July 5. She died three months later."

"I know. I think she must have known what was coming." James waited.

Agnes cleared her throat, then read.

Dear James,

I've enjoyed your letters over the years and the times you've stopped in to say hello. Each time, I wished I could give you the answers you were seeking, but Aggie had us promise. Today while I was lying in bed thinking about my life, I thought about what things meant the most to me. Funny how at the end of our lives we see things most clearly. Today the only things that matter are Howard and Aggie. Not the house, not our money or what our friends think of us. Just them. Just my family.

Aggie ran away because she didn't want you to lose any of those less important things or your family. She was well intentioned. It's good of her to care, but I've decided you should get to choose for yourself what things are worth giving up and what things are worth fighting for.

And so, I've decided to break my promise to her. I hope she'll forgive me and know my telling you is an act of love. When you see her, tell her I've missed her and prayed for her daily since she left. If my health had been better, I'd have followed her there and been beside her.

My girl is in Penance, a small town in the Dakota Territory. She is teaching school and doing a wonderful job of it. She writes us beautiful letters full of mishaps and adventure. But she is alone, and my girl should not be alone. Not when God designed a man so perfect for her.

I'd do it over differently if I could. I'd spare you both these years apart. My only solace is that I can tell she has grown and changed since setting out on her own. Perhaps she needed to go. But I think she's been alone long enough. Go to her now, and tell her that her mother said it was time to let you choose what you wanted in life. But as you ponder what it is you want most in life, remember that most things fade away with time. Only love, pure love, remains in the end.

Knowing Aggie, her eyes will light up at the very thought of it. She'll be angry, but then at least she won't have to wonder, and neither will you. Be gentle, though, and patient. She's built a wall around her heart. It's thick with reasoning she thinks is valid. Tear it down gently, if she'll let you.

I wish I could be there to witness it. To see her face when you stroll into town. I'll have to ask God if there is a way I can look down and watch. I'll find a way to be there—somehow, I will. I'll find a way to be there for everything. I'll be pleading from above for your happiness and for hers.

Take care of her,
Catherine Pratt

Agnes brought the paper to her heart. Her meddling mother—oh, how she missed her. "I wasn't there," she whispered. "I wasn't there when she died. I always thought I could go the next spring or the next, and then she was gone. I thought I'd go when you were married and there could not be something between us. I didn't know how bad off she was."

Quietly, she wiped a tear that had defied her and rolled down her cheek. "I wanted to do what was right. I thought I was, but . . ." She trailed off, overcome by the ache that twisted inside her. "I wasn't there to be with her. And you. I hurt you too, though I never meant to."

"She knows you wanted to be there," James said softly. "She knows where your heart was, even if you weren't beside her. She was proud of you too. When I'd stop to see them, she'd tell me that you were doing so well and working so hard. I'd wanted to come sooner, but I had to finish school. Then when I saw the advertisement, I knew it was time for answers."

Pulling her knees in tight, she buried her head in them. "I wish I could do it over."

He put an arm around her shoulders. Freddie, wise beyond his age, crawled over and worked his way into her arms. Then he reached up and put a hand on her cheek. "Mama."

She pulled him closer, and the three sat in the fall sunshine. The pain inside of her was eased slightly by the arms of the man and the child she loved. Her mother was right. This was what mattered. More than anything else. But would James agree?

"I hated leaving you," she said, not looking at him. "You know that, don't you?"

"Help me understand." He tilted his head so he could see her face. "Tell me what happened."

"I found out something. Something that matters a great deal to some, though I don't believe it should." Afraid to say the words, worried that she'd never again get to sit in the comfort of his embrace, she hesitated.

"What was it, Aggie?"

"When you asked me to marry you, I was the happiest I'd ever been. Everything I'd ever wanted was right before me." A terse chuckle escaped her as she stepped back to that day. "It was perfect, but . . ."

She was silent for a moment.

"What changed everything?" he asked in a quiet and earnest voice. A plea for answers.

"It didn't last. I ran to my mother and told her my news, and then everything fell apart." She inhaled slowly. "My parents weren't really my parents. Well, they took care of me because my real mother couldn't. They did their best to keep it a secret. They wanted to protect me from the cruel world."

"They should have told you," he said. "But why did you run? I would not have cared."

She looked at him. "There's more. I was shocked to know I wasn't born to them, but that did not change my love for them. I know that even more now that I have Freddie."

She paused, taking one more calming breath before saying, "But like him, like Freddie, I'm illegitimate." Agnes let the words hang in the air. The thumping of her heart was so fierce and wild that even the silence did not seem peaceful. "Don't you see? You are James Harris. A wedding with you would have been in all the papers. There were people who knew where I'd come from. It could have ruined you. I couldn't rob you of your family and fortune. I loved you too much to ask that of you."

When he said nothing, she rambled. "I knew your parents wouldn't accept me, that you could lose so much. And everyone would know, my parents may have become outcasts in their circle of friends. I thought running and starting over was the only way. I thought I was doing the right thing by you."

She dared a glance at him. His eyes were on Freddie.

"I don't expect you to still want me now that you know the truth. I knew that was too much to hope for. I came out here and tried to make a life for myself. And I have, and you'll have your own life too. Go back to Buffalo, find someone your parents will love. You'll have no trouble making a match."

When he still did not speak, she stood. Deep down she wished she could run somewhere so far away that it could be forgotten. But she'd done that already, and her past had followed. Pulling Freddie close, she started walking around the field, letting the tears come. Dear Freddie looked at her with inquisitive eyes as she sobbed.

A familiar hand reached around her and rested on Freddie's golden curls. James stood beside her. "It's only where he came from."

She looked up then and through her tears, their eyes locked. "It's only where *you* came from," he said. He spoke slowly, each word seeping into her heart. "It's not where you're going."

Then he wove his fingers into her hair. "I don't know what I would have said six years ago. I hope I'd have said it didn't matter. I hope I would have taken you in my arms and kissed you and loved you and never let you go. I can't go back to that time. The penance has already been paid. But I know what I'm saying now." He ran a thumb across her cheek, wiping one of the many tears. "Listen to me, Aggie. I'm telling you it doesn't matter. I pick you."

He pulled her closer, their faces inches apart. "It doesn't matter. It doesn't," he said again. "God has given us this second chance. Nothing will keep me from taking it. Not wealth or my family name. Nothing."

Sinking his fingers deeper into her hair, he moved toward her. "Aggie." His breath touched her skin. Then his lips touched hers.

So many nights Agnes had gone to sleep dreaming of his touch, but to have it, to be in his arms again, was more powerful than she had remembered. She returned his kiss and gave her own.

James grinned from ear to ear when Freddie's babbling drew them apart. "Freddie, do you think your mama is going to marry me now?"

Freddie took his chubby palms and smacked them together. "Bababa," he said, making little sense but bringing smiles to both their faces.

"She's made me wait long enough, don't you think?" James tickled him. "She can be a stubborn woman. But we men, we'll stick together."

Turning his attention from Freddie and back to the woman in his arms, he said, "Ag, you going to keep me waiting even longer? You did promise me you'd never love anyone else."

"I remember."

"Sam's a good man, but you promised me."

Agnes nodded. "He is a good man. He'll make someone a good husband." She paused. "But it's always been you. I kept that promise. I've loved you always."

He kissed her again, little kisses to her cheek and the tip of her nose. "Did you keep all your promises? I remember you telling me you'd never kiss anyone but me."

"James!" This time she rose on her toes and, putting a hand on his neck, pulled him toward her and kissed him on the lips. "I kept all my promises."

"Be my family? We'll live on the frontier, tending the sick and injured together, raising Freddie and all the other babies we can make." He winked at her. "We've already got a quilt to share. What do you say? Should we tell Clint he won, that he can keep me in Penance? We can get married today."

"What of Buffalo?"

He shook his head. "I'll stay. Someone else can go in my place. I don't ever have to go back. I'd give that up for you."

"For me." She pulled away, her breath caught in her chest. What she wanted was to stay in James's arms forever, never leaving, but was it wise? Inching farther away, she wrestled with what she wanted and what she felt compelled to do and say. "No, I can't marry you. For a moment I thought it was all so simple. That you loved me and I loved you, but, James, you can't marry me. You'll be giving up so much. For the rest of my life I'd wonder if you regretted it."

James's grin vanished. His hands fell to his sides. "I told you. You're all I want."

"You're going back to Buffalo. I want you to." She took a deep breath. "I can't agree to anything until you do. I want to, I want to so badly, but I can't. Not until you speak to your family. Tell them everything, listen to their arguments, then decide. Go back a free man with no obligations here. I don't want you to feel honor bound to return to me." She put a hand on his arm. "Go back, give your speech, see your family, and decide."

The romance that had been so thick in the air dissipated.

He spoke with a voice void of passion. "If going back will reassure you, then I'll go. I'll come back to Penance, though, and you'll see my heart will be as true then as it has remained all these years."

"James, you have to know something. When the new schoolteacher arrives, I'll have to leave my house. I'll have to make a new plan."

"I caught wind of that." He ran a hand through his hair. "Don't marry anyone else. If she gets here soon, stay with Hannah or Minnie. I'm coming back."

Agnes squeezed his hand. "I'll wait as long as I can. But if you decide to stay, then I'll marry so I can keep Freddie. It's not a threat, it's simply what I'd have to do."

"I'll come back." James kissed her cheek. "I will."

CHAPTER TWENTY-SIX

"You seem rather melancholy," Hannah said one afternoon not long after James left.

"He said not to worry, but I can't help it." Agnes picked at the tablecloth. "I'm sorry it took so long for me to tell you my whole tale. I wanted to, I just hated saying it all out loud. Being illegitimate is something I've hidden since finding out. And then the fevers and everything happened."

"Don't fret over that." She handed Agnes a hot roll. "I thought you and the doctor would make a fine couple. Even not knowing your whole history I would have chosen him for you. I liked him from the start."

She straightened. "For now, I have to find ways to pass the days."

Hannah passed her the butter. "He'll come back."

"Did you speak to him about bringing back children?"

"Yes, I did, and he's going to make all the arrangements. I

believe he'll have them travel by train sometime in the spring. I feel like an expectant mother, I'm so anxious."

"How will he know what children?"

"We told him to pick children who would get along with Ruby and to find children who needed us."

"That's all you told him?"

"He knows we don't care what our children look like or what their names are. It's exciting waiting. It just feels right. And I've learned that when God tells me something is right, I ought to do it."

"I don't doubt they'll be the perfect children then." Agnes smoothed a pleat in her skirt. "If he writes about the children, you'll tell me, won't you? If you hear anything at all?"

"That reminds me." Hannah jumped up from the table and ran to the other end of the house. "He left this and told me to give it to you when you started wondering if he was going to come back. I suppose now is as good a time as any."

Agnes took the letter and tore it open. Silently, she read his words.

Dear Aggie—

My affection for you is not a fleeting whim. My love and heart are yours today, tomorrow, and always. What began when we were children climbing over fences to be together will live on. I will be there when we marry, standing beside you making promises to love you and cherish you. I'll be there when you bring children into this world to be Freddie's brothers and sisters. We will name them together and watch them grow. And when you are in tears because they are growing too quickly, I'll cry with you because you and I both know I've no shame when it comes to tears. I'll be there when you need me, and I'll even be there when you're angry with me. I'll be there for it all. Don't doubt me. I'm coming back.

I'm going to tell my parents I have been reacquainted with my first and only love. I'll tell them I want them in my life, but I pick you and I pick Freddie, and they'll have to make peace with that. I'm going to see your father and tell him he need not worry about you. I'll promise him I'll do more than meet your needs. I'll promise him I'll treasure you. It's my wish he'll give me his blessing, because when I come back, I'm going to marry you. I'm going to share our quilt with you on cold nights. I'm coming back, Aggie. I've kept all my promises, and I'll keep this one too.

I love you. Distance will not change that.

Love and affection,
James Theodore Harris

Tell Freddie I love him too. Tell him it is my wish to be his papa.

"What does it say?" Hannah asked.

"He says he's coming back. Here, read it." She handed her the letter and waited.

Moments later, Hannah looked up from the letter with a wide grin on her face. "He's coming back, Aggie. I feel it in his words. He loves you as surely as any man has ever loved a woman."

The days passed slowly. Agnes did her best to fill them with teaching and visiting friends.

"You coming to gawk at the whale?" Minnie said two weeks later when Agnes and Freddie stopped by for a visit. She turned sideways so Aggie could see her rounded belly. "This baby needs to come. I don't think I've been this miserable in my life. I thought for sure I'd have a new baby in my arms by now."

"You do look ready." Aggie hoped she wouldn't offend her friend. Lately, Minnie had been easily agitated, very easily. Last week Agnes stopped by and offered to help her lift something only to have Minnie snap back about treating her like an invalid. And the next time Agnes saw her, she was angry because no one helped her with anything.

"I was more ready before the doctor left. Something is different this time. I toss around at night worrying something isn't right, and I don't even have McHenry to turn to. We need a doctor here, one who will stay and be here when we need him. Not that skunk James Harris."

Aggie nodded. She didn't dare tell Minnie that she'd insisted he go. Her heart ached. "Who'll come and help you with the baby?"

"Hannah said she'd come." Minnie arched her back. "I'm worried. It's just not right. I feel different this time."

"I don't know a thing about birthing babies. But if I can help, I will."

Minnie nodded. "Maybe you can help Lem with the other ones. If something happens to me, he'll need everyone to help."

"Nothing will happen." Agnes stood, anxious at the very idea. "You'll be fine."

"It's different, Aggie. I've walked this road before, and this one's not right. Call me crazy all you want—everyone already does—but I mean it when I tell you something is different. I don't know what."

Agnes swallowed hard. Minnie was serious. Agnes saw the worry written in her strained expression. "What can I do?"

"Well, for starters you can help me clean this house. You'd think I lived in a sty with pigs."

Grabbing a broom, Agnes set to work, grateful she could do something.

Everything felt different in Penance for Sam. He'd spent years working there and never worried about anything but saving the coins he earned. Now, working without thinking felt nearly impossible.

"Letter for you, Sam."

He nodded and took it. Then he stepped away from the counter and quickly read the words.

Dear Sam,

I've been thinking about you so much. You were always the best brother to me. Remember the fun we had growing up? I wish you'd come home and be with the family. You could meet my husband. I know you'd like him, and we could all be close again. The family misses you.

Besides, you're going to be an uncle and I want my baby to know you. There's land for sale here and new people moving in all the time. You said you liked making furniture. This town could use a good carpenter. It's not right—your staying away because of Ruth. Can you tell I'm trying to convince you? I know you have to decide for yourself, but I hope you'll come back.

Your Sister,
Rhoda

"Any mail for me?" He heard Aggie ask the postman.

"Nothing."

Sam shoved his own letter into his pocket. "Good to see you, Aggie."

"You, too, Sam. I haven't seen you in town much."

"I've been working long hours." He motioned toward the door. They stepped outside together.

"You're a hard worker." She smiled at him.

"I think hard work is in my blood." He gnawed on his cheek a moment. "The truth is, I feel out of place in town. I'm itching for something new, or maybe I'm itching for something old. I don't know where I belong these days." He patted the pocket with the letter. "Lots to think about."

"You don't have to stay away from town because of me. I never meant to make things hard for you."

"I know that. You heading home?" he asked. "I could carry Fred."

"I am." She handed Fred to him.

"I came out here hoping to find a future and to save money."

"Have you gotten what you wanted?"

"Well, I've been saving all my pay for years now, so I suppose I'm doing all right." He ran a hand over his scruffy jaw. "Truth is, I'm thinking of leaving."

She stopped in her tracks. "Where would you go?"

"Well, I haven't been home in a long time. My sister is married and having a baby. I think maybe it's time for me to pay them a visit. In a way, I have you to thank. You've been good enough to let me into your life." He paused, trying to find the words to explain the awakening of his heart. He felt it beating now, calling him to live his life more purposefully. "I've seen you and Freddie, and even you and James, and it has me missing my family and the people who care about me. I've been aimless for so long, but I don't want that anymore."

"Don't run away because of me."

"I was running away before. Coming to Penance was me floundering. But now I think if I left, I'd be going home." He smiled as he walked, bouncing Fred and making him giggle. "Maybe it's time."

"What about Ruth?"

"She's kept me away all these years. I don't think she meant to, and, well, my staying away only hurts me. It doesn't punish her any. Seems wrong for me to keep hurting myself over something I didn't do wrong. Something I can't change." He hadn't planned to act so quickly, but suddenly he felt like he couldn't leave soon enough. Looking at Aggie, he wondered why she seemed so pensive. He thought she'd understand. "Don't worry about me, Aggie. I've a good family back home, and I'm ready. My sister says they need a carpenter there. I've enough money that maybe I could open my own store and do what I love every day. Maybe I could find someone to share it with."

"I know you'll do well. Your family will be lucky to have you back. And I know you make fine furniture. I hope you build your sister a high chair for her baby." She gave him a half smile. "We'll miss you around here."

And then he remembered. He'd told her he'd marry her if James didn't return. They hadn't spoken of it in weeks. He'd been rash when he'd said it, but it had seemed so right before. He looked at Aggie's lovely face. The face that had always been kind but never full of love for him. He wasn't sure he wanted to be someone's second choice, not even Aggie Pratt's.

He cleared his throat. "I know I told you I'd help you keep Freddie." He looked at the baby in his arms. "I'll wait to go. I'll help you if James doesn't come back. I made you a promise."

"You go. It was never a fair plan. You deserve something more, someone more. I would never feel right marrying you, knowing I was keeping you from some girl out there who will be smitten with you. You deserve that, and I know she's out there. I think you should go find her. Things will work out for me and for Freddie." She bit her lower lip. "I know they will. I'll board with Hannah if I need to. I want you to go."

He nodded but not with the same exuberance he'd felt before. "I'll always remember you, Aggie. You were there for me when I needed it."

"I'm lucky to have met you, Sam. Send us all a letter sometime and tell us how you are."

"I will." He stopped then. "James is a lucky man. Don't let him forget it."

"If I see him again, I'll tell him."

He looked off toward the horizon. "He'll come back."

CHAPTER TWENTY-SEVEN

"Why'd the doc leave?" Tommy asked. "Don't he know we got sick people here?"

"He was invited to speak at an important meeting," Agnes answered him. "It was a great honor."

"Hmm. I still think he shoulda stayed. Besides, my ma said she heard from the postman that he heard from Minnie that you and the doc were going to get hitched. You can't get hitched to someone who ain't even here."

"You're getting married?" Charlotte asked. All the children started speaking at once.

Agnes put her hands in the air. "Quiet down."

The room buzzed a moment longer before they all waited, eager to hear. "Nothing was decided between the doctor and me. He is a grown man and has chosen to go East. It will also be his decision whether he returns to Penance or not. There's no formal agreement between the two of us."

"But don't you want him to come back?" Tommy asked.

"We'd all like him to return. He's an excellent doctor." Agnes began writing on the slate board. "We've a lot to do before we dismiss for the day."

"But I heard you were going to have to give up your job and your house soon. I heard the new teach is coming. What will you do—"

"Enough. No more questions."

Tommy's face fell. "Doctor Harris always answered my questions when I stopped by the clinic. I thought you—"

"No more!"

He closed his mouth and looked at his lap. The whole room quieted.

Sighing, she knew she had to say something. "Tommy, I *do* miss the doctor. And I do hope he comes back. I really do. But talking about it when we are supposed to be doing our schoolwork won't help. I can't bring him back, but I can teach you arithmetic while we wait. As for the rest, I'm still deciding what to do when the new teacher comes."

The afternoon wore on. Several more times she had to steer Tommy away from dangerous questions. Engaged in reading time, the students finally quieted only to be disturbed by a knock on the door.

What now?

She rushed to the door and flung it open.

Lem stood on the doorstep, his bald head beaded in sweat. "Minnie's having her baby," he shouted into her face. Instantly, the children started talking, wanting details. "Aggie, go over and help her. Go now, it's bad. I'll go for Hannah." He turned toward his school-age children. "Go home with Charlotte. I'll fetch you later."

"I'll go right over." Agnes's hands trembled. A baby. *Help us.*

She dismissed class, sending Osa to tell Mary to keep Freddie longer than normal. Her heart racing, she ran toward Minnie's. She'd never seen a baby come into the world before. If Lem didn't get back with Hannah quickly, she'd be on her own.

James, where are you? We need you here. Penance needs you. I need you.

Once she was at Minnie's, Agnes pushed the front door open and ran inside. She paused only a moment, just long enough to grasp for some composure, before stepping into Minnie's room. "Minnie, it's Agnes. Lem sent me."

She heard her friend moan in response, her body curled into a ball on the bed.

"Tell me what to do." She knelt in front of Minnie.

"Get me the doctor. Something's wrong." A long, agonizing groan followed.

Panicked, Agnes looked about the room trying to think what she could do to help. Wringing her hands together, she prayed silently for help. Surely she needed some sort of divine intervention. When the pull to do something became unbearable, she found a rag and wetted it in cool water, then put it on Minnie's forehead. "Is that better?"

"No, nothing helps," Minnie said between pains. "It's not right. It's never hurt like this before." Minnie grasped Agnes's hand. "You've got to do something." Then her hand tightened. Agnes bit her cheek as she tried not to cry out in pain. She silently counted the seconds, hoping the pain would pass and she could free herself.

"Hannah will be here soon. She'll know what to do for you. I'm sure she'll be able to fix everything." She glanced toward the door, though she knew Hannah wasn't there and wouldn't be for some time. Lem had only just left to fetch her.

Minnie sat, waving her hands in front of her face. "A bucket!"

Agnes ran to the kitchen and grabbed the largest pot she could. Just as quickly, she ran back and held it under Minnie. Looking away, she tried not to hear the sounds coming from her as she emptied her stomach.

I can't do this. I can't.

Pushing hair out of her face, she tried to get a handle on herself and think rationally. What had she heard about birth? Not much, as there had never been a reason to include her in such talk. Now she wished she'd asked someone.

"Help me!" Minnie reached out a hand. "You have to stop the pain. I'm going to die if you don't."

Agnes froze with her hand in Minnie's. Despite the woman's boisterous nature, Agnes loved her. The world would not be right without Minnie. "You want to get up?"

"I need to move, I have to do something, try something."

Grabbing Minnie's hand, Agnes heaved her to standing, then she wedged herself beneath her arm and the side of her body. Together they moved a few steps only to have Minnie double over in pain.

"I can't do this!" Minnie cried. "I can't! I just can't. Put me back in bed."

"You'll be all right," Agnes said, doubting her own words. "It'll pass."

Minnie turned her head and glared at her. "I'm going to die. You tell Lem I died cursing his name for getting me in this fix." She reached for Agnes. "No, don't. You tell him I love him. Tell him when I die."

"Please, Hannah, get here quickly," she said to herself, knowing she had absolutely no idea how to help a baby into the world.

Sam had a few more miles to cover before he reached his stopping spot for the night. It felt strange riding away from Penance, knowing he'd likely never return. He'd made memories and some good friends there. But it had been idle time, and now he had a destination. For the first time in years, he was deciding his fate.

Kicking his heels harder into his horse's sides, he picked up the pace. He was looking ahead for once rather than behind. He hoped his friends back in Penance would do the same, especially Aggie. She'd spent too long keeping herself from her own future.

James would come back for her, wouldn't he? He'd be a fool not to come back to a woman as fine as Aggie Pratt. Sam envied James for getting the chance to share his future with someone who also shared his past. He'd never get that, but Aggie believed a woman could love him. And today, with the crisp, fresh air and endless possibilities ahead, he believed it too.

He led his horse to the side of the road when he saw a rider approaching. Few people traveled this road. Only folks coming or going from Penance. The horse drew closer, and he sat up straight. He knew this rider.

"James?" he shouted, questioning his eyes. Could it be him? Back so soon?

"Sam, you headed somewhere?" James pulled his horse to a stop.

"I'm leaving. I decided I was done with Penance. It's time for me to go home."

"Did something happen?" He raked his hands through his hair. "I never should have left." James's face was flushed. He'd been riding hard. "I decided to come back tonight. You ever have one of those feelings you can't shake? I couldn't wait. I had to come."

"Everyone is fine. Well, they were when I left, but I heard Minnie was having her baby. I heard Lem shouting through the whole town about it. He seemed upset. You'd think by number nine you'd know how it worked."

"And Aggie?"

"She's been teaching school. Caring for Freddie. And worrying over you." He steadied his horse. "I thought you'd be gone longer."

"I made a promise to a girl." James laughed, relieved that all was well in Penance. "We'll miss you in town. I like to think we could have been good friends."

Sam stuck out his hand. "Let's part ways as friends. You back to Penance and Aggie, and I'm headed to my future. Somewhere out there." He motioned toward the horizon. "Things are as they should be."

"Take care of yourself."

"I will. You better hurry. Minnie's been fuming about you leaving before she had her baby." Sam flicked the reins, a new peace spreading over him knowing Aggie's future was about to ride into town.

James wanted to rush to Aggie's house and take her in his arms. Instead, he turned down the street bound for Minnie's. Before he even opened the door, he heard wailing from within. His pulse increased. Minnie and her baby must be the reason he'd felt the urge to rush back.

He quickly washed the travel grime from his hands in the large rain bucket on the front porch, then he stepped closer to the front door. When he pushed the door open a little, he saw Minnie doubled over, vomiting into a pot. Then he saw his Aggie bend and move the pot away.

"Do you want to lie down again?" she asked Minnie. "I'll help you."

Minnie only moaned and grasped for Aggie's arm.

When another pain overtook Minnie, Aggie reached out a hand and offered it to her. "Hold my hand, Minnie. We'll get through this one too." Aggie bit her lip as Minnie squeezed, pain evident on both women's faces.

He could watch no longer, and he walked into the room. "Mind if I help?"

Aggie's head shot up. She leapt to her feet and into his arms. "You're back, you came back. Oh, thank the good Lord, you're here."

She clung to him, and the last thing he wanted in the world was to pull away. Feeling her touch, smelling her sweet scent—she was home to him.

"I'm here." He almost said more, but it would have to wait. He stepped out of her arms and to Minnie's side. "Minnie, I want you to lie back in the bed. I'm going to examine you and see how things are progressing."

"I can't," she said.

He put an arm under her and helped her swing her legs onto the bed. With careful hands, he felt her stomach and then examined her progress. A few minutes later, he looked at both women. "This baby is close. It won't be long, and it'll be in your arms."

Aggie clasped her hands together, eager for the ordeal to be over.

Minnie curled in pain again. "You'd better do something," she said when the pain had passed.

Aggie looked at him with big eyes. "You're the doctor."

"I want you to listen to me, Minnie. I know you are in a great deal of pain, but we're going to get through this." He spoke confidently, remembering how his instructors had told him a woman in labor needed to believe she could do anything. "Remember, the pain will pass. You can do this."

Minnie's panic seemed to lessen some as he spoke. She nodded when he told her how to breathe through her pain. Somehow his words were the soothing balm she needed. No longer frantic with each pain, her agony became controlled.

When Lem arrived with Hannah, he practically fell at James's feet in gratitude and relief. Hannah told Agnes what she could do to help. They readied things for the new baby and brought fresh linens.

"Was it like this for you?" Agnes whispered. "Were you sure you'd die too?"

"I can't speak for Minnie, but with both Ruby and Grace, I was afraid I'd be torn in half." Hannah patted her arm. "Don't look so afraid. When the baby comes, the pain goes away too."

"I had no idea. I never knew it was so horrible. I don't feel like I'm any help at all," Agnes confessed. "I think I ought to get Freddie. After this, I think he's the only baby I dare have."

"Stay. You've seen so much already. Stay so you can see the moment that makes it all worth it. Soon Minnie will have a baby in her arms. She won't be screaming any longer, and she'll be making us look at how beautiful her baby is." Hannah had a twinkle in her eyes. "Besides, your James is back. He's back, Aggie! You're going to get married soon. I think you and the doctor will have fine-looking babies."

"My James?" Agnes looked over at him. "Babies?"

"I think it won't be long before everyone knows he's your James," Hannah whispered as they worked.

"This baby is ready to come. I'll need you both to help." James instructed them to each hold one of Minnie's legs, then all three encouraged the exhausted Minnie to push with all her might. Obediently, she pushed and groaned and pushed again.

When she declared she could push no more, James walked to the head of the bed and looked her in the eyes. His voice came slow and stern. "The only way to end this is for you to give all you've got and push when your body tells you to. You can't give up. Too many people need you and love you. Let's end this. Let's get this baby here."

Minnie said nothing, but when the next pain came, Agnes watched her grit her teeth and she knew Minnie was about to welcome a child. The baby's head emerged.

"Your baby." She patted Minnie's shoulder.

One more push, one more moan from Minnie, then into James's hands came a screaming newborn. Agnes stared, mouth ajar at the miracle of it all. "It's a boy," she said. "You have a new son, Minnie."

James cut the baby's cord and handed him to Agnes.

"Wrap him and put him in the cradle. Then help me."

"With what?" Agnes asked.

"The other baby."

Everyone looked at him.

"The second one isn't moving down on its own. Hurry, come and help." He turned his attention to Minnie. "I've heard this is the worst. The desire to push isn't as strong with the second one. You've got to help this baby come into the world, and it won't be easy."

Minnie looked near tears but nodded.

For several minutes, he encouraged her to use all her strength. "Aggie, when she pushes, I want you to put your hands here on her stomach and push downward. We have to get this baby out."

Their first attempt did little. The room felt dark and stuffy and dismal. The first baby cried, Minnie moaned, and she prayed for the second baby. With the next pain, they all worked together, and to their great relief, the baby crowned.

"We can do this," James said. "Minnie, you must give it your all. Aggie, Hannah, help."

And then a miracle like no other occurred. Another baby, slimy and blue, slid into James's waiting hands. James grabbed a cloth and rubbed the little girl's body. He turned her and patted her back.

Agnes held her own breath. She grabbed Minnie's hand and held it tightly while they waited. James shifted the baby and patted it again. This time the infant cried out, and everyone else breathed with her.

"You've a daughter." Agnes took the baby from James and held her near Minnie.

Hannah brought the little boy over. "Look at them."

Minnie sighed. The pain from before replaced by a look of

exhausted contentment. “Two.” Gently, she reached out and stroked his tiny fingers, then touched her soft head. “Have you ever seen babies so beautiful?”

Agnes stared in utter amazement. Minnie was no longer moaning or thrashing around. She was smiling.

“This is the moment I was telling you about,” Hannah whispered. “You’ve witnessed a miracle. Only God could take something so agonizing and replace it so quickly with a moment so sublime.”

“They’re perfect.” Agnes couldn’t take her eyes off the newborns. She swallowed. “You were right.”

James cleaned up, then stood to leave. Leaning against the doorframe, he knew he’d made the right choice. He’d given up a great deal in the last month, but what he’d gained he could put no value on. There before him he saw not just his career but his calling. He was a doctor in a town that needed him.

Quietly, he walked through the door, leaving the women to admire the babies. Lem sat in the main room, his knees shaking back and forth.

“You’ve a fine healthy son in there. And a perfect daughter.” James patted the man’s back. “Minnie’s going to be all right. She’ll be back to herself soon.”

The strong, quiet man bent over and buried his head in his hands. James heard one audible sob as he walked through the door and into the fresh night air.

CHAPTER TWENTY-EIGHT

"Don't leave!" Agnes's voice rang out into the street as she darted after him. "Don't leave!"

He turned and stepped back toward her. "Aggie, you didn't have to follow me. You can stay with Minnie and the new babies."

Ignoring his comments, she raced toward him. "James."

He stopped.

"Tell me everything. I want to hear." She'd longed for this moment. Dreamed of it. Desperately, she wanted to hear him say he was back for good.

He touched her arm. "I missed you."

Frozen in the moment, she waited.

"My parents aren't happy." He stepped closer to her. "They begged me to stay."

"Did you want to?" Doubts crept into her heart and mind. Like locusts, they devoured the hope she had. "You could have."

"Come with me." He held out his hand, and she took it.

James led her across the street and behind a store to a wooden bench the shop owner sat on when he needed a break. James patted the spot beside him. “I thought when I got there, I might be taken with the ease of life, but I wasn’t.”

“You weren’t?”

“I’d be lying if I said it was not a welcome respite from the toil of hauling water and cleaning dust from everything, but it didn’t feel like home.” His gaze wandered across Penance and landed on her. “This is home. I was there only a few days before I realized it. I heard conversations that sat ill with me. Talk of classes, people mocking poverty. My senses had been dulled to such talk before, but now each word pricked me, it angered me. I couldn’t run away soon enough.” He shook his head. “Penance isn’t perfect, I know that, but it’s home now.”

“You’ll stay for good?”

“Forever if it pleases you.” He took her hand. “The truth is, Buffalo has not felt right since you left.” He brought her hand to his mouth. The heat from his lips when he kissed her fingertips raced through her. “I told my parents I was coming back to Penance. I told them I was going to marry you and be a frontier doctor. My mother cried, and my father became cold toward me.”

“I’m sorry for that.”

“I wish it weren’t so. I do hope someday they’ll see value in the life I’m leading.” He smiled despite his losses. “Are you satisfied? I went home, I saw the house I was giving up, I listened to my parents’ arguments. My eyes were opened. I saw it all, and I’ve come back.”

Agnes put a hand on her heart. “Are you sure it’s what you want? You don’t have—”

He put a finger to her lips. "Shh . . . I'm positive this is what I want. I pick this dream of my own free will." He moved his hand to her cheek. "I pick you. I pick it not just for you but for me. It's the dream I want."

"You pick me," she whispered. "You're giving up so much for me."

He leaned closer and kissed her forehead. "You're only seeing what I'm giving up. I see what I'm gaining." He smirked, knowing he'd used her own line. "I see a whole life of happiness ahead of me. I'll be with you. I don't need anything else. Well, that's not entirely true."

"It's not?"

"We need to ride around Penance tomorrow and find a piece of land to call our home. We need a house of our own, and quickly. After all, we've already got a baby."

"And a quilt."

"I've thought of a few ways we could share that quilt." He grinned. "Where should we live?"

"Perhaps there is land toward Hannah's."

"We'll start by looking there." He rubbed his hands together.

"Oh, James." She leaned her head on his shoulder. "Is this real?"

She felt his lips press against her hair. They lingered. "It's very real and long overdue." He straightened. "I've brought you a gift." He grasped her hand and pulled her up off the bench and toward his horse. "Just a small one."

"What have you brought me? And tell me about your speech." She laughed. "I've so many things to ask you and to tell you."

"My speech was in a fine hall with prestigious doctors. It

all meant little to me. By the time I gave it, all I cared about was coming back here. I wanted to get back to Minnie and all my patients who needed me. Mostly, I wanted to get back to you." He pulled something out of his saddlebag and held it behind his back. "I wanted to get back to you and to Freddie. The whole time, I kept thinking about walking to Clint's door holding your hand. I couldn't wait to see the look on his face when we told him we were getting married and that I had no plans of leaving. Everything that meant anything to me was here, not there."

Just like pain from Minnie's labor vanished with the joy of the babies, the long winter of separation was over. Their spring had come. They could feel it in the air despite the late autumn chill. All the waiting, all the lonely years, all of it felt worth it for this moment.

"Let's go tell Clint. Let's tell Minnie and Hannah and everyone we see." The doubts were gone. The hope and happiness back. Agnes grinned. "Let's shout it from the rooftops. We've denied ourselves long enough. Let's wait no longer."

"Does that mean you're finally ready to marry me?"

She nodded. "It means I am ready to marry you this very day if you will have me."

"Let me give you my gift first." He pulled a rectangular object from behind him and placed it in her hands.

Agnes stared at it a long moment. She ran her hand back and forth across its smooth surface. "You brought my swing."

"I brought your swing."

"This is . . . " Her voice caught in her throat. "James, we really are going to have a future together, aren't we?"

"Yes. The best of futures." He took her hand and squeezed

it tight. "I'll push Freddie on that swing, and when he's sleeping, I'll sneak out and push you on it. It'll be for old times and for new times. When you've had your fill of swinging, we'll go inside and curl up under our quilt."

"Let's go get Freddie." Agnes started for Mary's house. "Let's not talk of the future, let's go and get it."

"I've missed him," James confessed as he followed her down the street. "I want to ask him if he's willing to have me for a papa. I figure a grin from him is a yes." He squeezed her hand. "Once I have Freddie's approval, let's sit and I'll tell you about your father and how he plans to visit in the spring. He's going to travel with Hannah's children."

"My father is going to come to Penance?" She gaped at him. "Honest?"

"He misses his little girl and wants to meet his grandson." James's dimple showed when he smiled.

"Is this real? It can't be." She wiped at the corners of her eyes. "Somehow I'm living a life I once believed I'd only ever live in my dreams."

"It's one of those rare dreams that actually comes true," James said as they walked to Mary's house. "Do you think he'll remember me?"

"Let's find out." Agnes knocked quickly. Excitement and anticipation swirled within her. "I've taught him a new trick."

"You have?" James asked while they waited. "What is it?"

"You'll see."

Moments later, the door opened. Mary held Freddie in her arms. He saw Agnes first and waved his arms toward her. She thanked Mary and took him. Then she turned him toward James. "Look who's back."

Freddie's already excited face lit up. He babbled in James's direction and leaned toward him. Agnes looked up from Freddie toward James. She'd expected him to take the boy. What she saw warmed her heart. James had tears running from his eyes.

Agnes pointed to James. "Your papa's back. Can you say it?"

"Paapaa." Freddie clapped his hands together. "Paapaa."

James put his arms around Agnes and Freddie. He pulled them close, kissing their heads and faces. "Papa's home," he said. "Papa's home, Freddie Boy."

Epilogue

The late summer sun sent rays of light across Agnes's face. She raised a hand to her brow to block them. "I've done it," she said to James when she saw him raise his head in her direction.

"All six of them are down for the night?" James leaned his garden hoe against the fence and stepped toward her. "You've worked a miracle."

"I'm lucky to have Freddie. He read to the little girls and helped me get them settled."

"I like that about him. There aren't enough twelve-year-old boys who'll sit beside little girls and indulge them in stories."

"We've been blessed indeed." She looked toward her swing, then back at him. "It's not dark yet."

"No, Mrs. Harris, it's not." He took her hand in his hand, and they began walking. "Come, let's swing. I'll see if I can push you as high as I pushed Catherine earlier."

"She's only a bitty girl. I doubt you can get me so high." Agnes scooted onto the swing.

"I'll get you high enough that you laugh like you did when you were just a bitty girl yourself." James reached for the ropes that hung on either side of the swing. Before pulling back on them, he kissed the curve of his wife's neck. "I saw Hannah today. Tommy came by too. It was a busy day at the clinic."

Agnes turned to look at him. "Is Hannah well?"

"She is. She was bringing Opal by so I could check the stitches in her leg. She's all healed up from her fall."

"Poor Opal. That cut was deep, and she cried whenever she saw it. Hannah's so gentle with her. She's so good with all of them." Agnes smiled as she thought of Hannah's large, happy family. "What did Tommy want?"

"He's sweet on Patsy and wanted to ask my advice. I thought he'd outgrow his quest for answers from me, but I think I'm doomed to be his lifelong confidant. I blame you. If you'd known a few more answers when he was a lad, he'd have come to you." James pulled back on the ropes, then let go.

"He looks up to you." Agnes soared into the air, laughing as the air rushed across her face. Up she went, not nearly as high as she'd gone when she was small but high enough that she could feel the breeze in her hair. She closed her eyes and pictured the life she'd had so long ago. She could see the trees of Buffalo, the brick houses, and the busy sidewalks. Then she opened her eyes and breathed deeply. This world they'd created, right here, was too beautiful to long for anything different.

Their cabin was not nearly as grand as the homes of Buffalo, but it was well built and full of love and tenderness, laughter and light. She loved this life, this town, and her family.

"James," Agnes said with her eyes still on the house. "Do you have regrets, even small ones?"

He said nothing but stopped the motion of the swing. He reached out his hand. She took it and walked with him on their stretch of land.

"No," he said as they passed their garden and then their barn. "I regret nothing. I'm tempted at times to regret that we were ever apart, but then we'd not have Freddie. And I don't know if we'd be here. Freddie's my boy. I can't imagine a life so fulfilling without him. That time of loneliness was our winter, and it led us to our spring."

"It's a good life." She pressed her fingers tightly against his and sighed. "Do you want to get our quilt?"

He raised a brow.

"I thought we could spread it out on the meadow and look up at the sky. Maybe play a round or two of Going to the Moon. Perhaps"—she pursed her lips—"we could play other games. The ones we don't play when the children are awake."

He pulled her toward him and put his hands on her waist. "I believe you became a much more assertive woman when you moved to Penance. You're bold and strong." He kissed her cheek, then her nose and forehead. "I have no regrets. None. I'd take this life, this houseful of children, and these horrible doctoring conditions any day to be here with you. Marrying you was the greatest choice I've ever made." His lips found hers. "I'll never regret it."

Discussion Questions

1. For six years Agnes has lived in Penance. Despite her love of the townspeople, she still feels unsettled about the past. Have you ever tried to leave something or someone behind and struggled to fully let go?
2. James and Agnes have a less-than-happy reunion. Could it have been handled differently? Was it fair for Agnes to deny him the answers he sought?
3. Hannah has recently suffered the loss of her daughter. She desperately wants an explanation of the cause of her daughter's death. How have you dealt with grief in your own life?
4. James doesn't plan to stay in Penance. At first, he sees the town's flaws, but with time his feelings change. Have you ever judged a place wrong initially?
5. Sam was jilted years ago and decides it's time to find someone new. If circumstances had been different, could he have had a successful relationship with Agnes?

6. Agnes feels a deep connection to Freddie from the start. Is it believable that love could grow so quickly?
7. Freddie is often scorned because of circumstances he has no control over. Have you ever judged someone based on one fact, only to change your opinion when you've gotten to know them?
8. Agnes and James share a history but have been apart for six years. What does it take for relationships to pick back up again after long absences? Do you have friendships or romantic interests that stay strong despite time and distance?
9. James is accepting of Agnes's secret when she finally tells him. Do you think his reaction would have been the same had he known sooner?
10. Penance is a common term and the name of the town. Would James and Agnes have ever truly gotten their happily ever after if they'd not gone through their season of "penance"?

Acknowledgments

Prior to writing this novel, I watched the old film *Blossoms in the Dust* that gives an account of Edna Gladney and her work and advocacy with illegitimate children. I was blown away by the cruel stigma society gave such children and knew I wanted to weave this real-life struggle into a novel. That idea became the catalyst for *A Life Once Dreamed*. The stigma today is not what it was before, but I believe we can all learn from that past discrimination and make sure we are mindful when we speak and interact with people with less-than-favorable pasts. I foster kids and have heard hurtful things said about them because of where they came from. I hope we can learn, like James did, that it's where we are going that matters most.

I wrote this story before I was ever published or even under contract to be published. Due to the long time from rough draft to publication, I know my thanks will not be as complete as it ought to be (blame my poor organizational skills and forgetful nature). My sisters, mom, and a few close friends read early drafts and offered great insights into what worked and what didn't. Thank you. Then I set it aside for well over a year. A few gracious readers I met online volunteered to read it when I jumped back in. I hope you know I am truly grateful for your time and feedback. I apologize that you aren't mentioned by name but hope you know your insights were valuable.

Lonnie Hull DuPont, my fabulous editor and friend, helped me as I began transforming this book into something readable. My new editor Rachel McRae took over when Lonnie retired (Love you, Lonnie!). I lucked out because Rachel is fantastic. Do you ever meet someone and think, *This is going to be great*? I thought that about Rachel. Editing is work, but with these exceptional women on my team, the process has been fun.

I want to also thank Amy Ballor, who helps me sort out my grammatical mess! Brianne Dekker and Karen Steele, who respond to my plethora of emails. I really just need to thank everyone at Revell. You're all the best. Thank you for making these novels a reality and for making the experience delightful. And of course my agent, Emily Sylvan Kim, who encourages me along.

No acknowledgment would be complete if I did not thank my family, who reads my drafts and cheers me on. What a blessing it is to be surrounded by all of you.

One of the most beautiful things about publishing a novel is that it allows you to connect with people you could not connect with otherwise. I thank God not only for giving me the love of writing but also for the good people who've entered my life because of these stories. Thank you, everyone, for reading my books, leaving reviews, reaching out to me, and enriching my life. I hope my stories entertain you and touch your heart.

Rachel Fordham is the author of *The Hope of Azure Springs* and *Yours Truly, Thomas*. She started writing when her children began begging her for stories at night. She'd pull a book from the shelf, but they'd insist she make one up. Finally, she paired her love of good stories with her love of writing and hasn't stopped since. She lives with her husband and children on an island in the state of Washington.

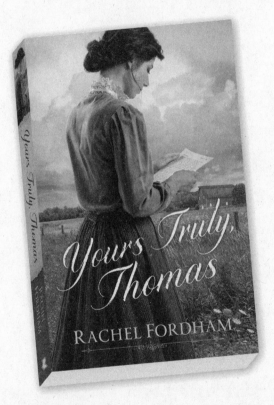

Meet

Rachel Fordham

RachelFordham.com

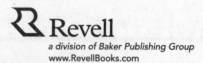

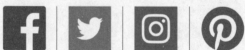